M000187450

WHERE DARKNESS BLOOMS

WHERE DARKNESS BLOOMS

ANDREA HANNAH

WEDNESDAY BOOKS
NEW YORK

This is a work of fiction. All of the characters, organizations, and events portrayed in this novel are either products of the author's imagination or are used fictitiously.

First published in the United States by Wednesday Books, an imprint of St. Martin's Publishing Group

WHERE DARKNESS BLOOMS. Copyright © 2023 by Andrea Hannah. All rights reserved. Printed in the United States of America. For information, address St. Martin's Publishing Group, 120 Broadway, New York, NY 10271.

www.wednesdaybooks.com

The Library of Congress Cataloging-in-Publication Data is available upon request.

ISBN 978-1-250-84262-6 (hardcover)

ISBN 978-1-250-84263-3 (ebook)

Our books may be purchased in bulk for promotional, educational, or business use. Please contact your local bookseller or the Macmillan Corporate and Premium Sales Department at 1-800-221-7945, extension 5442, or by email at MacmillanSpecialMarkets@macmillan.com.

First Edition: 2023

10 9 8 7 6 5 4 3 2 1

To Matt.
Thank you for loving me through it all.

And to my mother and grandmother.
I finally broke the curse.

Some of the thematic material within contains discussions of sexual assault (implied, later revealed), stabbing, death, sex (implied), and underage drinking.

WHERE DARKNESS BLOOMS

BISHOP

The land had always been parched but its thirst for blood was learned.

The people indigenous to the land could not stay as no crops would grow. Travelers exploring the west never stayed for longer than a fortnight. Frontiersmen swept through—first on horses and then by wagon. Each time they left behind only that which they no longer wished to carry. They left broken spindles and dried pinto beans and scuffed horseshoes, a trail of useless, forgotten things, in their wake.

Stay. A whisper in the dusty breeze. But they never heard the plea.

When the travelers attempted to pass through, the land called on the winds to lash their wagons and overturn their carriages.

Stay. Its yearning was laced into the wind.

But they mended their splintered wheels and reshoed their horses by dawn.

New travelers arrived, and this time, the land did not hesitate. Its winds roared across the honeyed plains, toppling carriages and basins, coaxing the flames of oil lamps toward the sun-dried fields. Burning up the opportunity to abandon it.

It held them hostage on its dry, cracked earth. The travelers regrouped, picking up what was left within the ash.

Stay. A rumble from its greedy roots.

But the mourners moved on, as they all had done, the bones of their dead marinated in its lifeless soil. Where blood had been spilled, sunflowers grew over the unmarked graves. They swayed in the wind, alone, roots drinking from the decay.

Until a traveler with a birthmark the shape of an ivy leaf arrived with his wife.

Stay, the land whispered, as it always did.

This time, the traveler paused.

The land shivered in excitement. The winds picked up to carry its words closer to the traveler's heart.

Keep me.

The traveler could feel the words at the edge of the wind, like the weight of a secret just before the telling. He grabbed his great-grandfather's weather vane from his carriage and placed it at the edge of the field. The wind rattled through the rusted metal. This time he heard them.

KEEP ME.

How? The traveler wondered.

The wind shuddered through the field where the sunflowers swayed, where the stolen lives of the dead lay. *Blood. Blood. Blood.*

The traveler told his wife about the whispers through the weather vane, the sunflowers calling. "There will be prosperity here. This place is different." There was only one requirement.

He reached for his wife's wrist and pulled his hunting knife from his pocket. "Just a few drops," he promised.

His wife refused. "No," she said, pulling away. "This is madness."

She ran, but it was too late. The cut to her wrist had been made, and it was much deeper than what the traveler had promised. She dropped into the dust like a sinking ship, the brittle grasses swallowing her whole.

The man buried her in the barren earth. When he rose the next morning, sunflowers with butter yellow petals surrounded the spot.

The land whispered, *More.*

"I will get you more," The man replied. Then he began to build.

As other travelers came to the wretched land, they saw what the man had begun to create. They saw the opportunity to start anew amid the golden fields. Finally, *finally,* they stayed.

Yet the land had tasted blood, and it wanted *more, more, more.*

The traveler did not tell his next wife before he brought out the knife.

CHAPTER ONE

The day Delilah's mom disappeared, there was a wilted sunflower on the bathroom sink. Two years later, all that was left was a smudge of yellow, a stain she could only see in just the right light.

On that day, she'd woken up for school and stumbled into the tiny bathroom on the third floor in this dusty old house, still achy from the night before. She'd spent a full minute poking at the bags under her eyes before she'd noticed the brown butter petals hanging limp over the faucet.

It wasn't necessarily odd for Indigo Cortez to leave bits and bobs around the house, soiled paintbrushes and rolls of washi tape trailing after her like breadcrumbs. But Delilah's mother was an artist. She had a taste for color, for light. She liked things that felt *alive*.

Delilah had held that half-dead sunflower in her palm for only a second before tossing it in the trash. Such a shriveled thing couldn't belong to her mother.

Now she knew to hold on to things a little tighter. A little longer. There were no more sunflowers—dead or alive—in the last house on Old Fairview Lane, except for the obstinate ones across the road that refused to stop multiplying. It shouldn't have annoyed Delilah as much as it did. Kansas *was* the Sunflower State. And in a town like Bishop, all wide open fields the color of corn silk even in the high heat of summer, it only made sense they continued to spread. Bishop was surrounded by them, a wall of aggressive yellow looming on the periphery with their empty, unreadable faces. They always seemed to be looking in, no matter which direction the sun faced. Delilah had always felt watched by them, but lately, something was different. It felt like they were *listening,* too.

At least she could keep them out of the house.

She stood at the kitchen window, watching the flowers lurch in the wind. It had started to pick up in the last hour, even though her phone said the winds wouldn't come in until later that night. The app was wrong, though, like it often was about Bishop's weather. The storm was already here. Delilah could feel it in the pea green sky hanging low overhead, the way static electricity in the air clung to her like a briar patch.

She bustled to the back of the house and yanked open the door to the storage closet. A riot of faded roof shingles, splintered patio furniture, oil cans and buckets rusted shut, and cardboard boxes—so many boxes—sat cluttering up the room. These were the things she had to choose from, a graveyard of broken things to prevent even more broken things. Flattened boxes to shore up the windows, shingles and old sheets and painter's tarps to drape over sharp objects. The furniture to push in front of the doors when it was going to be a really bad one.

She stared at the boxes, contemplating. The last thing Delilah wanted to do was call all the girls before the weather was even a thing. She could already hear Whitney's voice on the other end. *Oh my god, Delilah, chill.* Feel the breeze in the doorway as Jude marched past her, clearly annoyed. And Bo. Honestly, it didn't matter what Delilah told Bo. She had never been one to listen.

They already thought she was overprotective and that she'd only gotten worse with time. They weren't wrong, exactly. Once all the custody papers had been signed and their already-absent fathers had agreed to let them stay in Bishop, Delilah had been too grief-stricken to consider that maybe Whitney shouldn't try to do her own stick-and-poke tattoo in the crease of her arm, or that Jude should have a curfew, or that Bo . . . well, that Bo was always angry for a good reason.

But time had hardened her—hardened them all in one way or another. And now Delilah knew better than to leave too many doors open. There were too many ways for things to get in.

And out.

Just as she was about to close the kitchen window, a door on the other side of the house swung open, making the frames on the walls rattle. Jude bustled in first, her long ponytail spilling over her hoodie.

"Where's Whitney?" Delilah asked. "And leave—"

"—my sneakers at the door, I know." Jude kicked off her dusty purple sneakers with a little more force than was necessary before she plopped on the couch. "She's right behind me."

Delilah waited. The front door hung wide open, the scuffed brass knob making a *sh, sh, shhhh* sound as it rubbed against the wallpaper. She dug her fingernails into her hand to keep herself from slamming it shut.

A second later, Whitney threw herself through the entranceway. Where her twin's hair was always pulled back into a tight ponytail, Whitney's was as wild as a windstorm. Her soft curls, which usually hung well past her shoulders, puffed out like a dandelion. It had always been easiest to see the difference between them during a storm. When the weather turned feral, Jude turned in on herself. She became smaller, paler. The muscles in her jaw clenched until the worst of it had passed. Whereas Whitney became *more* herself in the thick of it. Something lit up behind her endlessly brown eyes whenever the wind kicked up.

"Made it," Whitney said, shoving the door closed behind her.

"Where's Bo?" Delilah asked, tilting her head to look through the small glass pane in the door.

"Dunno," said Jude, tapping the buttons on the remote. "Don't we get some kind of basic channels? I want to check the weather."

Whitney flopped onto the couch beside her sister, stretching her long legs out across Jude's lap. "I already have the radar pulled up on my phone. Look." She turned her phone toward them. The screen was blotted with red.

Delilah shifted to glance out the front window. The sunflowers were bent over now, their backs to the gray-green sky. The storm was getting worse. Her fingers twitched. A part of her knew she should just call Bo, tell her to get home quick. But the other part of her knew it wouldn't matter if she did. Bo barely even texted her back nowadays. There was zero chance she'd answer a call.

Delilah turned. "Where did you see her last?"

"In town," Whitney answered, not looking up from her phone. "She was talking to the event committee about the memorial."

Beside her, Jude continued to flick through the channels, all of which were blurry and unwatchable. "Looks like the satellite dish is out," she said, still absently tapping the buttons.

Delilah sighed. "Again? I'll fix it later. And I didn't know Bo was planning to do that," she added casually. But secretly, Delilah knew better. Even though she had begged Bo to just let it go, she knew Bo wouldn't listen. Bo would end up at the town hall to insert herself into planning the memorial anyway.

It wasn't that Delilah hated the idea of Bishop hosting a memorial. In fact, she was the one who'd proposed the idea to the committee in that relentless, fever-pitch month after the girls had come home to their empty house, the front door swinging in the wind. But no one had listened back then. Their mothers were missing, but there was also the aftermath of the windstorm to deal with.

Besides, missing women were as much a part of Bishop as the sunflowers and storms.

Growing up, it seemed like she'd attended some kind of haphazard memorial for women dead or missing at least once a year. Mrs. Rosen found cold in her pastel pink bathtub. Hailey Ramiro just up and gone, vanished from her bedroom in the middle of the night, not a trace of her left behind. The cops always came and investigated, like they were supposed to, but no one ever found anything other than a corpse that had died of natural causes or the stale air left behind in an empty house. Over time, the townsfolk had come to the conclusion that Bishop just wasn't the kind of place that could satisfy hungry, restless women with sharp edges.

Well, that woman was a little too wild, they would say, when one was found facedown in the garden.

She was always talking about leaving one day anyway, they'd said when a woman vanished in the midst of her well-worn life.

She never did follow the rules, they'd whisper, when another had tucked herself into bed only to never wake up again.

Delilah's stomach clenched whenever she let her mind wander in that direction. She knew those women had done nothing wrong—nothing to deserve that kind of fate—and there were no "rules" that would keep them alive and safe if followed. It was all rumors. Just people trying to make sense of this place.

Delilah *knew* that. And still.

There was a small part of her that believed if she could just keep them all in line, keep them smiling and obedient and whisper-quiet, maybe they wouldn't come across as girls with sharp edges. Maybe they'd somehow be spared from a similar fate as the others.

But another had gone missing just six months ago, and that girl had done everything right. Eleanor Craft had dropped dead in front of the oak tree in her yard at only eighteen—the same age Delilah was now. She'd been a model student, the kind the teachers always praised in front of everyone else and used as an example. With her flame-red hair and the sparkle behind her eyes, she instantly warmed everyone she came into contact with.

There had been no memorial for her. Eleanor's only living relative, her grandmother, hadn't wanted one, so the townspeople went about the business of getting on with their lives, just as Delilah had after their mothers disappeared. She'd combed through her mother's life insurance, cleaned out the bedrooms, and reorganized the pantry. *This* part had been Delilah's memorial in those early days. She had figured out how to care for them all because there was no other option.

For the event committee—and Bo—to want to bring this all up again, to drag her back into her own head, was cruel. And it didn't even make sense. Why a memorial and a big, flashy statue dedication *now*, two years too late? And why only to their mothers when there were so many missing and forgotten women?

"Got it!" Jude said, setting the remote in her lap. Through all the fuzz, Delilah could just barely make out a woman in a blazer, her hair pulled back into a tight bun.

"*This is a . . . for all of central Kansas . . . hang on tight and . . . evacuation . . .*"

The weatherperson's words were punctuated with white noise as the image wobbled onscreen. Delilah frowned. *Evacuation?* She was pretty sure she'd heard that right. Bishop was smack dab in the center of the state, in the middle of Tornado Alley, and the girls had faced down a million windstorms—both with and without their mothers. They'd never attempted to evacuate once. No one in Bishop had. It was almost like it was understood: storms came and went, but townsfolk always stayed.

Except for when they didn't.

Delilah looked out the window one more time. She tapped her fingers against the glass. *No Bo.* "We better start boarding up the house."

Whitney swiped the remote from Jude's lap and flicked off the TV. "I don't know why we don't use the storm cellar."

"Bo," Jude said softly, and they all settled into silent agreement.

They wouldn't go hide in the underground cellar because of Bo. That had been the agreement for two years, even though Bo had never asked them to do it. They all understood that it might feel safer between the damp asphalt walls of the cellar for three of them, but to Bo it would feel as dangerous as being swept up in a storm.

So they went to work.

Delilah trekked back to the storage closet and grabbed the boxes. Jude pawed through the toolbox for duct tape, and Whitney shot through the hallways like a feral breeze, slamming doors and windows closed in her wake. Together they slapped cardboard over the windows, silver tape streaking across them. They moved clunky pieces of furniture in front of the windows, blotting out the slivers of gray-green sky that were still exposed, just in case the storm still managed to bust through the glass. Their mothers might not be here to protect them, but their old, nicked-up furniture was still here to soften the blow from shattered windows.

The last thing to do was cover up the small panel of stained glass in the front door. Delilah grabbed a sheet of cardboard that she'd stacked on her mother's velvet reading chair and tugged at the roll of duct tape. As she began to place it on the window, she glanced outside.

Bo stood at the edge of the gravel driveway, her back to the house. The wind lashed at her honey blond hair so hard that it looked like freshly pitched hay. She was a fierce, tiny angel with a lopsided halo.

Delilah flung open the door and screamed, "Bo!" But the wind swallowed up her words before they reached the porch. She stepped outside, the door rattling behind her.

"Bo!"

This time, Bo heard. She slowly turned, her eyes glazed over. When she did, Delilah saw the puddle of blood at her feet, the sunflower the size of a dinner plate in her palm.

Delilah's heart picked up speed. She tried again. "Bo! Get inside!"

Bo didn't answer. Instead, her fist clenched around the flower until her fingertips turned white and every last petal dropped into the dust.

CHAPTER TWO

Bo held the sunflower in her hand, gently at first. And then, slowly, her fingers curled around the head. Her nails sank into the wet, seedy part in the center and the silky petals began to fall, one by one.

She liked the way it felt.

Bo had never really loved flowers—not like her mom had. Cori Wagner had wallpapered her tiny office with them. There had been delicate violets and full-blossomed daisies, ballet-pink lady's slippers and vines of sweet peas tangled up in them all.

But then everything changed. Cori's desk chair remained, worn and empty. And Bo painted the whole room navy blue.

"Bo!"

Bo blinked, and Delilah appeared in front of her, her light brown curls pulled back into a bun. Behind her, the old tire swing in the side yard creaked on its chain, metal grating against metal, and petals floated around her like dust. Bishop's warning sirens had already started to wail on her walk home, but now they were relentless.

Delilah clamped her hands on Bo's shoulders and squeezed. "Come on!" she yelled. "The wind's getting bad!"

Bo sighed. She tossed the now-dead sunflower back into the field it had come from and followed Delilah up the porch steps. A ribbon of blood ran down her knee and pooled at her shoelaces.

"Hey, what happened—"

But before Delilah could finish her sentence, Bo brushed past her, ignoring Whitney and Jude on the sofa, and stomped up the narrow staircase at the end of the hall.

She knew what they were doing. She knew what they were saying. It wasn't like Bo was oblivious to what the three girls she lived with thought of her. Bo couldn't remember how many times she'd overheard Delilah whispering words like *so mad all the time* and even *vicious*. And of course, there was Whitney's favorite line.

Why are you such a bitch, Bo?

Well, let's see, Bo thought as she limped into the tiny room at the top of the staircase. *My dad's gone, my mom's missing, and I have to live with the rest of you until I get out of here.*

And then there was the other thing. The thing that threatened to bubble over like a hot spring every time she walked back into town, or to school, or happened upon the wrong place at the wrong time. The constant hum of dread pulsing in her veins that she hadn't been able to shake since that night.

Bo flung open the door to her mom's old office and flopped on the bed. Well, *sort of* bed. When she'd realized that her mother was probably never coming back, Bo had moved out of the room down the hall she'd shared with Delilah and into this office. It was only a quarter of the size, but it had been her mother's, and that mattered. Plus, then she didn't have to share with Delilah and deal with her incessant poking and prodding.

What's going on with you lately, Bo?

Why won't you just talk to us?

Are you okay?

No, Bo answered in her head to no one. But it wasn't like she could talk to Delilah about it.

So instead of her old double mattress, Bo had dragged the camping cot out of the garage and set it up where her mom's desk had been. She'd layered it with old, musty afghans and pushed it up against the wall so she had enough space to close the door all the way.

She rolled onto her back and stared at the ceiling. Bo had painted that navy blue, too. When she had painted the wall where her mom's desk used to sit, she'd discovered little specks of black coffee in the corner, sprawling all the way across the wall, almost touching the ceiling like a watery constellation. She'd imagined her mom sitting in her chair, her favorite mint-colored mug in her hand, headset on, as she tried to explain to someone's grandma what a web browser was. Cori never complained about doing tech support, but the aggressive coffee splashes on the walls told Bo everything she needed to know about her mother's job.

Bo lay in the dark, listening as the tire swing outside began to slow. That was what storms were like in Bishop. It was like the winds knew right when someone was thinking too hard about a different kind of life. They'd pick up at the worst moment, pummeling her skin until it was red and raw. The storms pushed them all back into their homes. Away from the edges. Away from one another. Then they'd start to ease. And for a little while, everyone in Bishop would forget that they had ever wanted to try something different—*be* someone different—in the first place.

"Hey," Delilah said, tapping her knuckles on the door. She stepped into the room before Bo could tell her otherwise. "You should come downstairs."

Bo sighed again. "It's just another storm. I'm fine."

"Really? Why are you bleeding all over your bed then?"

Right. Bo had forgotten about her scuffed-up knee for one blissful second. She shrugged. "I fell."

"Where?"

"Up at school. I went to pick up my schedule."

Delilah went still, and Bo stole a glance at her. She immediately regretted it.

Bo hadn't hit Delilah—not once, not ever—but every time she lied to her, Delilah winced as if she'd been slapped.

"Juniors don't pick up their schedules until next week," Delilah said quietly. She glanced at the floor, the velvety blue walls, the pile of laundry festering in the corner. Anywhere but at Bo.

"Fine, fine, *fine*. I was in town. I was going over some stuff for the memorial tomorrow." Bo sat up and swung her legs over the bed. She had to get out of here before more questions came hurtling toward her. "Are we done here? I have to clean out this scrape."

"*Bo*," Delilah huffed. That was it. No more nice Delilah. No more tender Delilah who talked to her like she was a preschool teacher trying to spoon-feed her the alphabet. Bo had reached her max allotment of patient, saintly Delilah. She pushed a limp pillow out of the way and sat on the edge of the cot.

"Why are you doing this to yourself? To *us*?" Delilah said.

Bo scoffed. "What you really mean is why am I doing this to *you*, right, Delilah?"

She opened her mouth to reply, but it was too late. The embers that had been licking at Bo's insides all day erupted into wildfire. If Delilah wanted to have this conversation again, then Bo was going to have it, and she was going to burn everything to the ground.

"I don't want to hear it," Bo said through gritted teeth. Delilah pursed her lips. "You're just going to tell me to let it go, that our moms are gone and we're going to 'move on.'" She curled her fingers into air quotes. "But I don't know how you expect any of us to move on when we never even figured out what happened!"

"Bo." This time when Delilah said her name, that single syllable, she said it so gently that it almost made her crack around the edges.

Almost.

"They never even found them!" Bo erupted. She jumped off the bed and started to pace in a tight circle like a cat trapped in a cage. "No one even knows what happened. So if some ridiculous event committee wants to build statues for them, and they want everyone to sit in the sun and tell stories about them for an hour, then why *not*? Who knows? Maybe we'll find out something and—"

Delilah stood. She grabbed Bo's shoulders and squeezed, just like she had beside the sunflower field. "It's been *two years,* Bo," she said, her face crumpling. "There's nothing to find."

If it wasn't Delilah standing in front of her with her doe eyes and perfect skin, she might have broken. She might have softened enough for Delilah to see the fault line that split Bo right down the center, into the Before Bo and the After. The crack that had spread like a spiderweb, starting with the night their mothers had disappeared.

It was only supposed to be a party.

It was just supposed to be some meaningless night out, a bonfire on the very edge of town where the sunflowers crested a dead-end road. And it *was* that, at first.

When Bo had come home from a run that afternoon, no one was there. Not their mothers, not any of the other girls. It wasn't uncommon for them to go their separate ways throughout the day, but as the sun began to wane, they would all find their way back to the house before dinner. Bo had hopped in the shower, letting the steam settle into her skin, and gotten dressed.

The house was still empty.

She didn't like being alone in the house. The way it was tucked into the dusty corner of the street, how the sunflowers always stared ominously at her through the windows in spite of the weather. She texted Whitney, Where are you?

Bonfire at the clearing, she replied.

Meet us.

And even though Bo had thought she'd finished sweating for the day, she jogged across town in the late-summer heat. As she cut through the center of town, more and more people began to pop up like dandelions in front of the small-town shops and in spaces between buildings. A couple of them waved, but most quickly looked away and continued shuffling down the sidewalk. That happened a lot to Bo. People would catch her eye and then look away, pretending she was a ghost instead of a girl. She never knew if it was because of her, or if seeing her churned up some kind of uneasiness about her missing mother, or if it was something else entirely.

She had just started to catch her breath at the clearing when Whitney slipped a red plastic cup filled with something that looked like honey and smelled like fire into her hand.

Bo drank it down. It was as thick as syrup.

The boy appeared as she finished the last drop. He was summer in human form, with hair so sun bleached it was almost white and freckles all over. He towered over her, which wasn't saying much considering Bo was one of the shortest girls in her class. The lip of his plastic cup brushed her shoulder.

Hey, he'd said. It was one trivial word, and it made Bo's skin flush.

She hated that.

He reached for Bo's wrist, his calloused fingers cupping it, his thumb pressing into the soft skin where her pulse thrummed.

It was the first crack.

The rest of the night unraveled like a spool of thread. Bo never caught the end again before the whole thing came undone. She'd been trying to smooth out the tangled remnants of her life ever since, and a second-chance memorial had felt like a way to wind everything back into place. But now that the memorial was only a day away, Bo had started to think that nothing—not even a permanent stone statue—could fix what had been broken inside of her.

"Sit," Delilah said, her voice cutting through the memory.

Bo blinked, suddenly woozy. She sank back onto her bed.

"What happened?" Delilah asked, softer this time. She leaned forward, careful to avoid the angry wound on Bo's knee.

"An accident."

Delilah stiffened. She glanced up. "Try again."

"I just . . . something happened when I was leaving the planning meeting. Just a little, um." Bo winced as she swung her legs back onto the bed. "Fine, I kicked Evan Gordon's ass on my way home."

Delilah pressed her hands to her face. "Bo, why—"

"Trust me, he's way worse off than I am." She glanced over at Delilah, who had squeezed her eyes shut like she was trying to force herself to teleport out of this room—or out of this life. Bo sighed. "He was right outside of town hall and he started saying stuff. And I couldn't ignore it. I didn't ignore it."

"You can't go around kicking people's asses every time they say something you don't like," Delilah said softly, but even as she said the words, she couldn't hide her mouth from creeping up in the corners.

She touched Bo's knee, which was already puffing up. In the last few minutes alone, a throbbing knot had taken over her entire kneecap, turning the skin the color of a ripe plum. "That has to hurt."

Bo shrugged. She knew it should hurt, but honestly, it didn't. Still, Delilah would think she was lying again if she told her she could barely feel this wound that cut to the bone.

It wasn't that it didn't *hurt,* exactly. It was that everything else hurt so much more. In some ways, the scrapes and cuts and bruises made Bo feel more alive than anything else. Like maybe she wasn't just a walking ball of hellfire.

Bo had lost so many things she loved that night at the bonfire. Her love of late-night runs, the protection of the storm cellar. The way she felt around the other girls. The way she felt in her own skin.

Her mother.

"I'll go get some things for it." Delilah hopped off the bed. She didn't look at Bo. "Be right back."

She watched Delilah trudge toward the door, searching for a way to soothe this wound, despite the fact that she had spent most of the afternoon staring out into the storm, waiting for Bo to come home.

"Hey, Lilah?"

It was a nickname the girls had called Delilah when they were growing up, when they all still had fathers and their mothers were best friends instead of roommates, and they lived in separate houses on a different, dusty street in Bishop.

Delilah slowly turned. "Yeah?"

"Thanks," Bo said softly.

Delilah's eyes shone. She blinked quickly and swept out of the room as if the wind were pushing her out.

Bo leaned back onto her bed and stared up at the navy ceiling. If she imagined hard enough, it almost looked like Evan's blue jeans as she'd kicked him into the dirt after he'd said those words.

Your mother never wanted you.

He never wanted you.

She squeezed her eyes shut, but nothing happened. She patted the skin beneath her eyes. Still dry.

Bo had forgotten how to cry, but she still knew how to bleed.

CHAPTER THREE

I t wasn't that Whitney had a death wish. It was just that there were more important things to do than wait for a storm to pass through.

Plus, she was tired of listening to Delilah and Bo argue.

Whitney listened to the hum of their voices between the wind's lashes and the old house's groans. There was a certain rhythm to their conversation, the crescendo of Bo's anger and the lulls of Delilah's disappointment. It was a symphony of unbearable tension and it never freaking stopped.

She'd heard the groan of Bo's makeshift bed and that was her cue—time to get out before Bo inevitably pounded down the stairs, rattling Whitney's mother's knickknacks all clotted up together on the TV stand.

Whitney uncurled herself from Jude on the couch. Her sister sat up. "Where are you going?"

"Out," Whitney answered, and before Jude could protest, she slipped through the front door and down the gravel driveway, letting the wind push her all the way to the end of the street.

Considering there was an evacuation order, no one was actually *evacuating*. Whitney took the long way into town, purposely avoiding the straight shot down Main Street to loop through the gravel side streets. There were still cars nestled in dusty driveways, each kissed by the buttery yellow petals of blooming sunflowers. The houses were still, windows boarded up with cardboard boxes, like Delilah had done to their house, or with crusty cooking sheets, rolls of wire meant for enclosing chicken coops, or behind precarious glass panes and old furniture that could bear the shatter that was sure to come.

Bishop never listened.

It didn't matter if it was a massive storm or a Main Street parade, the people who lived here treated this town more like a holding cell than home. Even though there was an "event committee," Whitney couldn't remember the last time there had been an actual event to go to. The storms pushed people away from one another. The deaths and disappearances made them weary. It seemed like everyone had one eye on the weather radar and the other on one another.

Which was extra unfortunate because Bishop was its own world in the middle of nowhere that no one would ever find on a map. Surrounded on all sides by sunflowers that grew taller than Whitney herself, it always felt like they were all being watched while they lived their lives. And sometimes lost them.

And once something was lost in Bishop, it was never found.

The wind raged as Whitney made her way past faded brick shops and tiny cafes to the clearing on the other side of Main. It was the place where Bishop all of a sudden stopped. Like whoever had settled this place had decided they didn't need a road out of here— just the one that cut through downtown. Like they just . . . gave up on the idea. Stopped pouring concrete and called it a day, tucking themselves back into their warm little houses like mice in a nest.

It was the same clearing she'd brought Delilah to on That Night.

At sixteen, Delilah had never been to a party; she had been too busy planning to be the youngest woman elected to the US Senate or an astronaut for NASA or whatever audacious ambition she'd carved out for herself that week. While Whitney, a year younger, had been to every party, even if it involved only herself, a half-empty bottle of whiskey, and an inky sky speckled with stars.

That Night, the clearing had been full of people. They all orbited around a bonfire while avoiding the rusty old weather vane that also occupied the space, their bottles full of jewel-colored liquor that glinted in the light. Whitney had drunk until her cup was empty, again and again, and all the while her mother was already missing and she didn't even know it. She drank until her throat burned, and she had never even known that her mother hadn't come home from teaching her last English class at the high school.

Now the space was empty. Except for the weather vane.

Whitney stepped into the clearing. The weather vane poked up from the center, squealing under the strain of the wind. It was an ugly thing, this bent-up rooster that had turned a pale, sickly green over the hundreds of years since Bishop had been founded. But no one ever dared to touch such a "historic relic."

The story went like this: before Bishop's founder ever laid a single brick, he had jammed the weather vane into this very spot, declaring that this would be a place for all. An opportunity for men and women alike to "grow and thrive."

Right. Just like her mom had "grown and thrived" here. And now Bishop had the audacity to throw them a memorial like it was some sort of jolly send-off, two years too late? In Whitney's opinion, this place could fuck right off.

Whitney went up to the weather vane and flicked it.

It jerked to a stop. The wind settled and the clearing went silent.

She held her breath. This was the part that always stung, like ripping off a bandage. Just for a second.

She reached into her back pocket and pulled out a bracelet.

It probably used to be gold, but all the shine had been rubbed away from years of wear, leaving behind a dull metal finish. Two charms tangled together in the center of Whitney's palm—a horse and a flame—hooked so close together that their clasps clicked, and a third clasp hung off to the side. Whichever charm had been attached to it had long since broken off.

Carefully, she looped the delicate little bracelet around the tip of the rooster's tail. The tarnished horse charm glinted under the milky white sky. The wind began to churn again.

And now came the balm.

Whitney closed her eyes and let the wind curl itself up her jacket sleeves, thread itself through her hair. She pretended it wasn't the breeze at all, that it was her hands, as delicate as the bracelet she always wore. Just for a second.

Whitney pulled in a shaky breath. The weather vane slowly began to turn.

She opened her eyes. "Eleanor?"

But Eleanor Craft did not materialize in front of her. She never did, and Whitney had learned not to expect her to over the months that languished on. No matter how much Whitney pleaded to the sky, the stars, the bottom of a whiskey bottle.

Only the whisper of Eleanor's voice carried on the wind.

More, she said. Like she always did.

"More what, Eleanor?" Whitney whispered back.

More what?

It had felt like forever since Whitney had first brushed her frigid fingers against Eleanor's at a bonfire. It had been almost six months since Eleanor had wrapped her arms around Whitney's waist and pulled her so close that her lips brushed against Whitney's while she whispered.

More.

Eleanor had been the kind of person who was never satisfied—

not with Bishop, or a teacher's exasperated responses when Eleanor asked *why*. And not with stolen kisses behind a shield of bonfire smoke.

Whitney had given her more on That Night. She'd given Eleanor everything: a commitment, a charm, and a kiss carefully planted on her collarbone.

This time when their fingers touched at the bonfire, Whitney had slipped the bracelet from Eleanor's wrist. "I have something for you," she'd whispered, hooking the small silver charm onto the bracelet. It glinted in the firelight as it slid to meet the horse.

Whitney had felt something bump into her back as she lurched forward. "Whoops!" A guy with dark hair stumbled, a splash of something that smelled like an oak barrel leaping from his cup onto his jeans. He pawed at the stain before glancing up at them.

She blinked in surprise. Whitney had only ever seen Evan Gordon when he was looking for a fight, but tonight, his eyes were unguarded and tender. His gaze bounced between her and Eleanor. "Sorry," he said almost wistfully.

"It's okay," Whitney said slowly, but Evan's attention was already elsewhere. He gazed longingly across the bonfire to where Delilah stood, a plastic cup pressed to her lips.

Eleanor's hand had brushed against hers, pulling her back in. Whitney would never forget the way her hand, raw and pink in the cold, looked beside Whitney's olive one as Eleanor held the delicate charm in her palm. She looked at Whitney. "A flame."

"That first night at the bonfire—"

"When you held my hand the first time," Eleanor finished, her voice shaky. And her face softened into something so gentle that it almost scared Whitney.

That was the moment she'd decided that she loved Eleanor Craft.

She'd threaded her fingers through Eleanor's, the old charm and the new pressed together between their palms as Whitney planted a constellation of kisses on Eleanor's collarbone. Around them, everything else melted away like wax on a candle. The acrid scents of alcohol and smoke dulled until all Whitney could smell was Eleanor's floral soap. Colors muted. The tinny music blaring from someone's cheap speaker floated away, one note at a time, and all that was left were Eleanor's shallow gasps as Whitney left a trail of kisses on her neck.

The next day, she was gone.

Whitney never saw Eleanor again. No one did.

They found her body facedown beneath the old oak tree in her front yard. There was no memorial, no funeral service. Eleanor just ceased to exist to everyone.

Except Whitney.

To the rest of Bishop, Eleanor was just another dead girl. To Whitney, she had been the only reason left to hope for a future better than the painful past lingering behind her. She'd already lost her mother, but at least falling in love with Eleanor had given her a reason to keep going. Six months later, losing Eleanor still felt like slivers that refused to work themselves out from under her skin.

The entire world kept spinning on its axis anyway. Time ticked on, deliberate and unbearable. The rest of Bishop went on cleaning up their yards and doing their errands, and for the most part, Whitney did, too. Her body went through the motions of long days and even longer nights, of fingers typing out English essays she barely remembered writing, of eating canned soup that tasted like nothing at all. Her memories of Eleanor were the only things that held her fragile heart together. At least she still had those.

Somewhere along the way, Whitney no longer saw Eleanor as the tiny silver flame she'd slipped onto her bracelet months ago. The fire vanished.

Now Eleanor was the wind.

Whitney gritted her teeth as the wind churned up the dust around her. "Come on, Eleanor. *More what?*"

She had started coming to the clearing shortly after Eleanor had vanished. This empty space, pressed in on all sides by sunflowers, had felt like the end of the world. It *was* the end of the world. It was the place where Whitney had fallen in love and the place where that love had been taken away.

It wasn't so much Bishop itself that she had to be afraid of. It was at the edges where bad things happened.

The first time she came here, nothing had happened. Eleanor had only been gone for three days, and the clearing had remained abandoned since the party. Whitney had circled through the dust like a vulture searching for ... what? Even now, she still wasn't sure. All she knew was that the hitch in her gut wouldn't let her *not* do it. So she kicked through a riot of broken bottles and plastic cups, finding nothing, before heading back to the house.

The next time she came, a week later, the last remnants of the party had been cleaned up. Whitney had curled up beside that wretched weather vane that had lied to her yet again about "growing and thriving," dust clotting up her curls, and wished she could just disappear, too.

The wind had picked up. The weather vane had creaked.

More.

That was the only word the weather vane, or Eleanor speaking through the weather vane, had uttered ever since. It demanded and it took, even though Whitney had nothing more to give. Even though most days, Whitney felt like an echo of her former self, all dampened and muted.

But she had made a promise.

Whitney had promised Eleanor that night that she could have her. So she had come back to this desolate clearing, again and again, waiting until the day that Eleanor decided there was nothing left she wanted.

It had been months, and still, Eleanor never whispered what she wanted on the wind.

More what?

The weather vane whipped in circles, blurring to a mess of sickly green.

Whitney's hair whipped against her face. "I'm going to have to stop doing this eventually, Eleanor!"

I'm not going to do this anymore, she thought.

This time the wind screamed.

CHAPTER FOUR

Jude had always hated the storms.

Her mom used to tell her that Jude and Whitney were born in the middle of the biggest tornado that Kansas had ever seen. That the entire house rattled on its frame as Ava Montgomery pushed, and that every window shattered the moment the twins were born. Whitney first, followed quickly by Jude.

But, as Ava had told it, Whitney didn't cry. It was Jude who screamed as loud as a siren.

Even now, seventeen years later, Jude wanted to scream every time the wind picked up. It wasn't that the wind *hurt*, exactly, but there was always the echo of something lingering on the breeze. Like the murmur of a word, the whisper of a phrase that she couldn't quite catch. The only difference was that as she got older, she figured out how to ignore the almost-words and the shaky feeling they left her with.

Jude had figured out how to ignore a lot of things.

When Delilah retreated upstairs to her room, she hooked her finger beneath one of her makeshift cardboard fortresses and peeled back a layer from the front window. The sky had decided on a pale coral as the clouds began to part and the wind wound down. It had been more than an hour since Whitney had left the house, and what her mother used to call Jude's "worry knot" in her stomach had started to flare up. She pressed her palm to it and tried to breathe.

It wasn't the first time her sister had walked straight into a storm, and Jude knew it wouldn't be the last. But every time Whitney walked out the door, Jude couldn't help thinking of their father.

Silas Montgomery had walked out of their old house on Cranny Street in the middle of a storm. Jude never saw him again. Her mother had told her it was for the best. Over the years, she'd been able to puzzle together pieces of the story, or their origin story, as Bo liked to call it. All three of them—Indigo, Cori, and Ava—were loved by men whose attention was as transient as the Kansas sky. Eventually, they all trickled away from Bishop like withered leaves carried off in the wind. And their mothers, best friends and the ones left behind, moved into the house at the end of Old Fairview Lane with their daughters.

Until they disappeared, too.

With the memorial hovering over her like a bad dream, she knew the knot in her stomach would only get worse. It was a constant, lingering reminder of everything she—they—had lost.

Jude slowly peeled away the cardboard until watery light shone through. She pressed her cheek to the window and looked down the driveway. No sign of Whitney.

It's because I love her. Because I loved them, she told herself. It had been the one piece of advice she'd taken away from the single therapy session she'd attended right after her mom disappeared. Jude had been trying to explain the worry knot, and how it hadn't unclenched in weeks, even though she knew her mother was probably never coming back at that point.

Love is deeper than worry, her therapist had said as her long, delicate fingers fiddled with a loose string on her sweater. *You love so deeply, Jude. That feeling in your stomach is tied to how much you care. Maybe you need to start calling it a "love knot" instead.*

It was like Jude was always trying to hold on to her people so tightly that her whole body clenched.

Everything outside had fallen into a slumber. There had only been one casualty: the already crooked mailbox in front of the house. That last feral blast of wind had snapped its rotting post in half, taking it out for good, before the storm calmed. Now the sunflowers hung their heads, what was left of their petals exhausted and limp as night started to close in. Jude had never minded the sunflowers. They didn't freak her out like they did Delilah, and they didn't enrage her like they did Bo. But she wasn't ambivalent about them like Whitney was, either. More than anything, Jude just felt *sad* when she saw them, and she didn't know why.

Jude turned away from the window. She closed her eyes and thought, *Whitney, come home.*

She waited.

Nothing happened.

The only sound came from somewhere upstairs, where Bo and Delilah had retreated into their separate spaces after yet another argument. Their fights were just part of the daily landscape now, just as commonplace as Whitney's favorite coffee mug or the scuff marks in the hallway from Bo's boots, though she never admitted they were hers. There were no more muffled voices; just the soft pad of Delilah's footsteps pacing the hallway, and the creaking reply of Bo's cot.

Jude sighed. In all the shows she'd watched and books she'd read, having a twin meant you were supposed to have telepathic superpowers. But if Whitney ever heard her pleas to come home, she never said as much.

In fact, Whitney hadn't said much to Jude in person, either. She'd always kept her secrets to herself, for the most part, but as the years stretched from the night of the disappearances to where they were now, Whitney had curled more and more into herself, like a flower with rotting roots. And as time passed, Jude had stopped trying to unfurl her sister's petals. Not because she didn't want to, but because she didn't know how.

Maybe Whitney was drinking again.

Maybe Jude should look for the empty bottles again.

She had just started down the hall when there was a sharp knock on the front door. Jude turned. There was a blurry silhouette on the other side of the stained-glass window.

Whitney surely wouldn't knock on her own door. But who else would brave the last angry breaths of a windstorm to show up at their house?

The knock came again, sharp and impatient. Jude opened the door a crack.

Bennett Harding stared back at her from the other side. His eyes flickered. "Oh. Hey, Jude."

"Hey," she croaked. *Damn it.* She cleared her throat and tried again. "Hey, Bennett. Come in."

"Thanks." Bennett slid his arm across the door and followed her inside. Pink bloomed on his cheeks and nose, coloring his smattering of freckles. His hay bale–blond hair had been raked through by the wind. It looked like someone had pulled their fingers through it.

Jude blinked the thought away. She pointed limply toward the staircase. "Uh, Delilah's upstairs."

Bennett shifted from side to side. "Actually, I was hoping I could talk to you."

Jude froze. With just one sentence, all the blood rushed to her head, and suddenly, she felt hot.

I was hoping I could talk to you.

She cleared her throat again. "What about?"

But Jude knew what it was about. Ever since the night at the bonfire, she'd known this conversation would happen. At some point. Even if it was two years too late.

That night had been burned into her brain, and not just because it was the last time she had seen her mother. Because it was the last time she'd kissed Bennett Harding, too.

It wasn't supposed to last longer than the summer. Jude knew that. Bennett had been up-front with her right from the start. Bennett would jump headfirst into his senior year, and all the frivolous details that came with that: football under the flicker of rusty lights, an after-school job out in the cornfield, dancing to the last song at the homecoming dance with someone other than her.

They met in the storm cellar behind Bennett's uncle's house, tucked themselves away in Jude's room when no one else was paying attention. They met in the middle of the sunflower field at the end of Old Fairview Lane. They'd both emerge—Bennett first, and then Jude a few minutes later—covered in petals.

She wasn't supposed to fall in love. But like her therapist had told her, *You love so deeply, Jude.* Before she knew it, she found herself double-checking her phone before she drifted to sleep each night while the crickets hummed their mournful summer song outside her window.

And then July spilled over into August. As night began to swallow up daylight and a chill hung in the air like an omen they were all trying to ignore, there was a final summer bonfire out in the clearing.

Bennett had agreed—they'd meet one last time in the storm cellar before the party, then they'd go their separate ways. *Think of it as a blessing, really,* Bennett had told her as they made their plans. *I'm going to be all over the place senior year.*

By *all over the place,* Jude was pretty sure he meant *all over other girls.*

But maybe not? She'd told herself as she'd made her way to the cellar before sundown. She could have been wrong. Maybe Bennett had changed his mind.

Jude pulled out the musty old gingham blanket they always used from the shelf. Laid it on the cement floor. Laid herself on the floor.

This would be the time she would say it. She would tell him that she craved his kisses, that she touched her mouth to stop her lips from tingling long after he'd left. That she thought about the way his brown eyes changed to caramel when the sun dipped low in the sky, and how she knew he was self-conscious about that one crooked tooth, but he really shouldn't be.

She would tell him that she loved him. That she wanted to be together. Like, *together*-together.

Jude waited. The sun waned through the windows and the wind picked up, just like the weatherman had said it would.

But Bennett never showed. Like he said he would.

By the time Jude showed up to the party, it was too late. Jude could see it happening even as she approached the clearing. The way Bennett's head dipped low, his lips brushing her cheek. His eyes full of honey and longing.

Bennett had fallen in love with Delilah.

"So, um, this is probably going to come out wrong," Bennett said, cutting through Jude's thoughts. He smiled the farm-boy smile that had gotten him into—and out of—trouble so many times before.

Here it comes, Jude thought. Her stomach lurched.

I'm sorry about that night.

I'm sorry I stood you up.

And maybe even: *I still love you.*

Bennett raked his hands through his hair again. A nervous habit. "You haven't been back to the cellar recently, have you?"

Jude blinked slowly. "Excuse me?"

"Never mind," Bennett said, shaking his head. "It's just, my uncle William was saying that someone had been snooping around in there recently. Like there were all sorts of things out of order, and he found, um, that blanket on the floor."

"The blue gingham one?" Jude asked softly.

He nodded. "That one."

Heat crawled up Jude's neck. "You think I'd just go through your uncle's stuff like that? That I'd go back to that cellar for, what, Bennett? For fond memories?"

"No, I—" Bennett let out a long, low breath. "Let me try again here. Okay, it's just that I know things ended kind of abruptly and that you may . . . still . . . have feelings? And wanted to go back there?" He said the last part with a shrug of his shoulders and a half-hitched smile, which mortified Jude even more.

A voice cut through the tension between them. "Bennett? Is that you?" Delilah called from upstairs.

Jude glanced toward the stairwell and then back at Bennett. "I've never been back there since that night," she whispered. Her throat felt like it was going to close up when she said the next words. "You're with Delilah."

"Sorry, I asked, but—"

"Maybe you should ask your uncle if he knows anyone who may want to ransack his cellar."

"Bennett?" Delilah called again.

"Yeah, I'm here. Be right up." Bennett looked down at Jude, and for a second, Jude saw something she hadn't seen etched into his face before: remorse.

Without another word, he passed by Jude, his hand accidentally brushing the back of hers as he moved toward the staircase. She shivered.

As much as Jude wanted to hate his fingertip brushing against her skin, she didn't. And she hated that even more.

CHAPTER FIVE

Delilah followed the sound of Bennett's footsteps up the stairs. When he came over, it was never a straight shot from the front door to the long, crooked hallway at the back of the house. There was always a pause, a hesitation. The floorboards creaked as he circled through the entryway, orbited around the living room. He never came directly to *her*.

It had been like that the night of the bonfire, too. Bennett had already been there for a while before she'd arrived. She'd watched him from over the rim of her plastic cup as he'd weaved through the party. He swayed through the crush of bodies and music like a slow-moving river with no sense of urgency.

Until he finally happened upon her.

And when he did finally settle, his dust-covered shoes bumping up against hers, the hem of her skirt billowing up against his jeans, Delilah knew.

She knew that Bennett Harding had been worth the wait.

Even now, almost two years later and despite the mess they found themselves in, she still thought he was worth the wait.

Outside, the wind blew half-heartedly, almost as if it were worn out from all the screaming it had done earlier. Footsteps creaked on the old wooden stairs. "Bennett," she said when he reached the landing.

He grabbed Delilah's hands, cupping his own calloused ones around hers, and kissed each knuckle. Delilah gritted her teeth. She tried to force down the shock of pain that bloomed on her skin every time her boyfriend touched her.

Bennett's eyes flicked up to hers as he kissed her pinky. He whispered, "Does it hurt?"

It did hurt. It always hurt now, but the way he looked at her from under the windswept hair that hung across his forehead, how his expression was always stained with hope, like maybe this time, this touch, would be different, hypnotized Delilah into trying again, every time.

It really did feel like some sort of spell, too. That night, Delilah had only had half of whatever was in her cup, but her insides had felt like they were full of little bubbles the second she'd touched Bennett's hand. The bubbles had fizzed through her fingertips, spilling into her arms and then her heart, making her feel as light and effervescent as her mother's laughter.

It was a feeling that hadn't dulled as the days grew shorter and Bennett's overnight stays grew longer. It had only grown stronger.

Now whenever Bennett slid his warm palm over her stomach in the middle of the night, the bubbles felt like little zaps. Sharp streaks of lightning that stung in the spot Bennett's fingers or hands or lips grazed, only for a second, until they dimmed. She knew it was weird, but it wasn't like Bishop was exactly a normal place. And besides, couldn't it just be some explosive kind of chemistry between them? Didn't all the great romance stories talk about how a lover's touch felt like lightning in their veins?

Delilah smiled, gently untangling her hands from Bennett's. "What are you doing here? It's still pretty windy out there."

"I just wanted to make sure you were all okay." His head dipped between his shoulder blades as he planted a kiss on Delilah's bare shoulder. She winced, but she forced herself not to budge. Whatever this was, it wasn't going to ruin what she had with Bennett. She wouldn't let it.

Bennett gently untangled himself from her. "It doesn't look like there was any damage done to the house this time, though."

"I haven't taken a look around yet," Delilah said, leaning back ever so slightly. "I've been up here with Bo."

Bo.

She'd forgotten. It only took the sound of Bennett's approaching footsteps to dissolve all her plans. Delilah gently touched his arm through his shirt, dampening the pain. "I have to grab something for Bo really fast."

It was as quick as a snap of thunder. So quick that Delilah surely would have missed the look that crossed Bennett's face if she hadn't been staring right at him. And after two years together, Delilah knew that look, knew all of Bennett's looks.

It was disgust.

It was no secret that Bo hated Bennett, but until recently, Bennett had at least pretended to tolerate Bo. Delilah wasn't sure what had changed over the long, dwindling summer, but she was pretty sure it wasn't anything good. All she knew was that every time she said Bennett's name in front of Bo, she could see the muscle in Bo's jaw clench from the other side of whichever room they were in. And when she had tried to bring up Bo to Bennett, he had tenderly caressed her cheek before changing the subject.

But still, the look on Bennett's face never crossed paths with his words. He nodded. "Okay. I'll go wait in your room, if that's okay."

She laughed. "Of course it's okay." Before she left the landing to cross into the bathroom, she stepped onto her tiptoes to plant a kiss on his nose, careful to kiss more air than skin.

Bennett's mouth softened into a smile. "See you in a minute." And he disappeared behind her bedroom door.

Delilah rushed into the tiny bathroom she had once shared with her mother. She hooked one finger under the mirror over the sink and started to pull. It made a groaning sound—everything in this house seemed to groan, like it could barely stand being a part of this hundred-year-old lopsided colonial—but it didn't budge.

Delilah muttered to herself. This happened sometimes, especially after a storm. It was like the wind pushed so hard against the house that all of its joints shifted, the nuts and bolts and ancient hinges. When she tried to open a cabinet or a door again, the wood no longer remembered what it felt like to be in its proper place.

Delilah caught her own eye in the mirror. It was the first time her reflection had taken shape in it in a very long time. She had done her best to avoid looking at herself in this particular mirror, and for a while she told herself it was because the lighting was bad in here, and she'd rather brush mascara over her lashes in the oval-shaped mirror above her dresser. But it had been years, and she knew why she wouldn't, she *couldn't*, look at herself in this mirror. She just couldn't say it out loud.

She stopped pulling and set her hand on the edge of the sink. There was still a stain near the faucet, the faintest trace of yellow where the petals had already started to rot on the porcelain before she found the flower two years before.

How long had it been waiting for her there?

It was a question that Delilah had been asking herself since she'd woken up the morning after her mom had disappeared, and she never found an answer.

There had been one split second when everything could have been different.

While Bennett had been circling around the fire, slowly making his way to her, she had been standing beside Whitney, their shoulders flush and sticky with summer heat, honey-colored liquor stinging the back of her throat. She'd felt someone staring at her.

Evan Gordon was watching her from under his mess of black hair, his sleepy eyes filled with something she couldn't quite identify. He smiled at her. It was a tepid thing, like he was trying it out for size. And, even though she definitely should *not* have felt this way looking at Evan, who had been in more fistfights with Bo than she could count, a sort of white-hot curiosity stirred within her. A what-if.

But Delilah would never know what if. Bennett eventually found his way to her. As the bonfire had dwindled and the rest of the party broke apart like ice in the spring, she had stayed with him. And when a chill had started to creep in, Bennett had weaved his fingers through hers and led her to the small storm cellar behind his uncle William's house, where there was a picnic blanket waiting for them.

They hadn't even kissed that first night. Delilah had been so entranced with the dips and pauses in Bennett's voice, how his laugh rose from somewhere deep in his chest, like it was always there, waiting to erupt until someone helped him release it with a few well-timed words. She'd lain beside him all night on the concrete floor, whispering secrets as moonlight streaked through the crack between the doors.

She'd come home late in the morning to an open front door and a wilted sunflower on the bathroom sink. That was the last time she'd really looked at herself in this mirror.

Delilah quickly blinked and pulled harder. This time, the mirrored door popped open, revealing a riot of medical supplies—gauze, tape, boxes of bandages in every size. She pawed through it all.

Finally, there it was: the dusty bottle of hydrogen peroxide. Delilah grabbed it from the back of the shelf and twisted off the cap. She looked inside. Nothing.

She shook the bottle. A few pathetic drops rolled around the bottom.

Delilah sighed, tossing the bottle in the trash. That was one thing about her mother that she didn't miss. Indigo constantly left a trail of disaster in her wake: makeup sponges on the countertop, translucent cheese wrappers on the cutting board, dabs and splashes of rainbow-colored paints around her bedroom, her studio, Delilah's room. Everyone in the house always knew where Indigo had last been and what she had been doing by the trail of multicolored breadcrumbs she left in her wake.

Until that one day. Until the last day, when she left nothing behind at all.

Delilah clicked the mirrored door back into place, thinking. She'd given the rest of her mom's old healing balm to Jude a few months ago after she'd burned her hand baking banana bread. But maybe there was more.

Delilah marched across the hall. When she reached the closed door of her mom's old studio, all of her courage withered like a flower in the rain.

Delilah stood with her hand on the doorknob, heartbeat thrumming. She tried to avoid her mother's art studio as much as possible. The last time she'd been in here was at least six months ago, when she'd been forced to go in to find some embroidery floss in one of the desk drawers for Whitney, who had randomly taken up cross-stitching curlicue swear words onto cloth. Her latest creation still hung in the hallway outside of the room she shared with Jude.

FUCK THIS, it said.

Yep, Delilah thought, and she pushed open the door.

She noticed the smell first. It was like the air particles in the room had clung to the scent of her mother, refusing to release her from the past. It smelled like watercolors and winter sunlight, like a mixture of melted glue and incense.

It smelled the way Indigo had smelled whenever she crawled

into Delilah's bed in the gray hours before dawn after working on her art all night.

Delilah swallowed down the knot rising in her throat. Even though she'd been in the studio a handful of times since the disappearance, she felt a little woozy every time she stepped inside. The discarded paint tubes, crusty brushes balanced on forgotten palettes, canvases stacked against the wall, waiting patiently to be used—it was all a snapshot of her mother's last days. It denoted a life half finished.

Delilah tiptoed across the studio toward the desk in the corner. Her mother almost never sat at this desk—she was a blur of curly hair and eighties dance moves in the studio. But this was where she kept all the little bits and bobs she otherwise wasn't sure where to place, including her homemade healing balm.

Indigo had mostly used her balm—a blend of coconut and tea tree oil that she'd melted into a circular tin—for all the nicks that ended up on her fingers while she was making paper art, but sometimes she used it for Delilah's cuts, too. She'd rush to her studio while Delilah bled, or cried, or both, and come back with the tin in her palm, her fingertips swiping through the balm—once, twice—before sliding them gently across the wound.

Now Delilah stared at the paint-streaked desk, fingers lingering on the top drawer knob. There wasn't a balm for this kind of wound. At least not any kind that she could find.

But Bo needed her, and this was what she had to do. So she did it. Just like she always did.

She yanked open the top drawer.

Inside was a mess of trinkets—sticky notes, Sharpie markers, a small wooden box shaped like a crescent moon, tufts of unused yarn and thread, sparkly paper clips scattered through it all like snowflakes. She dug through the drawer. When she had finally pushed aside enough of the chaos to get to the back, she found what she was looking for: a small circular tin.

There was a box she'd never seen before next to it.

Delilah set the tin on the desk, followed by the box. It was small and square, and there was still clear tape sealing it around the edges. She immediately recognized the black rose stamped onto the lid. It was from Rose and Rain, the eclectic little shop in town that her mother frequented.

She slid her nail through the tape and popped off the lid. Three pristine tubes of acrylic paints stared up at her from their tissue paper nest inside.

She knew what these were for.

Slowly, Delilah turned to face the table near the door. Her mother's last art project sat there, untouched and dust-laden.

Indigo had been working on it all summer, but she wouldn't tell Delilah what it was supposed to be. Even now, Delilah had no idea. It still looked like a series of some sort of papier mâché, like her mother had started molding human busts from clay and paper clippings and glue, but she got bored halfway through.

But Delilah remembered. She remembered the last words her mother had told her before she headed into town that day.

I'm going up to the store to get some paint, Indigo had said, planting a kiss on Delilah's head as she set her half-empty coffee mug in the kitchen sink. *I want to get started on those paper busts.*

But they're not even done, are they? Delilah had said.

Indigo had laughed, a wind chime sort of sound that was both soothing and jarring. *Oh, love. Something doesn't have to look the way you think it should for it to be finished.*

Delilah stared at the misshapen heads, slivers of dried paper still dangling from their chins, necks, ears. They still looked unfinished, unfocused, and that made her sad.

But the paints . . .

She looked at them again. Their perfectly white caps were still firmly in place, no divots in the tubes where her mom had applied pressure to release the paint. These paints were brand-new. Her mother had planned to be around at least long enough to finish painting these sculptures.

Delilah sighed. She wanted it to be true so badly. She wanted to believe her mother hadn't just up and left her here, alone, to take care of the house and the girls and everything she no longer wanted to deal with. She had tried, over and over again, to push down the feeling of being left behind, telling herself it was just an aftershock of grief, but it always bobbed to the surface like an apple in a barrel. Delilah rubbed her neck, staring at the paints. But really, how long had they been sitting here, waiting for Indigo to apply her brushes to them?

Delilah grabbed the lid and began to place it back on the box. As she did, a slip of paper fluttered out and fell to the floor.

She scooped it up. It looked like a receipt from Rose and Rain, the ink now faded. She held it carefully between her fingers and tilted it toward the last dregs of sunlight streaking through the window.

There was a date at the top. It was the same day as the disappearance.

Delilah's pulse picked up as she scanned the rest of the receipt.

Paints purchased at 3:55 PM. According to the police, her mom had already disappeared by then.

And then, at the bottom, a note scrawled in messy handwriting.

A phone number, and a message.

Call me, it said.

CHAPTER SIX

There was a thunderstorm raging in Bo's head as the early morning light streaked through her room.

She'd spent all night trying to calm the aching at her forehead as she tossed and turned on her cot, thinking about the impending memorial. She'd even swiped a streak of Indigo's healing balm between her eyebrows, praying that whatever supposed magic was in it would help.

It hadn't. Bo had reached for her mother's old pain meds instead.

And now as morning dew clung to the window, Bo's head felt like an anchor pinning her to the murky depths of her bed. She pinched the bridge of her nose.

A door on the other side of the hallway creaked open and a parade of footsteps marched down the stairs. The light pattering of Delilah's, followed by the clomping of Bennett's.

Ugh, Bennett was still here.

Bo rolled to her side. Of course he was. Of all days, he had to be here on *this one*. There was the clinking of plates and the murmur of voices as they moved around the kitchen beneath her. Delilah laughed.

Pain zipped through Bo. She couldn't imagine what a real, genuine laugh felt like anymore. She could barely remember the shape her lips used to make, the sound that used to float out of her mouth like a chime.

And maybe that was for the best, really. The less Bo laughed, the less she had to hear how much she sounded like her mom.

That was what everyone in Bishop used to say from the very first giggle that left Bo's throat as a toddler. Cori Wagner's laugh paralleled her daughter's, so much so that you couldn't tell which was which if you weren't looking straight at them.

But when you were looking, it became instantly apparent. While Cori had hair the color of cattails, Bo's was butter melting in the sun. She hadn't inherited her mother's cobalt eyes, either. Bo's were brown, the same color as the dust that coated every surface in Bishop.

The only things they had in common were their traditionally masculine names (*That's the most ridiculous rule,* Cori had said when people had told her Bo was a boy's name) and the sound of their laughter.

Her mother had still been laughing the day before she'd gone missing.

It had been a Friday, and Bo had left her mother at her desk. She could hear Cori laughing into her headset as Bo double-knotted her running shoes in the hallway outside the office. *Honestly, Janet,* she'd said. *How do you even explain what the cloud is to someone who still has a flip phone, for goodness' sake?*

Bo fiddled with her laces a bit longer as she listened to the lilt of her mother's voice. The rest of the house was empty. Ava had been up at the high school for most of the day, getting her classroom ready for the new school year, and Indigo had blown through the house like a storm, saying something about picking up fresh paints downtown. Delilah and Jude had followed shortly after to shop for school supplies, two weeks early, which was extremely on brand for them both. And Bo hadn't seen Whitney all day.

It was just her and her mother and the clunky air conditioner groaning under the summer sky. She listened to it whir, blurring the edges of Cori's phone call.

It was almost two o'clock. Her mother would be off work soon for the weekend. Bo really should stay a bit longer. Cori had been asking her to help in the garden all week, to yank up weeds and harvest the cucumbers that had grown as long as Bo's arm.

But as the minutes ticked on, and Bo had tied and retied her shoelaces more times than she could count, she finally stood. *I'll help her tomorrow,* she'd thought.

"Mom, I'm going for a run!" Bo had called.

"Bye! Be safe!" her mom had called back before returning to her headset. The last sound Bo had heard was her mother's laughter as it trailed her out the front door.

Be safe.

Like there was anything to be afraid of in a place like Bishop. It was a speck on a Midwest map, a dust-laden town trapped by windstorms and sunflowers. Women went missing sometimes, sure, but if she had to guess, Bo figured they'd packed up and left for something better before someone could hold them back.

Still.

There was this feeling that Bo had never been able to shake since she was little. It settled into her like fog over the fields whenever she stepped out of the house. Like someone was watching.

But it was more than that. It had *become* more than that.

Bo had started down the gravel driveway, her shoes kicking up pebbles behind her.

Now it felt like someone was *plotting.*

She had clung to her favorite path that looped around the town's perimeter. It was a withered thing, mostly overgrown and covered in patches of weeds, but it was abandoned, and it was the only place where her heartbeat fell into a slow and steady drumbeat and the thoughts constantly swirling in her head dulled to a low roar. When her feet drummed the earth, she could almost forget the way the sunflowers pushed up against the path, how they seemed to bob in time with her own personal rhythm.

Almost.

But as she ran past the sunflowers on that day, Bo still couldn't shake that feeling of watching. Of plotting. It reverberated through her bones. She swore she felt their heads dip toward her as she passed, their spindly leaves reaching, whispering against her sweaty skin.

Bo jerked off the path.

Her breath quickened as she picked up the pace through the neighborhood. Every place worth going to in Bishop was propped up along Main Street—the grocery store, the post office, the single "fashion boutique"—and the rest of the town was composed of snakelike side streets that slithered around the perimeter, each adorned with its own pocket of houses. These were painted in faded reds and sunburnt oranges, and despite the graveyard of toys in the yards, no one seemed to stir.

She cut across the street and through Bishop High's parking lot, weaving through the few cars left baking in the late afternoon sun.

"Wagner!"

Bo stuttered to a stop. She squinted across the lot.

Three silhouettes stood beside a cherry red truck. They approached slowly.

Evan Gordon stood to the left, the tallest of the three, his dark hair slick with sweat and pushed back into a ponytail. He quickly opened the truck door and tossed his backpack inside, reminding Bo that she should pick up her textbooks this week, too. The other two looked almost identical—like Whitney and Jude—only they weren't twins. These boys were two years apart.

Caleb and Bennett Harding.

It was only now that Bo knew they weren't really coming closer to have a friendly conversation.

They had been watching. Plotting.

The rest was a blur. The way they'd smelled like summer heat, how Bennett's voice had sounded like it was underwater, how Caleb's teeth had glinted in the sun when he laughed at some terrible joke Evan made. The way the sunflower petals had felt like sandpaper against her skin as she ran back home. And the words Evan had hurled at her, planting roots that had spread like ivy over the years.

You'll never leave here.

By the time she had flung open the front door, her mom was gone. All their moms were gone. And they weren't coming back.

And what Evan had said to her had come true. Bo had never left Bishop.

There was a knock at her door, making her jump. "We've gotta get going soon," a voice said from the other side. *Jude.*

"I'm up. Be down in a sec." Bo listened as Jude's footsteps faded. She laid back down in bed and pressed her hands to her eyes, trying to force the truck and the heat and the three dark silhouettes from her mind.

She sat up. A sharp pain ricocheted through her head. That was nothing compared to her knee. She winced as she limped around a pile of dirty laundry and headed to the dresser in the corner. Bo fumbled through the drawers, searching for something acceptable to wear to her own mother's memorial.

It wasn't that Bo had actually wanted a full-blown memorial. It was Caleb and Bennett's uncle, William Harding, who'd mentioned it after Bo had heard rumors about paving over the clearing.

The committee's been talking, and there really is no good use for that space, he'd said to Bo outside of town hall. *We could easily move the weather vane and pave over the spot.*

It had been one of Bishop's rare days when the wind was still and subdued, and the first breath of summer hung heavy in the air. Bo had heard rumors flying around the hallways about how there were plans in motion to pave over the clearing. Everyone was convinced Mr. Harding, who doubled as a history teacher and Bishop's part-time mayor, had heard about all the parties and hookups that happened in that gravelly cove and wanted to put an end to it. There was low-level panic coursing through the student body.

But not Bo. She couldn't care less about the parties. She only cared about her mother.

So on the last day of school in late May, Bo had run straight from the front steps of Bishop High to the town hall. She was still catching her breath when Mr. Harding had walked out the door, a file tucked under his arm.

Then let's build something there instead of paving over it. Maybe statues or something? Finally hold a real memorial for my mom? she'd added quickly. Anything to stall. Anything so she could preserve the space.

She had never really believed what the cops had told her, even though Delilah insisted they knew more than she did. Maybe that was true on some level. Maybe Sheriff Ableman and the two lonely officers under him had experience in searching for missing women. But Bo was an expert in *her mother.*

It was late Saturday morning when the girls realized they hadn't seen any of their mothers since the previous day. Their gray sedan was back in the driveway, but Ava was nowhere in the house. Indigo's studio was a mess—which was more than normal for her—but she'd left behind a sunflower on the bathroom sink. And Cori had left behind nothing at all.

In the frenzied days that followed, the cops concluded that their mothers had disappeared sometime Friday afternoon. That they most likely left the house on their own, at first, as there were no signs of struggle. And then, most likely, someone had taken them, dragging them into the graveyard of sunflowers and maybe even beyond. But the only evidence they found was an eyewitness account from an anonymous source that swore they saw all three women in the clearing around one in the afternoon, and some footprints left behind in the dust.

None of it made sense to Bo. Her mother hated the clearing. She always told Bo that it was the place where "used condoms and future plans went to die." If she was there, in the middle of the day with Ava and Indigo, something wasn't right. Bo knew it in her bones.

So when Mr. Harding had mentioned paving over the clearing where her mother had last been seen, something in her churned. She needed to preserve the space. To really look at the clearing again, look for anything that could possibly point to where her mom had gone.

She had to be there one last time before she could finally let it go.

Everything in Bo had screamed *no* as soon as she had suggested the idea of a memorial to Mr. Harding.

No, she wouldn't help plan it.

No, she wouldn't relive that horribly shitty day over again.

No. No.

Nope.

But a deeper, more urgent part of her knew this was her very last chance to find out what had really happened to her mother.

Bo yanked a forest green dress from the bottom drawer. Did it matter that it wasn't black? She shuffled over to the mirror propped against the desk and smoothed out the fabric.

No, it doesn't matter, Bo decided, and she slipped it over her head.

Today Bo would be the one watching, plotting. She'd watch as the committee wheeled out some rickety statues on rusted dollies. Where they placed them. She'd search the crowd, watch their faces, witness the beads of sweat collecting at the backs of their necks.

If anyone knew something about what had happened that night, she was going to find out.

"Bo, we're leaving!" Delilah called. The front door creaked. "We'll meet you outside."

"Okay, coming!" She flung open the door and rushed into the bathroom. Tied her hair into a bun as she shoved her toothbrush in her mouth. Two quick swipes of red lipstick—one, two—and she was out the door.

By the time Bo reached the front porch, the rest of the group had started down the path heading into town. Whitney's and Jude's arms were tangled up in each other as they dodged the ash tree at the end of the driveway. Delilah's and Bennett's fingers swung so close together that they might as well just hold hands, but they didn't. Like there was some kind of invisible force field between them that no one else could see. Bo lifted an eyebrow. She didn't know what *that* was all about, but in her opinion, the less physical contact anyone had with a Harding, the better.

As if on cue, the wind picked up as they approached the memorial site. Bo pushed the loose hairs back from her face and scanned the scene. Rows of plastic folding chairs sprawled out in front of them, mostly empty except for a few stragglers who had just arrived, with a fresh pallet of wood smack in the center of the clearing. On top of it sat three hulking statues wrapped in burlap bags.

"Is it supposed to storm?" Jude asked nervously as they continued walking, tucking her hair behind her ears. She glanced up at the sky.

"When doesn't it storm?" Delilah sighed.

It was a good question. Bo could vaguely remember clearer skies and tepid breezes when she was younger. More sunshine on her skin, more freckles on her shoulders. She wasn't sure when the storms had started to lash at Bishop with increasing ferocity. All she knew was they could barely go a day without having to board up the windows again.

One by one, Delilah and Bennett, then Whitney and Jude walked down the center aisle to the empty row of chairs in the very front. Bo started to follow when two shadows stepped in front of her.

"Hey, Wagner."

Evan Gordon and Caleb Harding stood in the aisle, blocking her path to her seat.

If Delilah thought Bo's knee looked messed up, she should have seen Evan's face. There was a deep cut beneath his right eye, where Bo's fist had made contact. The skin around it was so puffy that his eye was swollen shut, patches of purple and blue blooming around it.

And Bo didn't feel bad about it at all.

She'd left town hall after talking with Mr. Harding about the final setup plans. Caleb and Evan had been standing outside in the sun, leaning up against the brick wall, probably waiting for Caleb's uncle. Caleb had been looking at his phone, but Evan noticed Bo right away.

"Wagner," he'd said.

Bo hadn't answered. She kept walking. She wasn't going to do this. Not today. Not ever again.

"WAGNER."

Bo stopped. She turned slowly. "We aren't on speaking terms."

Caleb had glanced up from his phone. Evan slinked toward her, a cocky grin spreading across his lips as he moved in closer. "We are if I say we are."

Bo let out a sharp laugh. "Oh, did the Hardings allow you to speak for yourself, huh? Or did they just tell you what to say to me since you're just their pathetic little follower? You can tell them I said to shut to the hell up." She spun around to leave.

"You wanted it."

Bo froze. She swallowed the sick feeling climbing up her throat.

"Your mom didn't want you, so you found someone who'd deal with your shit." His eyes blazed with fury. "I heard you're a good time, though, Wagner."

Evan touched her face.

Bo slammed her fist into his.

They'd scuffled right there on the sidewalk in front of the town hall, Bo swinging at any part of Evan that was available, until he threw her off him. People weaved around them as if they were just puddles on the sidewalk, careful to avoid getting between them. It was true that Evan and Bo had been doing this sort of thing since they were kids, and people were used to it, but it still made her stomach drop every time they passed by. Like no one cared what happened to her. Bo's knee hit the ground first, tearing open her jeans and staining them with blood.

"That's *enough*! Stop!" Caleb had rushed toward her. He reached his hand out. "You okay?" There had been a gentleness in his voice that definitely hadn't been there the night in the cellar. And now, at the memorial, Bo saw him walking toward her, inserting himself into yet another argument with Evan. He'd say the same words, with that same fake gentleness, she just knew it.

It made Bo want to rage.

You okay?

No. She was not okay.

"What do you want?" Bo snapped. She was talking to Evan, but looking at Caleb as he approached.

Evan leaned toward her. "When this is over," he whispered, "we're going to have another 'talk.'"

Bo huffed. "Is that a threat or a promise?"

Whitney spun around from the front of the aisle. "Can't you just drop it for a single day, you asshole?" Her hands balled into fists at her sides.

"Okay, just stop." Caleb took a step forward, but when he saw the look on Bo's face, he thought better of it. "Just let it rest, Evan."

Caleb lifted his eyes to hers. There was something else in his expression, something she hadn't seen before. Not in the parking lot or at the bonfire and definitely not in the storm cellar.

Fear.

Like maybe Caleb could finally see all the raw and shattered parts of Bo, all the unfinished pieces that stuck out at jagged angles. And it scared him.

Good, she thought, brushing by him and trudging toward her seat to join the others.

A fierce wind ripped through the clearing as she scooted in next to Whitney. It coated her entire body with a damp chill, even though heat still radiated through her from her exchange with Evan and Caleb.

Tinny organ music began to play, the notes quickly swallowed up by the wind. Beside her, Whitney threaded her fingers through hers. Bo turned to look over her shoulder, carefully loosening her fingers from Whitney's just a bit as she did. Just so she could breathe. The seats were mostly full now, and the low hum of shifting bodies and polite conversation had softened.

Together the four of them stood, hands entwined. So much had happened in the last two years. They had all lost so much.

But no one had lost all that Bo had.

No one wanted to be found as much as she did.

CHAPTER SEVEN

W hitney could barely hold on to Bo's hand.

Her sweaty fingers entwined with hers, and even now, even during one of the worst days of their lives, Whitney knew Bo would rather not be touched.

She hadn't always been like that.

In the Before, Bo had practically lived in the sliver of space between Whitney and Jude. She called herself their "honorary triplet" and would squeeze between them on the lopsided sofa, even though she constantly complained she was too hot.

Whitney had thought Bo's knee-jerk reaction to being touched had to do with her grief—like maybe sympathy hugs felt like sharp edges against her skin. But as time dragged on, and Bo's aversion only got worse, she had started to wonder about That Night when everything went wrong.

The organ music stopped. Bo dropped her hand.

Plastic chairs squeaked as people sank into them. From behind the statue, Mr. Harding appeared, carrying a couple of papers as he walked toward a makeshift podium, his salt-and-pepper hair worked into a tangle by the wind. Behind him, at the edge of the clearing, the weather vane slowly circled.

"Hey everyone," he said warmly, tapping the mic. He gave the crowd his sheepish teacher grin. "Glad to see all you here despite the weather."

There were a few chuckles from the crowd. Whitney rolled her eyes. Mr. Harding could say he kicked a puppy and the rest of Bishop would smile and nod. He was their golden boy, their homecoming king of the nineties, their beloved history teacher whose soft eyes crinkled in the corners when he smiled.

Everyone had loved him. Especially her mother.

But looking at Mr. Harding now, with his faded tie and hair that stuck up at odd angles—even when it wasn't windy—Whitney couldn't piece together the image that had been burned into her brain for the past two years.

Her mom kissing Mr. Harding in the staff parking lot the day before she disappeared.

"We're here today to remember that treacherous August night, on this day two years ago, when three women of this town disappeared: Cori Wagner, Indigo Cortez, and Ava Montgomery."

At the sound of her mother's name, Whitney's insides flip-flopped. The way he said it, with that lilting undertone reserved for tragedies, made Whitney want to crawl out of her own skin. She glanced over at Jude, who was staring at her fingernails.

Whitney didn't want pity.

She just wanted her mother.

"While we may never know what truly happened that night, it's safe to say that the lost women of Bishop are gone for good." Mr. Harding cleared his throat. "Which is why it's time to commemorate them with a permanent memorial."

Whitney's heart started to pound as a couple people off to the sides began to move. This was it. This was where they pulled the burlap cover from whatever mess they'd made of her mother's image. Because no matter what they did, there was no way the committee could possibly capture all the dimensions of Ava Montgomery in something as lifeless as stone.

Please don't let it be books. Please please please.

Ava had been Bishop High's favorite language arts teacher. And, of course, she loved books, and not only the ones written by old white men. She read books about Black girls with magic and graphic novels about mermaids, and when Whitney had started to realize that maybe she *only* liked girls, her mother had gently set a book about lesbians who hunted sorcerers into her lap.

But her mother was so much more than just her books.

Ava Montgomery was the kind of person who woke up early to feed the single fat squirrel that hauled itself onto the porch, even though it clearly didn't need any more food, let alone the spoonfuls of peanut butter Ava would leave in the frostbitten morning. She was the kind of mom who woke Whitney and Jude by stroking their hair instead of yanking them out from under their covers, no matter how late they were. She liked citrus tea with a big glob of honey and watching Indigo's Pilates videos while sitting on the couch, eating popcorn so buttery that it literally glistened.

She knew how Whitney felt about her first official girlfriend before *Whitney* knew how she felt, and the only thing she said about it was "Be sure to bring her by for dinner," before planting a plum-colored kiss on her forehead.

As a burlap cover wafted to the ground, a sharp wind cut through the aisles. Whitney tried to smooth her curls, but she knew it was pretty much a lost cause. Wind was like water here—it was just a necessary part of living in this place.

The weather vane picked up speed. Whitney's heartbeat picked up speed. *Eleanor.*

She strained to listen, but the only sound she could make out was the lashing of the wind.

One of the men from the event committee jogged in front of the statues, chasing the windblown burlap that looked more like a tumbleweed than a sack. Murmurs rose up from the crowd behind them as a particularly urgent gust of wind cut through the clearing. Whitney glanced at Jude. Both of Jude's palms covered her eyes as she stood beside Whitney. She couldn't even bear to look.

But Whitney could.

She stood on her tiptoes as the last covering blew off the third statue and floated away. There they were. The statues of the lost women of Bishop.

There she was, the stone version of Ava Montgomery, standing on top of that same plywood pallet. Dead eyes. No smile.

And she was holding a book.

Jude groaned, peering between her fingers. "When they said they wanted to do a 'real' memorial, I didn't think they'd make it look so ridiculous," she mumbled.

Whitney sighed. "That doesn't even look like my mom."

"Not at all," Bo whispered.

"Mine, either," Delilah said softly. Whitney glanced over at her. Unlike the rest of them, Delilah actually had tears in her eyes as she surveyed the mess they had made of her mother. Indigo's long, curly hair that she always wore loose in real life was pulled back into a severe bun in her statue version. And of course—*of course*—she held a paintbrush.

Delilah winced and started to dig through her purse. She pulled out a small blue bottle of antacids and popped a chalky tablet into her mouth. "This is just . . ." she started, chewing furiously. But she didn't finish the sentence.

The last statue, the one of Bo's mother, was the worst of all. Cori Wagner stood between Ava and Indigo, her arms outstretched toward the rows of seats. She didn't hold a book or a paintbrush in her hands, and honestly, that would have been better than nothing, even though those objects were unimaginative as hell. Instead, her statue was the only one smiling as she reached toward the crowd for an awkward stone hug.

There were no violets or ripe summer tomatoes in Cori's arms, no baskets of the rainbow-colored yarn she used to knit into lumpy scarves. There was nothing in her fingertips at all.

And yet, claps erupted from behind them.

Mr. Harding's face broke into an easy smile. "Thank you, yeah. They did a nice job. So on the left here we have Indigo Cortez, our town's resident artist of sorts. And on the right, there's Ava Montgomery, who we all know loved her stories." With that, a soft echo of laughter rose up from the crowd. Whitney curled her fingers into her palm until she broke the skin.

Another gust of wind streaked through, whipping Mr. Harding's hair into a messy soufflé on top of his head. Around the clearing, hundreds of sunflowers shivered in unison. "Whoa, wind's picking up again," he said, patting it down. He turned back to the statues. "And here in the middle we have Cori Wagner, always with a smile on her face, always willing to offer a neighbor a helping hand. Even her job was helping people with their computers! Cori was the epitome of kindness, the helper of our great community."

Beside her, Whitney could almost hear the sound of Bo's muscles clenching. She reached down to grab her hand, but Bo's fingers were white-knuckled around one another.

The wind made a whistling sound as it swept through the nooks and crannies among the three stone women. The mic in front of William crackled. He cupped his hands around it to protect it from the wind. "Does anyone want to come up and say a few words so we can close this out before a storm rolls in?"

Another echo, this time whispers instead of laughter. Whitney closed her eyes. Someone would go up there, right? Say a few words? It wasn't like their mothers were hated—after all, hadn't Mr. Harding obnoxiously called Cori "the helper"? But they were loners, Whitney knew. The three women had lived together at the edge of town with their vegetable garden and raucous paintings and piles of books stacked so high that they almost reached the ceiling. They were polite and friendly enough, but they had one another, and that was clearly all that mattered.

Whitney opened her eyes. Mr. Harding had disappeared off to the side.

The podium was empty.

This whole thing was pointless. Whitney stared at the statues, chiseled and erected two years too late. She had long come to the conclusion that her mother, wherever she was, was never coming back. That she would never have the chance to bring her girlfriend home for dinner to meet Ava.

But someone else had gone missing only months ago. Where was *her* memorial, the commotion over another woman lost too soon? Whitney's eyes pricked with tears. She just couldn't understand why Eleanor had dropped from Bishop's memory like dead autumn leaves, while the town went ahead and erected blank-eyed statues for their mothers years later.

Whitney tapped Bo on the shoulder and motioned for her to move. She lifted an eyebrow before stepping out of the way.

By the time Whitney had reached the podium, it was barely standing. The whole thing creaked and groaned as the wind lashed at it. She cupped her hands around the mic like Mr. Harding had and started to speak.

"My mom was a beautiful person and the best mom," Whitney said. She cleared her throat. "And I think it's great that you all felt like she needed a statue to honor her, but I'm not up here to talk about her. I want to talk about Eleanor Craft."

Whitney! Delilah mouthed from the front row, only the wind had picked up so aggressively that Whitney couldn't tell if she'd just made the shape of her name or if she'd actually called it out loud.

Whitney shook her head. *Not today, Delilah. Not just going to be calm and quiet.* She pressed her lips close to the mic. "What about Eleanor Craft? She was only eighteen when she disappeared, and it happened only six months ago. No one gave *her* a memorial. Is it because you don't think she was important? Is it because she wasn't 'a helper'? Is it—"

The wind pummeled her so hard that it left her breathless.

Her fingers shook as she squeezed the mic. "Eleanor deserves to be remembered, too! You can't just forget about her and—"

"WHITNEY!" Delilah yelled. This time Whitney heard her.

"No!" she yelled back. "Let me do—"

There was a massive groan behind her. Before Whitney could turn around, she felt a shock of pain in her shoulder that made her vision sear white.

And then everything went dark.

CHAPTER EIGHT

"Move!" Jude yelled as she pushed through the knot of people that had started to crowd around her sister. Her heartbeat roared in her chest.

She slipped between two older men who had rushed forward as soon as the statues had started to wobble. Jude hadn't even noticed it at first. She had been too busy looking at her hands clasped together so tightly that her skin had turned white.

She couldn't bear to watch Whitney take the podium. It seemed like every time her twin decided to stand up and say something, the opposite happened within Jude. Her throat closed up and her voice raked against her tonsils. Like Whitney sucked up all of the courage in their shared DNA, leaving Jude shaky and dry. It had happened when Whitney had told their eighth-grade teacher that "feminist" was her second-favorite *F* word, and when she'd told their ballet teacher that pliés weren't doing it for her, and now, as she talked about their mother and Eleanor Craft.

Eleanor Craft.

It was like the winds had heard Whitney. The second Eleanor's name left her lips, the wind cranked up another notch. Another *ten* notches. It rattled the tin awning on the little shop that Delilah's mom used to frequent. It slapped so hard at Jude's skin that it actually made her ache, and the whisper of words she couldn't understand pressed in around her.

And then there was the crack of stone separating from stone.

That was when Jude had looked up.

Just in time to see Cori Wagner's stone likeness fall forward, her open right hand jamming its fingers straight into her sister's neck.

"Move, please!" Jude mumbled again as she wriggled between a mother and her young daughter. The little girl stared up at her, her lips stained purple from the grape sucker in her tiny fist.

Whitney lay on her side, her hair splayed around her head like a dark halo. Her eyes were pinched shut, but even from here, Jude could tell she was conscious.

Barely.

Jude dropped to her knees, careful to avoid the slivers of stone that had broken off from the statue. Her heart was beating so fast that she could barely breathe. "Whitney?" she whispered.

Delilah skidded into the tight space beside her. She swung her purse so it settled in her lap and began pawing through it. "Okay, okay, okay," she said, trying to conceal the fear in her voice. "It's gotta be in here."

"It's not a goddamn show, get out of the way!" The crowd that had started to gather rippled as Bo emerged on the other side. She picked up a chunk of her mother's stone arm that was next to Whitney's head and heaved it into the grass without looking twice.

Bo sank gingerly to her knees and scanned Whitney. She reached toward her, brushing a tangled curl from Whitney's face.

Her neck was already starting to swell. The soft curve where her collarbone met her shoulder was concave, and a bruise the size and color of a plum had started to form in the spot where there should have been bone.

"Here it is," Delilah said shakily. She whipped out a roll of gauze bandages and started to pull at the mesh.

Bo slapped the gauze out of her hand. It bounced in the gravel and rolled away. "Are you serious right now? Does this look like a gauze-level injury?"

"Is she okay?" someone yelled from the crowd. "Should we call an ambulance?"

"Mmmmph." Whitney groaned.

Jude's heartbeat hitched. "Don't move," Jude whispered into her ear. "We're going to get you some help."

"Incoming!"

Jude's spine stiffened.

"Coming through." Bennett dropped beside Jude and everything inside her stilled.

But he didn't even look in her direction.

"What do you think, Lilah? Should we take her to the hospital?" He looked up at Delilah from under his lashes, his calloused thumb pressed to Whitney's wrist. "Her pulse is up and down."

Delilah's lip quivered. She pressed the heels of her palms into her eyes. "I don't know. I don't know what to do."

And then Bennett turned to her. He looked at *Jude* from under those matchstick lashes, pink blotches blooming on his neck, his lips sunburnt from the summer sun. She watched the soft spot just under his chin as he swallowed, remembering what it felt like to kiss it.

Jude swallowed. She looked down at her twin.

In the three seconds Jude had been distracted, Whitney's entire shoulder had blown up to the size of a grapefruit. She wasn't moving anymore.

"We have to take her in," Jude whispered.

Bennett nodded. He turned around and shouted, "Caleb, get the car!"

The crowd broke apart like a biscuit melting in gravy. When

Jude stood up and brushed off her knees, she glanced around. Delilah still hovered over Whitney, knuckles pressed against her lips, face chalky white. Bo was nowhere to be found. Jude gritted her teeth. *Where is she?*

A flurry of people pushed past her as the rumble of a truck engine ignited. Jude stumbled. The heel of her shoe caught on the plywood pallet and she fell back.

When she hit the gravel, what was left of the plywood groaned until it snapped. A lightning bolt streak cut through the center where Indigo's statue had toppled sideways and pierced it with her stone paintbrush. Jude's fall had been the last push; the entire base cracked in half, revealing parched soil beneath it.

Something glittered in the sunlight beneath the plywood.

"Jude! Are you okay?" Delilah yelled.

"I'm fine!" She sat up, brushing dust from her dress. Behind her, Jude heard the snap of gravel under car tires. People were shouting directions, but the tail end of their sentences kept getting swallowed up by the wind.

Take her—

Turn the wheel to the—

Move over to the—

Jude turned back to the tiny glittering thing. She pulled back a shard of wood and dug her fingers deep into the soil. Something hard scraped her skin.

She grabbed it, setting it into her palm and brushing off the dirt. A charm.

Jude looked closer. It was a tarnished silver acorn with a clasp, like something that belonged on a bracelet. By the dull sheen to it, it looked like it had been marinating in the soil beneath these statues for a long while.

There was something on the clasp.

Jude held the acorn charm so close to her face that she could smell the metal and dirt.

And the blood.

There was a dark crimson-brown stain that ran down the clasp and pooled on the top of the acorn. Jude rubbed her thumb over it. She'd seen something like this before. Not the blood, but the charms. Tiny silver things sparkling in the light streaming from the front window.

Dangling from Whitney's wrist.

This charm belonged on her sister's bracelet.

So what was it doing here?

"Okay, you open the door," Bennet called, jolting her back into the present. A door slammed as Caleb hopped out of the front seat and swung around to the back. The crowd parted as Bennett slowly lifted Whitney and carried her toward the open back door.

Jude watched as the boys worked from both sides of the truck to position Whitney on the seat. One door slammed shut. Then the other. Caleb hopped back into the driver's seat.

Bennett spun around, his palm lying flat on the roof. "You coming?"

He was looking at Jude.

Delilah stepped forward. "I can come with—"

"No, don't worry about it, Lilah. It should probably be Jude," Bennett said, not taking his eyes off her. "She should be with her sister."

Delilah's face crumpled. "Right," she said, clearing her throat.

Jude's heart pounded. She wasn't sure if it was from the bloody charm or the way Bennett was looking at her, the hum of her name on his sunburnt lips.

Jude.

She curled her fingers around the charm and tucked it into her pocket.

And then she headed toward the car.

CHAPTER NINE

Delilah tried to stop looking at her phone, but she couldn't help picking it up from the kitchen table every three seconds. Still, it never rang.

Bennett had left with Jude hours ago, and she hadn't heard from either of them. That wasn't like Jude.

And it definitely wasn't like Bennett.

Ever since that night at the bonfire, Bennett had been attached to Delilah like a burr on a sweater. And honestly, she didn't mind. Bennett was soft on the inside with an exterior that was easy to break open with a little effort. To Delilah, it was barely any work at all. She'd just taken the plastic cup from Bennett and that was it. Almost like that cup had the same weight as a promise.

They'd been together ever since, and Bennett had never once forgotten to call or show up. But still, she wondered.

At first, Delilah could thread her fingers through his for long enough to pull him close, heartbeat to heartbeat. She could work through the pain of kisses planted all over her like little snowflakes. But as time wore on, the pain had only grown. She knew the rumors about Bennett. She knew he had gotten around before they found each other.

And now Bennett's kisses felt like a storm.

She paced the living room, her bare feet padding over the hardwood. *Where are they?* she thought. *They should be back by now.*

She dialed again.

Bennett's phone went straight to voicemail.

"Ugh!" Delilah tossed the phone onto the armchair by the window. "Why won't he just answer?"

"Because he's *busy*," Bo said. She sat on the sofa, legs dangling over the edge. When Delilah shot her a look, she closed her eyes and pinched the bridge of her nose. "Not everyone's available to be at your beck and call twenty-four seven."

Heat crawled up Delilah's neck. It was annoying enough that Bo had just disappeared when Whitney got hurt, but it was even worse that she had popped back up as soon as Caleb and Bennett took off for the hospital. And now she was being extra cagey. "I don't expect him to be at my beck and call . . ."

Bo let out a mean little laugh. "Sure, Delilah." She tipped her head back onto the armrest, eyes still closed.

Was it so much to ask to hold people accountable? To make sure they were safe?

Her mother had always done that, at least. Delilah specifically remembered her mother with a phone pressed to one ear, her fingertips stained with rainbow paint. Calling Ava. Calling Cori. Checking on her friends. Asking them what she should pick up for dinner (because Indigo was a lot of things, but a good cook wasn't one of them).

And the night she'd disappeared, well after the cops said she must have already been gone, she'd called Delilah, too.

A cacophony of rings that went to voicemail because Delilah had been too busy following Bennett into his uncle's cellar, hypnotized by the sway of his gait. She'd been transfixed ever since.

But last night something strange had happened.

As Delilah lay curled up beside Bennett in her bed, he'd shifted ever so slightly so the very tip of his nose brushed her forehead.

Her whole body snapped on like a streetlight.

The fleeting bubbles and zaps were replaced by something much, much darker.

It felt like a shadow and stung like a needle.

Delilah had jerked away, but Bennett hadn't woken. He'd just mumbled something in his sleep about toothpaste and rolled onto his side.

But the ache stayed.

It had been there, nestled between Delilah's ribs all day. No matter how many antacids she chewed, or which bra she wore, she couldn't escape it. And it was starting to scare her.

She just needed to see Bennett again and everything would be okay. The ache would dull, the tolerable little love zaps would return. They would figure this out—together.

"I'm going upstairs," Bo said, rolling off the sofa.

"Wait."

Bo looked at her.

Delilah winced. She wasn't exactly sure why she said it. All she knew was she didn't want to be left alone in this empty room, with this relentless ache. And Bo was the only one here.

"Yeah?" she said slowly.

"I just . . . what do you think they're going to do about the statues now?"

Bo sighed heavily and sank back onto the sofa. "Honestly? I hope they just toss the stones into the sunflower fields and forget it ever happened."

"But how could you let them do that?" Delilah said softly. "You wanted this. You went to the committee."

"Only when I heard they were planning on doing something!" Bo pulled a loose string hanging off her dress. "I just . . . I thought if I got close to the planning I'd hear something, or see something, and I don't know. I just want to know what really happened."

It was a conversation Delilah and Bo had had a million times over the past two years. Bo had always insisted that something strange had happened to their mothers, that the evidence the cops had presented didn't add up. There had to be a coverup.

Yes, they'd left their purses and IDs back at the house, and yes, even the old gray sedan they all shared was still in the driveway. But what the cops had told them hadn't made sense either—at least that was what Bo had insisted. That there was no way someone had just taken all three of them. Dragged them into the ocean of sunflowers and left them to drown in the soil.

It was a theory all four of them had rejected. Even though the evidence pointed to a hasty departure, there was still the fact that Ava had a black belt in Taekwondo and Indigo always carried a pocketknife.

They all knew that blood would have been spilled.

There had been a second theory.

The cops told them if their mothers hadn't been taken, then it was just as likely that they'd left on their own.

Bo had outright rejected it. "My mom would *never*," she'd told the cop, who was at least a foot taller than her. "She'd never just leave me."

But Delilah wasn't so sure about her own mother.

Indigo loved her friends and daughter with a fierceness that was sometimes thrilling, but she also hated it here. She felt trapped within Bishop's sunflower walls, and by the cornfields on the other side of those, and by the tepid townspeople who really only came together for funerals. Her mother was an artist, a visionary, and she insisted that real art was inspired by living. A place like Bishop was only filling the cracks inside her with dust.

If Delilah could have added something to her mother's statue, it would have been wings instead of a paintbrush.

She'd never told the other girls that. When Whitney, Jude, and Bo had written off the runaway theory as nonsense, she'd just nodded her head in agreement. They were all so certain that their mothers couldn't possibly leave them. Delilah had to trust that her mother wouldn't want to, either. She couldn't—no, she *wouldn't*—let her mind go to that place for too long. There were people relying on her, and she couldn't let a tidal wave of grief wash her away.

The conversation had ended there for everyone except Bo. She had never been able to drop it, while Delilah wanted nothing more. If they could all just let it go, move on with their lives without ever knowing for sure what had happened that night, then Delilah wouldn't have to look so hard at the idea that maybe her mother had left on her own.

But then there were the paints.

Why would her mother buy a new set of acrylics, untouched and unopened, the same day she disappeared? Indigo protected her supplies like a magpie hoarding coins. If she'd really left on her own, she was going to take those paints with her.

And the receipt. *Call me.* Those two words gnawed at her.

Delilah let out a long, slow breath. "I want to know what happened, too."

Bo sat up a little straighter. "Do you think someone's covering something up?"

"I don't know . . ." she said slowly. It was best not to add too much fuel to Bo's fire. "But I found something in my mom's drawer yesterday that has me thinking more about it."

"What was it?"

"I found—"

There was the sound of a car door slamming, followed by the quick procession of steps up to the front porch. The door groaned open.

"We're back," Caleb said breathlessly. His freckled face was raw and pink from the wind.

Bo swung her legs over the couch and scrambled toward the kitchen. Delilah would have to talk to her about this later. She rushed to the door and flung it all the way open.

Whitney stood on the porch, one of her arms draped around Bennett's broad shoulders, the other tied up in a sling. Her eyelids were so heavy that Delilah wasn't even sure they were open. Jude stood on Whitney's other side, fingers lightly hooked onto her sister's elbow as she guided her through the door.

"Oh, Whitney!" Delilah said, her voice shaking. She tried not to look too hard at the ring of dried blood staining Whitney's collar, or the brace around her neck that was the color of a dirty dishrag, or the splotchy patch of purple skin blooming just beneath it. Instead, she gently cupped Whitney's face in her palms. "Why didn't they clean you up at the hospital?"

"I'm fine," Whitney slurred. "It's just a fractured collarbone. Nothing they could really do about it but wait for it to heal."

"They gave her some pain meds," Jude piped up.

"Yeah, sorry we didn't call," Bennett said, guiding Whitney toward the sofa. As he slid her onto the cushion, Whitney's brace snagged his shirt, pulling the collar loose and revealing the small birthmark on Bennett's chest. Delilah used to trace her fingers over the patch of brown skin that looked like an ivy leaf. It'd been months since she'd been able to do that.

Now the birthmark was red.

A fierce, angry red that looked more like a fresh burn than a birthmark.

Delilah stared at it. Bennett glanced up at her and quickly adjusted the collar. "I wasn't getting great service. You know it's all cornfields until you hit the city."

Delilah watched as Jude hovered close to Whitney's side. She hooked her arm beneath her sister's sling as Whitney slowly settled onto the sofa. Once she was there, Jude turned. Not toward Delilah. To Bennett.

Jude's fingers settled into the crook of his elbow and slid like raindrops off his skin. And Bennett didn't pull away. In fact, he *leaned* into it. His body swayed toward Jude's, but he was careful to avoid her gaze.

Delilah's eyes fluttered. She lifted her chin. "You could have tried to send a text or—"

"It really was a mess there," Caleb interrupted. She'd almost forgotten he'd swept in the door with them. "Hey, Lilah," he said, reaching for her arm.

Pain radiated from Delilah's elbow up her arm, almost as if someone had banged on her bones like a drum. It was a pain deep and raw, like something was being taken from her at the same time it shook her.

She ripped her arm away from whatever had hurt her.

Caleb froze, his arm outstretched, his fingers grasping for something that was no longer there. His eyes were as wide as moons.

"Lilah?" Jude said. Her eyebrows were knitted together with concern.

"Delilah?" Bennett stepped toward her. "Are you okay?"

"I don't know . . ." She glanced down at the spot on her arm where Caleb had touched her. There was no mark or bruise. Her skin wasn't splotchy or red, even though it felt like razor blades were slicing up her skin.

Whatever was hurting was coming from the inside.

She slowly wriggled her fingers, waiting for the ache to dull. It had been *Caleb* who had touched her. Not Bennett. And it had felt just as painful.

"Delilah?" Bennett leaned down to look in her eyes, his eyes stained with worry. He placed his palm against her cheek.

She screamed.

The pain seared through her skin like the summer sun on asphalt. It felt hot at first, and then it felt like she was being cut open from the inside out.

She grabbed Bennett's hand with hers and yanked it away. Jude rushed toward her, wrapping her thin arms around Delilah's neck. Jude's skin felt like cool water against her own.

But the only word that flitted through Delilah's mind was *Bo.*

Delilah didn't understand why or how, but being next to Bo was the only thing that mattered. Bo and her gritted teeth and fierce eyes and the wrinkle between her eyebrows that never fully smoothed itself out, even when she was laughing. That was who she needed.

She untangled herself from Jude. "Where's Bo?"

Jude blinked. "She mumbled something about going into town when she was walking toward the kitchen."

Bo.

Delilah hadn't called for her, or reached for her, ever since the day after the disappearance when she'd found Bo on the front porch sobbing her eyes out. Delilah had sat beside her and scooped her in her arms like a pile of laundry, holding her close to her chest until Delilah's blouse was soaked through. Bo had grown thorns since then. It was best not to touch.

But all Delilah wanted right this second was to reach for Bo. She needed her like a balm.

And Bo had left again.

CHAPTER TEN

Bo slipped through the kitchen and out the back door when no one was watching.

It was so obvious the way this was going to play out. Bo could see it the second they all stumbled into the living room. The way Jude looked at Bennett. The way Bennett refused to look at Jude. How Delilah looked at them both. And Whitney was hardly conscious to witness any of it at all.

They'd all pretend that everything was fine, that Jude didn't have extremely obvious feelings for Bennett, that Delilah didn't notice the way Jude hovered around her boyfriend the same way the wind always seemed to hover over Bishop. The whole thing was painfully awkward, and Bo was done bearing witness to that.

Plus, Caleb was in her house.

He was *in* her house, and she hadn't invited him.

Bo walked down the gravel driveway and toward the dirt path that looped around the outskirts of town. The last light of the day dissolved into darkness. Even though she was out of the house, and she was technically in the open air, she never felt completely free. The sunflowers reached toward her with their velvety petals as she approached. She stopped and looked up.

"What do you want from me?" she asked through gritted teeth.

The sunflowers stared back at her with their unreadable faces, bobbing slightly in the wind. And then they *lunged toward her.*

Bo was sure of it. They leaned in even though the wind was lightly blowing in the opposite direction. A chill ran down her spine.

She swung at the flowers so hard that a riot of petals fluttered to the ground. Bo's pulse rocketed through her veins as she veered off the path and ran toward Main Street. One by one, people came into view as she crossed through downtown. The sky was now as dark as ink, but milky light spilled from the bar on the corner, the crackle of tinny music wafting into the street. There was laughter and clinking glasses.

Bo only slowed when she reached the clearing, letting out a long breath. She glanced back at the sunflowers pressed up against the town borders.

What the hell was that?

She was probably just imagining it. The sunflowers had always been eerie petaled things, but *sentient?* Bo shook her head. It had been a long day.

She took in the scene at the clearing. Whatever cleanup had taken place after Whitney had gone to the hospital seemed to have stalled out shortly thereafter. Some of the larger pieces of the statues had been hauled away, but there was still a web of smaller fragments lying in the dirt. Even some of the plastic folding chairs from the memorial were still stacked in lopsided piles, waiting to be collected.

Bo kicked through a pile of rubble. She wasn't sure what she was looking for, exactly. Just that something in her tugged her toward this spot. It always had, ever since she'd found out that this was the last place where anyone had seen her mom. And now here she was, standing in a pile of stone from this half-hearted attempt at honoring their mothers. She let out a sharp laugh. It was almost funny. Like this damn town would rather knock them down over and over again than celebrate them.

Bo glanced at the fragments at her feet. She couldn't tell the difference between most of them—which were Ava's fingers or Indigo's nose—but there was one larger chunk staring up at her from the ground.

It was her mother's face.

Cori's dead stone eyes looked at her, unblinking. Her stomach sank. Whoever had made this thing had tried to emphasize the crinkles in the corners of her eyes, but they had ended up looking like whispery scratches instead. Or maybe that was the best they could do. No one could replicate with stone the kind of sparkle Cori had in her eyes.

Bo reached for her mother's face. Her fingers brushed against something just beneath it. She pushed the stone to the side.

The edge of a black garbage bag poked out from the ground.

There was a garbage bag buried under the statues.

There was a garbage bag buried under the statues.

Bo had seen enough true crime documentaries to know that a garbage bag buried in the earth for no one to find wasn't a good thing. Her heart started to race.

The pallet. The event committee had insisted on putting down that rickety plywood over a big chunk in this clearing months ago. Said it would help "level off" the already flat land to keep the statues safe from the winds, but that had to have been a lie. The plywood hadn't done anything; the statues had fallen over anyway.

Maybe the pallet wasn't there for the memorial at all.

Maybe it was there to hide something.

Bo sucked in a breath. She was getting ahead of herself. This garbage bag was probably leftover from the cleanup crew after they packed up for the day. It had probably gotten buried while they were shifting around the rubble.

Slowly, she pulled. The bag crinkled as the dirt and stone slid from the plastic. When most of it was aboveground, she opened it.

There was only one thing in it, settled into the creases at the very bottom, but it was too dark to see what it was. Bo pulled in a shaky breath and reached her hand inside.

"Hey, did you check over here?" a voice cut through the dark, making her jump.

Someone was coming.

Bo yanked her arm out of the bag and tried to stuff it back into the earth, but it was too late. Two sets of footsteps quickened as they approached. She quickly scurried through the stone and behind a stack of folding chairs.

"I checked *everywhere*, William." A second man. Bo squinted in the dark as they both paused at the clearing. The second man stumbled as he bumped up against the pallet.

William Harding patted the man on the back. "You've had a lot to drink, Jeff. Is it possible you left your phone back at the bar?"

Jeff Ableman. Bo recognized him. He was Bishop's sheriff, although it seemed like he was almost never on duty, except for when someone went missing or he wanted to bust teenagers drinking in the clearing. He lived a few streets down. His son, Henry, had been in Bo's geometry class last spring.

"'S not there," Jeff mumbled. "Maybe I dropped it here earlier?" Mr. Ableman started to drop to his knees, both hands reaching to brace himself for impact. "I'm gonna look a lil in here . . ."

Bo's heart rocketed in her chest. They were so close to the garbage bag. So, so close. They couldn't find it, not before she could see what was inside.

"Wait, wait, wait." Mr. Harding hooked his arm around Sheriff Ableman's and lifted him upright. "Come on, Jeff. The memorial was hours ago. You would have noticed if you'd dropped your phone then." He let out an awkward laugh. "Let's get you back to the bar."

Ableman rubbed his eyes. "Maybe you're right. It was a long time ago." He dropped his hand from his face and looked around, as if he suddenly noticed exactly where he was. "Why's this place such a mess still, huh?"

Mr. Harding wrapped his arm across his shoulder, gently guiding him away from the clearing. "Oh, I let the guys go early, you know. They'd been working so hard. I'm going to finish up here myself."

Sheriff Ableman said something, but their backs were turned to her hiding spot as they walked back toward town. Their conversation wafted away with them.

She let out a breath.

Bo hopped to her feet and rushed back to the pallet, to the bag. Mr. Harding hadn't said when he'd be back to clean up the mess, and she needed to know what was hidden here before it disappeared for good.

She dropped to her knees and ripped open the bag. Without thinking too hard about it, she stuck her hand inside and reached until her fingertips brushed something cool and metal.

She knew what it was.

Her fingers shook as she wrapped them around the handle and pulled.

A knife. It was a knife.

Bo was sitting on the stone remains of her mother's statue, holding a knife covered in rust-colored blood. Her entire body shook as she pulled herself to her feet. Someone had tried to bury this knife. They didn't want it to be found.

Bo had always known that this town was creepy around the edges. The whispering sunflowers and hellish windstorms. The missing mothers. Eleanor Craft found dead two feet from her front porch. "Natural causes," they'd said.

How does a teenager die of "natural causes"?

Bo's fingers curled tighter around the knife. She stuck the blade into her back pocket and headed toward the dirt path.

Something wasn't right in Bishop.

And she was going to find out what it was.

CHAPTER ELEVEN

When Whitney was twelve, she snapped her wrist like a twig while she was doing cartwheels in the high school parking lot.

Her mom had been tucked in her classroom, finishing up her paperwork for the day, while Whitney and Jude waited on the blacktop. Jude had taken to picking the puffy dandelions that grew in the cracks between parking spots, carefully holding the whisper-thin seeds in her palm like a secret. Whitney had timed her cartwheels perfectly. When the wind kicked up, scooping the tiny puffs from Jude's palm and launching them into the air, she tumbled through the floating parade of seeds with glee. But she didn't notice the crack zigzagging beneath her feet.

Her mother had scooped her off the asphalt and driven her to the only clinic in Bishop, where the only doctor there, Dr. Egart, molded a cast to her arm. *You're lucky it wasn't worse,* she'd said, smoothing out the x-rays on the countertop. *You would have had to go to the hospital. They have other doctors, specialists, there.*

Whitney had hated the cast more than the pain. While that was excruciating, for sure, she knew it was also temporary. Once the source was properly treated with iodine and gauze and plaster, the pain dulled to a low roar, and then nothing at all. But the cast was hell. It was itchy and constricting, and it held the wound hostage long after the pain had subsided.

She would have preferred to feel the pain—all of it, all at once—so it could finally end.

Whitney shifted the ice pack closer to her collarbone as she sat in bed. The meds the hospital had given her were definitely working. She could barely feel the cold snap of ice on her skin, but she almost wished she could.

The pain had stitched the memory into her bones as they mended back together, making it a part of her now. The way Jude had rushed over, skinning her knees on the blacktop. How her mother smelled like sweat and pencil shavings as she lifted Whitney into the sedan that still sat with a broken engine in their driveway now. How being completely free was a little too dangerous. How it scared her and the people she loved.

Whitney curled into a ball in her bed and closed her eyes, even though it was already dark in her room. Maybe she should skip the meds tomorrow. Maybe if she could sink into the pain of her messed-up collarbone, *really* let it sear through her like a wildfire, it would finally burn away the rest of the pain that refused to let her go.

It was there, a knot just under her ribs, every time she visited Eleanor in the clearing, spoke to her through the weather vane. No matter how much Whitney begged the wind to let her feel something else besides *this,* it was always there, permanently stitched into her DNA. That whole "time heals all wounds" thing? She was thoroughly convinced it was absolute bullshit.

"Whit?" Jude's soft voice wafted through the dark.

"Hey," she replied from the cocoon she'd made of her bedding. "You can turn on the light."

But instead of flicking on the overhead light and drowning them both in an uncomfortable glow, Jude shuffled over to the tiny lamp propped on top of the stack of books between their beds. She sank onto the edge of Whitney's bed. "How are you feeling?"

Whitney rubbed her face. "Foggy. I barely remember going to the hospital."

"It's probably for the best. Bennett said there was only one doctor there. They couldn't even clean you up all the way."

Whitney frowned. That didn't seem right. There *had* to be more than one doctor in an entire hospital. She touched the ice pack on her neck, wondering why there hadn't even been a nurse there to clean her wound. "Jude, what kind of hospital did we go to?"

Her sister shrugged. "I don't know? A small one? I didn't even get a good look at it, really. Bennett asked me to wait in the truck."

Whitney sat up straighter, and the pain in her neck sharpened. She winced. "You didn't go in with me?"

Even in the dimness, she could see Jude's eyes grow wider. "I mean, no. Bennett said he wasn't sure what they would do to you in there and that it might freak me out to watch, so it would be best to wait until you all came back."

Something hot and sour curdled in Whitney's stomach. Her sister hadn't even bothered to go into the hospital with her? Just because some completely mediocre guy told her to wait? It hurt almost as much as her fractured collarbone.

Whitney opened her mouth to say as much, but Jude's voice cut through the dark. "Delilah's still up," she whispered, even though they were an entire floor away from the other bedrooms in the house. "She's freaking me out a little."

Whitney frowned. It was clear that her sister was trying to change the subject, and honestly, Whitney was too foggy to try to push any further. She turned her head slowly toward her sister so as not to disturb the ice pack. "What's Delilah doing?"

Jude shrugged. "I don't know. Just like, sitting on the couch with her hands over her face. Talking to herself."

"Talking to herself? About what?" Whitney tried to keep the sharpness from her voice, but the hospital situation rubbed against her like sandpaper, and now Jude was bringing up this thing with Delilah, when her sister was more than capable of dealing with it herself.

"I couldn't really tell." Jude let out a slow breath. "Something about Bennett, maybe."

Jude wasn't telling her everything. Whitney knew it the moment the words left her twin's mouth. That was the best and worst thing about Jude. She was so earnest that even the brush of a lie changed the whole texture of her words, and Whitney could tell the difference. Their mom had been able to tell, too. That had been the worst thing. Jude could never get away with lying to cover for Whitney for "borrowing" their mom's best lipstick, or sneaking out to go drink in the clearing, or anything in between.

Jude's eyes met hers. "She's not even worried that Bo hasn't come home."

Oh. Oh no. Whitney's heartbeat hitched. She winced as she pulled herself up.

After Delilah had recovered from whatever had hurt her earlier, promising Bennett that she'd get checked out by the town doctor tomorrow, she'd seemed okay. Well, okay *enough* for Whitney to take a pain pill and spoon with an ice pack in bed without worrying. But this was weird. The mumbling to herself Whitney could almost understand. Not incessantly calling Bo's phone to get her to come home?

Something was definitely wrong.

"Fine, I'll go talk to her." Whitney carefully kicked off her covers and swung her legs over the bed. "Coming with?"

"Yeah," Jude said, pulling a loose string on Whitney's blanket.

There it was, that rough texture around the edges of her words again. Something she was holding back.

Whitney sighed. That was the other thing about Jude—she'd never talk about something until she was ready, no matter how much Whitney prodded. She picked up her watered-down ice pack and shuffled gingerly toward the door. Her head felt like a slab of cement.

"Whit, wait."

She turned to Jude. "Yeah?"

Jude squeezed her eyes shut. She reached into her pocket and pulled out something small and silver. "I need to tell you something."

"What?" Whitney turned back and sat on the edge of her bed. Jude sank into the nest of blankets beside her. Slowly, she opened her palm.

There sat a small tarnished thing. Whitney leaned in.

An acorn charm. With a rust-colored stain etched into it.

"What's . . ." she started. She knew the answer before she finished the sentence. Her mouth went dry. Whitney's eyes snapped to Jude's. "Where did you find this?"

"At the memorial," Jude whispered. "In the clearing."

And just like that, Whitney was thrown back into her twelve-year-old body, palms scuffed from cartwheeling across the blacktop. Jude's small hand outstretched in front of her, the wisps of dandelion seeds folded into the creases of her skin. Whitney had loved to watch the way the wind lifted the seeds from her sister's palm, like it was alive and hell-bent on freeing them.

She blinked, and she was back in her room. The air was stale. There was no wind to breathe new life into the charm in Jude's hand.

This was a dead thing.

"It looks like it goes with your bracelet?" Jude said tentatively.

Whitney touched the spot on her wrist where the bracelet

usually lingered. The doctor must have removed it to do x-rays, and suddenly she realized she had no idea what had happened to it.

"It was Eleanor's bracelet." Cold panic swept through her. "Wait, where is it?" She stood up and started shuffling through the blanket nest. "Did I have it on when I got home?"

Jude shook her head. "No, they put it in a baggie. Your nose ring is in there, too."

Whitney touched her nose. *Damn it.* "Where's the baggie?"

A pause. She spun around to look at Jude, who was suddenly extremely interested in the skin around her fingernails. "Oh. Um, I think they gave it to Bennett. He must have forgotten to leave it."

Whitney chewed the inside of her cheek. "Let me see it," she whispered.

Slowly, Jude stood. She slid the charm from her palm to the center of her sister's.

Whitney tilted her hand toward the dusty lamplight. The acorn in her palm was the exact size and shape of the other charms on Eleanor's bracelet. It was the same dingy silver that had probably once been gold, and it was missing the clasp. And Jude had said she'd found it in the clearing, where Eleanor used to hang out for bonfires and parties.

She picked it up between her fingers and examined the stain. It almost completely covered the cap of the acorn, and was even darker on the clasp.

Jude cleared her throat. "Where did you . . . even get her bracelet, Whit?"

"I found it." She swallowed, still staring at the charm. "After."

It was half true. After the kiss and the promise at the bonfire, Whitney had woken hungover and lovestruck early the next morning. She'd texted Eleanor: Morning, sunshine.

A smile had played on her lips as she'd sent it. Eleanor hated mornings. To her, there was no point of being awake until the sun hung straight overhead like a ceiling fixture.

Whitney had set her phone on the makeshift nightstand and rolled over. Eleanor wouldn't be up for hours, she figured, so she might as well dream of her until she could see her again. When she woke again an hour later, there was a message.

Morning, beautiful, it had said. Meet me in the clearing? I need to tell you something.

Her heart fluttered. Eleanor had sent it almost immediately after Whitney had sent hers. She'd missed it.

Are you at the clearing? I can meet now.

She hit send. And waited.

But Eleanor never responded.

There had been this feeling knotted up right behind Whitney's ribs as she stared at her phone. It was like she already knew that Eleanor wasn't going to text back. She'd never text Whitney again.

Eventually, Whitney had decided to go up to the clearing to see if Eleanor had somehow, miraculously, stayed there to wait for her. But it was empty. All that was left was the weather vane, the ashy remnants of last night's bonfire, and something sparkling in the soil.

Eleanor's charm bracelet.

Whitney had held it in her palm for a good long minute, trying to remember if Eleanor had left it last night, and if it was warm to the touch now because of the sun or because it had recently been on her wrist.

She looked around. The clearing was eerily quiet, the wind non-existent. Even the sunflowers' heads drooped, completely ignoring the sun. Like it was satiated. Like *they* were satiated.

Whitney went back home.

It was Delilah who told her the news a few hours later, standing in their kitchen.

Eleanor's grandmother found her this morning, she'd said, threading her fingers through Whitney's. *She was outside in the front yard.*

Whitney had pulled her hand back. *Okay, so? Where is she now? Can I call her?*

Before she'd even finished the sentence, Whitney knew. That same knotted-up feeling reemerged and she suddenly felt sick. The way Delilah's expression broke confirmed it.

No, she couldn't call Eleanor.

She'd never be able to call her again.

Natural causes, the cops had said. Just flat dead, face-first in the flower bed next to the porch steps.

But this charm. This buried relic Jude had found in the clearing. It was covered in blood.

It was covered in blood.

The house shook under Whitney's feet as the front door swung open. "Family meeting!" Bo called as she stomped through the kitchen.

Jude snapped up to look at Whitney, eyes wide. "What's wrong, Bo?" she yelled.

"Everything," Bo yelled back. "We have a huge problem."

CHAPTER TWELVE

When Bo told them all about the knife in the clearing, it took everything in Jude not to throw up. It wasn't that there was a knife buried in Bishop. Or even that she might have walked over it in her dusty purple sneakers a million times, never knowing that something sinister was soaking in the soil beneath her feet.

It was that Bo had been the one to find it.

Something had been wrong with Bo for years now. She knew it. They all knew it. But only Jude knew that it had to do with Bennett's brother, Caleb.

It wasn't long after their mothers had disappeared that Jude had found the Allwell's Pharmacy bag in the kitchen trash, stuffed toward the bottom. Bo had been the only one home that day since Jude had taken out the trash. She knew she shouldn't look, but Bo had barely spoken to any of them for a week, and Jude was desperate.

She'd plucked the bag from the can and peeked inside.

An empty box for the morning-after pill.

And a receipt. Jude had scanned it, feeling increasingly ill by the second.

Plan B.

Bandages.

Bo hadn't been dating anyone. That much Jude was sure of. She used to tell them things, and Jude was certain she would have spilled. But hadn't Jude seen her with someone at the bonfire that night?

Caleb.

Jude had crumpled up the bag, shoved it deep in the trash can, and never spoken of it again. At first she thought Bo would eventually spill, like she always did. But then she didn't. And Jude never figured out how to bring it up.

Bo had been through something that had made her crack. Finding a bloody knife in the clearing was just one more horrible thing. This time she might break.

The girls sat around the dimly lit living room. Delilah was still tucked into the corner of the couch where Whitney had found her earlier, only she wasn't whispering to herself any longer. She stared at the crack in the floorboards, her lips parted slightly. Whitney was curled up beside her, head on Delilah's shoulder. Bo hovered over them all, pacing like a caged animal. She hadn't sat down since she stormed through the door.

"So what are we supposed to do about it?" Jude said after a moment. "Someone hid a knife under the statues and I'm guessing they didn't want anyone to find it. But now what?"

Whitney lifted her head. She reached into her pocket. "Here's something else."

"Whit," Jude said softly.

"No, it's okay." Whitney didn't look at her as she held the tiny acorn in her palm. "Jude found this in the clearing, too."

Bo lifted an eyebrow. "The same spot?"

Jude nodded. "I found it on the ground after the statues broke."

"It was Eleanor's," Whitney whispered. "I think there's blood on it."

Delilah's eyes fluttered as she snapped back to life. "Oh, Whitney," she whispered, wrapping her arms around Whitney and pulling her closer. "I'm so sorry."

"That settles it!" Bo slammed her hand on the coffee table, making a trio of succulents quake in their pots. "A knife in the clearing. Eleanor's charm in the clearing. They both have blood on them. Anyone else seeing the connection here?" She paced. "And the memorial. Did they want to put those statues up because they knew? Those assholes—"

"Hold on a sec." Delilah gently touched Whitney's shoulder one more time before letting her arms drop. "Of course they wanted to put up the statues in the clearing. That's where our moms were seen last, remember?"

"Then explain this to me." Bo was pacing so furiously now that Jude was positive the soles of her feet would wear through the threadbare rug. "Explain to me why they put those statues up *two years* after our moms disappeared. Yeah, I know they said they'd do it because I wanted it, but they were originally going to pave over the clearing. I begged them not to. Is there something else they don't want us to find?"

Is there something else they don't want us to find?

Bo's words rang through Jude like a church bell, transporting her back to the stifling cab of Bennett and Caleb's truck as it rolled to a stop on a makeshift dirt path. Sunflowers pressed in on all sides, almost completely blocking out the sun. *Where is this hospital?* She'd laughed nervously. *It's almost like they don't want us to find it.*

Bennett's eyes snapped to Caleb's before he glanced up to look at Jude in the rearview mirror. His eyes crinkled at the corners as he let out a laugh. *Right,* he'd said. *Hey, Jude, I was thinking. You should probably stay back here until they're done with Whitney in there, okay? I just don't want you to have to see anything you don't want to.*

Jude had glanced down at her sister, who was curled up beside her on the seat, head propped in her lap. Whitney had been whimpering in pain the whole way to the hospital, and the colors on her neck had turned to a pulsing, electric blue. The thought of someone poking needles into Whitney, stringing her up to glossy saline bags and beeping monitors, made Jude's stomach roll.

But still. Whitney was her sister.

I can do it, she'd said.

Bennett hopped out of the truck and opened the back door. He leaned into the cab and hooked his arms under Whitney, his face so close to Jude's that she could smell the sweat on his skin. *Trust me on this, okay? We'll get Whitney better, and then I was thinking maybe you and I could go somewhere tomorrow to talk.*

Jude had watched his lips caress every word, lulling her into a lovestruck slumber. He had chosen her. He *was* choosing her.

Okay, she'd said limply. Bennett and Caleb lifted Whitney out of the car and shut the door behind them.

But now, back in their living room, Whitney had found her voice again even as Jude had lost hers. "Pssh, I wouldn't be surprised if they put those statues up to hide the blood," she said. "And especially the knife."

"The evidence," Bo added.

"Wait a sec, this is too much," Delilah said, rubbing the skin between her eyebrows. She sighed heavily. "Some of this could be a coincidence. We could be getting ahead of ourselves."

"Lilah, *listen* to me, please! Just trust me on this. Something isn't right here." Bo finally stopped pacing and faced them. "I know it in my bones."

Bo and Delilah began to bicker, while Whitney attempted to play referee. Jude let the familiar rhythm of their arguing carry her further into her thoughts. More than anything, Jude wanted

Delilah to be right. She wanted things to just be *normal* for a minute. A gap in all the darkness to finally take a breath.

But Delilah was wrong.

This was not a coincidence. There were too many unlikely variables that had ended up in the same place: the knife, the charm, the last place Eleanor had been seen alive.

And then there was Bo.

Jude knew, more than anyone, that Bo protected her secrets like a fortress. And she never asked them to help her hold them. She never asked anything of any of them, really.

Except for this.

Jude cleared her throat. None of them noticed.

She slammed her hand on the coffee table.

It wasn't as dramatic or forceful as when Bo had done it. The succulents didn't even budge. But it was enough.

Delilah, Whitney, and Bo stared at her. She felt heat blooming on her cheeks. "I believe Bo," Jude said.

Delilah sighed again, but this time she sounded more tired than exasperated. "What are we going to do about it?"

"This could be our chance," Whitney said softly. "This could be the only shot we get to figure out what happened to Eleanor."

"And our moms were in the clearing, right?" Jude added. "What if there's more there? What if there's more"—her eyes cut over to Bo's—"evidence that we haven't found yet?"

Bo let out a long breath. "Come on, Lilah. We can't live like this anymore. We have to know what happened, one way or the other."

Delilah's shoulders slumped. She squeezed her eyes closed. "I have to tell you something."

Jude's stomach knotted, tighter and tighter, as Delilah told them about the receipt and the message she'd found in her mother's studio. This wasn't right. None of it was. Something had gone very, very wrong around the time their mothers had vanished.

"We have to figure out what happened," Bo said after a moment.

Delilah sighed. "Okay, we do a little bit of poking around. Nothing huge. And then we drop it—for good—if we don't find anything, all right?"

Together, the girls nodded. Bo immediately launched into her plan, doling out things to research and places to visit as if she'd been waiting for two years for this moment. According to Bo, Whitney and Jude should dig deeper into Eleanor's last days, starting with her last living relative: her grandmother. Bo assigned herself the task of digging around town hall to figure out what the plans were for the clearing. Delilah, she said, should figure out what happened with the receipt from Rose and Rain.

But Jude already knew where to start.

She excused herself to go to the bathroom while the girls plotted. When she slipped into the tiny petal-pink bathroom on the main floor, she locked the door behind her. She pulled her phone from her pocket and began to dial.

It only rang once before it connected.

"Hey, Jude," Bennett's voice said from the other end. "What's up?"

CHAPTER THIRTEEN

Delilah had always thought that secrets were evil little things, capable of bringing down an entire empire, or even a rickety home at the end of Old Fairview Lane. Until she decided to keep one of her own.

It wasn't that she didn't think Bo's theory had merit. How many times had Delilah woken in the dead of night over the past couple of years, convinced Indigo's ghost was staring at her from the other side of the room?

Find me, it said at first.

Find my body, it said more recently.

But Delilah had never been sure that her mother was dead, no matter what her nightmares told her. As much as she told the girls they should just give up the search and move on, even she knew that was impossible.

Especially since the feeling that she was missing something had never left her.

She'd known that receipt was important the second she found

it. She just knew it, the same way Bo knew deep in her bones that something was wrong.

Delilah listened to the sound of Bo's footsteps padding through her room the next day. She clomped through the kitchen, and then back up the stairs as she grabbed something from her room. "Be back later!" Bo yelled as she slammed the front door closed behind her.

She let out a breath as the house settled around her. Whitney and Jude had already left for their Bo-appointed mission. She was alone.

Even still, she couldn't help tiptoeing across the upstairs hallway and carefully, slowly opening the door to her mother's studio as if the girls were still on the floor below her. She breathed in the dust that always kicked up whenever she entered, not bothering to let it settle before she sank into Indigo's chair. She pulled open the top drawer.

The fresh box of paint and the receipt with the phone number were still there.

Delilah dialed the number. Her fingers shook as she pressed Enter.

But nothing happened.

Almost as soon as Delilah placed the phone to her ear, there was a click on the other end, followed by a robotic voice listing the digits. Then, a beep.

She jabbed the End button before it could record anything.

The phone at the other end of the number was clearly turned off. That was the best-case scenario. It could be a line that no one used anymore. Delilah might never know who was on the other side of that number.

Who was one of the last people to talk to her mom before she vanished.

She held the receipt between her fingertips for a long time. The ink had faded, but the paper was wrinkle-free and folded in a crisp, pristine line down the center. The handwriting, though, was haphazard and rushed. And it wasn't her mother's.

Delilah closed her eyes, trying to picture the scene at the store. Her mother orbiting the art supplies, removing the lids of sample paints to smell the oil and acrylic. Indigo had always insisted there was no better scent on the planet than fresh paint and the promise of a new project.

Grabbing the box. Taking it to the checkout counter in the back. Someone behind the register printing out the receipt and taking the time to fold it, carefully, precisely.

And then racing to write down a phone number?

It didn't make sense.

Unless.

Delilah opened her eyes. *Unless someone else saw them. They had to move quickly.*

She glanced at the receipt one last time before slipping it into her back pocket and heading toward the door.

Rose and Rain had been a centerpiece on Main Street since Delilah could remember. It was started by two old women, Rose Salwart and Gale-Ann Greenwich, who were married and lived in the brick house around the corner from the shop. Delilah imagined they'd made the conscious choice to go with Rain instead of Gale-Ann for the second part of their shop's name, which just sounded more poetic. The two were *still* married, in fact, and Delilah recognized Gale-Ann's pale lavender hair as soon as the chimes rang on the door. She stood on the top platform of a stepladder, draped in a gauzy white dress that made her look a little like a dusty angel.

"Delilah?" she said from the back of the store. She waved a feather duster at her. "Delilah Cortez?"

"Hi," Delilah said, waving back awkwardly. "I just wanted to . . ." She paused. Even though she had practiced what she was going to say at least a million times on her walk over, the words suddenly clotted up in her throat.

"Well, I never thought I'd see you back in here," said Gale-Ann with a warm smile. "Your mother always said you weren't the artistic type."

Delilah forced her mouth into a smile. "Yes, I haven't been in since . . . well, since a long time ago. But speaking of my mother, I was wondering if you could help me with something." She pulled the receipt from her back pocket and thrust it toward her. "Do you know whose phone number is written on this receipt from your store?"

Gale-Ann plucked the slip of paper from Delilah's hand like she was picking a particularly stubborn weed. She grabbed a pair of tortoiseshell reading glasses from her dress pocket and slipped them onto her nose. Delilah watched as she mouthed the numbers before saying, "Sorry, hon, don't recognize it." Gale-Ann gave her a wistful smile before shoving her glasses back into her pocket and turning to the shelves she had been in the midst of dusting. Delilah's heart sank.

"Wait," she said. "Is there any way to look it up?"

She hated the way the words sounded when they came out. They were rough around the edges, hungry and desperate. The fact was, Delilah didn't like not having options. She'd gone the past two years without any other option but to bear the storm, to batten down the windows, to survive. For her, but for them all, too.

This slip of paper was the only option left. It was the only thing in Delilah's life that hadn't been planned and predestined.

It was the only way she would ever really know if her mother had planned to leave her all along.

It was easier for the other girls. Of course Bo's mom wouldn't have left her favorite person in the world on purpose. And Delilah was almost certain that Ava Montgomery would rather cut off a limb than leave her twins behind in a place like Bishop.

But Indigo? Indigo was different.

Delilah saw it in the white space in her paintings, heard it in the lull between her mother's sighs and sentences.

More than anything, Indigo wanted out of this place.

Maybe even more than being with Delilah.

It was a painful thought, but one that she had gotten used to hearing in her own mind over the past two years. Over time, she had convinced herself that it must have been true, that her mother had run away from here. From her. In some ways, it was easier to bear that thought than imagining her dead and decaying in the sunflower fields.

No matter what had happened, Delilah had to find out the truth. It wasn't just about her anymore. It was about the other girls, too.

"I could help," Delilah added. "Like, if you needed me to look up contact numbers on a computer or something?"

Gale-Ann let out a laugh so forceful that it felt like a slap. "Hon, you think I know a lick about looking up numbers in a computer? I order the art supplies. The numbers are Rosie's territory, and she's out for the day."

"Please," Delilah said. She winced as she clasped her hands together at her heart. It was a little pathetic. She knew it, Gale-Ann knew it. But it was all she had. "I'll do anything to find out whose number that is. That receipt is from a box of paints my mom bought the day she disappeared. And someone wrote down that phone number on her receipt hours before she vanished into thin air." Delilah reached for Gale-Ann's arm. "I need to know who she was going to call."

Gale-Ann's face softened. She sighed. "Well, there's one place we can look. Come on." She grabbed Delilah's wrist and pulled her toward the back room.

Room wasn't quite the right word for it, actually. It was more of a closet. And it was stuffed full of broken things—window screens torn down the center, yellowing canvases with puncture holes at the edges, even a terra-cotta rooster statue with the head broken off.

Gale-Ann shoved the dusty rooster head over and reached to the back of the shelf. Dust floated in the air like the inside of a snow globe as she dragged a heavy black book toward her. "Here." She coughed, plopping it into Delilah's arms. "This is what we used to use for our old register. Customers used to write their information for when we would send out sales calls."

"Sales calls?"

"Pre-internet days, before you were born. Rosie and I'd call up customers whenever I was gonna teach a pottery class, or when there was a big sale or something." Gale-Ann must have noticed the look on Delilah's face, because she added, "It's not like there are *that* many people in Bishop to call. We used it all the way up until a couple years ago. Anyway, that's your best bet. Good luck."

"Thanks." Delilah pulled a wobbly step stool close to her and sat with the book in her lap.

Gale-Ann opened the closet door. She hesitated. "I just want you to know, um, that you aren't the only one who misses your mom. I do, too."

When Delilah looked up, the look on Gale-Ann's face made the knot in her throat grow bigger. "She taught here, with you, sometimes, right?"

"Yes. Tuesdays and Thursdays. Painting. The kids from the high school all loved her. I swear, they only ever took after-school jobs here so they could take her classes for free. But even more than that, your mother was a good friend to me when I was first transitioning. She sat with me in front of this old shop's bathroom mirror and taught me how to do perfect winged eyeliner. I still use her tips sometimes." She cleared her throat. "Anyway. I just wanted you to know . . . there are more people who want her found than you might know."

Gale-Ann gave her a small smile before sweeping into the store, leaving Delilah in the dimly lit closet. She tried to swallow, but the knot in her throat burned.

She let out a breath and opened the book. It was an old address book, the kind that was separated by yellow inserts marked with each letter of the alphabet. She flipped through. Most were written in careful script, the slot for email addresses left blank next to most of the phone numbers. Delilah flipped to the front page and scanned the tiny print. PUBLISHED IN 2003.

This address book was ancient. There was no way she'd find a phone number from only a couple of years ago in here.

As Delilah started to close the book, the pages began to flip to the last section, which didn't have a lettered tab. EMERGENCY CONTACTS, it read. Delilah scanned the list. Rose and Gale-Ann were at the top, of course, but beneath their phone numbers someone had scrawled *Employee contact info.*

She ran her finger down the list. She recognized most of the names, had seen them or met them at some Bishop function at one time or another. Then there was the very last name, all the way at the bottom.

Evan Gordon.

The Evan Gordon? The same Evan who was best friends with Bennett and Caleb?

The one who'd given Bo a bloody knee a few days ago?

Her heart picked up speed. She checked the number on the receipt.

It matched.

Evan Gordon had hastily written his phone number on her mom's receipt.

And now she was going to find out why.

Chapter Fourteen

Getting into Bishop's town hall was easy for someone like Bo. She was a tiny thing, barely taller than the clerk's counter, and fortunately for her, she had inherited Cori's softness around the eyes. The feral part was hidden well enough.

"Take a left at the staircase, sweetheart," the woman at the front desk told her with a toothy grin. "The public records are in the cabinet by the window."

Bo bared her teeth in what she hoped was a decent enough attempt at amiability and scurried down the hallway to the left. It was almost impossible to get lost in here; there was literally only one hallway she could go down. But Bo figured the more polite she was, the more likely it was that the woman at the front desk would allow her to dig through records before getting suspicious.

She wasn't lying about looking up Bishop's property records. She just didn't mention what *else* she was looking up.

She pushed open the wood-paneled door to the records room and instantly sneezed. It was so dry and dusty inside that she felt like she'd inhaled a mouthful of sand as soon as she stepped over the threshold. She wiped her mouth, half expecting to find specks of dust lingering on her lips.

There was exactly one file cabinet in the records room, and it was just to the side of the open window. The rest of the place was stuffed with extra chairs, dented-up tables, and what looked like a box of deranged Santas for the annual Christmas display in the lobby. She kicked the box out of the way. Somewhere inside, a warped version of "Jingle Bells" started to play.

"Gross," Bo whispered, heading to the cabinet. She would make this part quick.

She yanked open the top drawer and thumbed through the records. *Water main line, property taxes, event committee.* Nope, nope, no. She shut the drawer and opened the next.

The first file in the second drawer read *Bishop property ownership.*

Yes.

Bo slid the folder out and flipped it open. There was a single document inside. She held it up to the sunlight and read:

The Town of Bishop
Property Deed

The four square miles of the town of Bishop is unto itself, owned by itself. There will be no proper owner of any land within this square footage, and all homes, ranches, and farmland are considered to be "rented" from the land itself. All land used for the public is, and will continue to be, owned by the town itself. The 8,332-square-foot clearing at the west end and the 597-square-foot clearing at the east end MUST remain clear at all times. No home may be built upon them at any point.

Bo flipped to the second and final page, but there was only a map of Bishop. It was old and whisper-thin, and the pencil lines around the perimeters were so light that she had to step closer to the window to really see them. She tilted the paper.

A burst of wind rushed through the window, blowing her bangs across her face. Bo swept them back and blinked. She blinked again.

A sunflower bent in through the window. It stared at her with its endless, shadowy face, buttery petals fluttering in the wind.

"How did—"

The wind blew again, harder this time. She swore she heard a single word, or the echo of a word, float in on the breeze.

Look.

Bo stumbled back. The sunflower lurched, just an inch, but it was enough to make her blood run cold. She balled her hand into a fist at her side.

But before she could swing, the flower *moved*. Almost as if it could sense Bo's rage, or maybe even an underlayer of fear, and it slowly retreated out the open window, a light breeze massaging its petals as it stared at her innocently.

Bo shook her head. "No." She closed the window so hard the glass panes rattled. "No. Nope."

She dragged in a breath through her nose and released it from her mouth in one long stream, just like she had learned to do when her heart rate got too high on a run. She squinted out the window.

The sunflowers were so close to the building that their petals made a *shh, shh* sound against the brick. They bobbed in the breeze as if they were swaying to a song no one else could hear. Maybe they *were* listening to something she couldn't hear.

Bo felt the chill of the almost-word the flower had whispered. *Look.*

She shook it off, sliding the document back into its folder. *The clearing.* Nothing was supposed to be built on it, ever, according to these documents.

So why did they insist on erecting the statues there?

Look. Bo wasn't sure if she heard the word in her own mind or if it had somehow seeped through the closed window. Her eyes settled on a signature at the very bottom of the second page.

Edward J. Dingal.

"Edward Dingal," Bo said slowly. She tried to make out the date beside the name. *1861.*

Bo chewed on the inside of her cheek. There was something about the name that itched at the back of her brain, something she could feel but didn't quite understand. She closed the folder and slipped it back into the drawer.

She yanked open the rest of the cabinet drawers, one by one, thumbing through manila folders and stacks of old flyers for memorials and ice-cream socials. But she couldn't find anything on Edward Dingal, and nothing on the other thing she had come here to look for.

"They have to be here," she mumbled to herself, clicking the last drawer shut. She half-heartedly combed through the box of deranged Santas, but she knew the records she was looking for weren't in there.

They had to be somewhere else in this building.

Bo poked her head out the door. The woman she'd met at the front was still clacking away at her keyboard. Other than that, the rest of the building was silent.

She tiptoed toward the room at the end of the hall. It was technically the mayor's office, but honestly, Mr. Harding didn't have a lot of duties in a place like Bishop. He was rarely behind the old oak desk, signing papers or talking on the ancient office phone. No one was there now.

Bo crept into the dust-laden office, careful to avoid the window where the sunflowers silently watched. She sidled beside the desk.

The phone rang. Bo jumped. She held her breath as the little red light on the handle blinked.

"Hello, Bishop Town Hall," the woman from the front desk said. Her voice echoed from down the hall. Bo exhaled.

And then she went to work.

She pulled open all the drawers, quickly scanning the contents. There were pastel sticky notes and pens with bite marks on the caps, rusty paper clips and packets of gum that looked about a hundred years old.

And in the bottom drawer, dozens of empty manila folders. Bo shoved her hands inside and flipped through the folders, just to be sure that there was nothing of importance. Her fingers snagged on what felt like a stack of papers near the bottom. She tugged. Several pieces of cream-colored paper jutted out from the pile, but Bo could see there were plenty more still tucked into the last manila folder in the stack.

Her hands shook as she pulled it free. Before she even opened it, somehow, she knew. This was exactly what she'd been looking for.

No one kept a file in a separate place unless they didn't want anyone to find it.

Bo held her breath as she flipped through the documents. Death certificates, or at least photocopies of them. One after another death in Bishop, nothing left of these women but faded ink.

Bo's eyes blurred as she scanned through the names. *Olivia Alvarez. Helen Worchesky. Ashley Goddard.*

Mary and Elizabeth and Tasha and Lillian and Sarah. The corners of Bo's eyes stung as she flipped through them all. It seemed like anyone who identified as a woman was as good as dead in this dusty, barren hellscape.

She stopped near the top of the pile. She squinted at one of the names. Harriet Jones. She had lived down the street from Bo and her mother at one point, before her daughter had died in a farming accident. At least, that was what Belinda Jones's death certificate had said. Harriet had died, alone, in Bishop's only nursing home two years ago.

She turned the page. Jasmine Wright. Died of a "cardiac event" eighteen months ago. Jasmine had been in the grade below Bo. She'd been a distance runner, faster than Bo out of the gate but more likely to lose steam in the last mile.

The next one was Cara Carter. Another cardiac arrest, almost exactly a year ago. She was only thirty years old.

And then there was the last paper at the very top of the pile. The ink hadn't had a chance to fade yet.

Eleanor Craft, "natural causes." Six months ago.

As Bo stared at Eleanor's name, the edges of the paper began to go fuzzy. She swallowed the sick feeling climbing up her throat. *The dates.*

When she'd combed through the older certificates, the time between deaths had been *years*. Sometimes Bishop would go as long as half a decade before another incident. But as Bo had turned the pages, the heart attacks and accidents and unknown causes had started to bleed together. The years between them began to shrink.

The last four: *Two years ago. Eighteen months ago. One year ago. Six months ago.*

"Can I help you?" a voice cut through Bo's thoughts. She dropped the folder on the desk as if it had burned her fingertips.

The woman from the front desk narrowed her eyes. "Why are you here? I told you the public records—"

"Gloria, it's no problem." Another voice wafted into the stuffy room, followed by William Harding. He broke into an easy smile when he saw Bo. "Oh, Bo! Good to see you again."

Bo swallowed. "So, I didn't know—"

Mr. Harding waved his hand as he slid behind the desk. "Really, it's no big deal. I'll just put this back." He reached for the bottom drawer and dropped the file inside. As the drawer clicked shut, he clapped his hands together. "Was there something you were looking for that I can help you with?"

She shook her head. "No, no. I'm good. I just got mixed up." She pressed her mouth into a smile and looked at Gloria like she had when she'd first arrived. This time Gloria didn't smile back. "Okay. So, I'm gonna go. Thanks for your help."

Bo wove through the room, careful not to make eye contact with Gloria. As she reached the door, Mr. Harding cleared his throat. "Hey, Bo?"

She froze. "Yes?"

"Make sure you're careful out there, okay? It's going to be getting dark soon. Don't want anything to happen to you."

"I'll be careful," she said slowly.

Bo pretended that everything was fine as she walked down the narrow hallway back to the lobby. But inside, her heart rocketed in her chest. She had to curl her fingers into her palms to stop them from shaking.

It wasn't Mr. Harding's words that scared her.

It was that he knew exactly where to put the folder back in the drawer.

CHAPTER FIFTEEN

Whitney's shoulder throbbed as she climbed the crumbling steps to the Bishop Nursing Care Center, but it was Jude she was still thinking about. The way she had stared at her fingernails when Whitney had asked her about the hospital. How she'd softly answered, *I didn't even get a good look at it, really. Bennett asked me to wait in the truck.*

Whitney tried to calm the hurt that curdled in her stomach. It was fine. It was probably for the best that Jude didn't end up going into the hospital, anyway. She had always been sensitive about that sort of thing.

Something in Whitney softened as she watched Jude reach for the front door. In a lot of ways, Jude was more like an exposed nerve than a human. She'd never been able to watch an animal in pain, and whenever Bo came home, scraped up and bloody yet again, Jude always pretended to pick at the skin on her palm. If there really was such a thing as kryptonite, Jude's was someone else's pain.

And while Whitney had never spent more than a couple hours

inside the Bishop Nursing Care Center when she'd volunteered last summer for Cross-Stitch Day, she'd spent long enough in the dank recreation room to know this was the kind of place that would rub Jude's soft heart raw. Now that Whitney thought about it, it was probably one of the reasons why she'd taught Mary Porter to stitch a curlicue *I'm a fucking delight* onto her Aida cloth. She *was* a fucking delight, even in a place that didn't have room for that kind of joy.

But if Jude didn't want to be there with her, she never let on. Together, they entered the front lobby, which was painted the color of cement and smelled faintly of dish soap. A gray countertop jutted out from the wall, and behind that, a girl sat with her earbuds in. She glanced up when she saw them come in. "Hi, can I help you?" she said, pulling out her earbuds.

"Hi. Um, I'm here to see someone." Whitney smiled, trying to force the shakiness from her voice.

She hadn't been nervous until right this second, until she'd placed her hands on the Formica countertop and peeked over the edge at the girl sitting behind the clunky old computer. Whitney recognized her from Bishop High, although she was pretty sure she was a couple years older than Delilah. Her long black hair was woven into tight braids that flowed down her back, leaving only her bare shoulders exposed under the dim lights.

The girl leaned on her forearms. "Oh yeah?"

"Yeah," Whitney said slowly. There was a scar, still fresh, on the girl's right arm, the puckered mark disrupting her deep brown skin. The rest of her arms, and her hands, looked as soft as linen. Whitney imagined running her finger from her scar to the crook of her elbow in one long sweep.

Something poked her side. Whitney blinked and found Jude's fingers jabbing her stomach. She swatted them away and turned her attention back to the girl. "Susannah Craft. We'd like to visit with her."

The girl lifted an eyebrow. "Susannah? She doesn't get many . . . well, any visitors."

Whitney watched the way the girl's wine-colored lips formed around Susannah's name. Slowly, deliberately. She was still watching her mouth move when Jude's voice cut through her thoughts.

"We're friends of the family," Jude said quickly. She pulled her mouth into a nervous smile. "Can we see her?"

"Sure," the girl responded. But she was still looking at Whitney. "She's in the rec room. Just grab a couple of visitor badges before you go back."

Jude plucked two orange badges from the wicker basket on the counter. "Thanks," she said, and she rounded the corner toward the hallway.

"Thanks," Whitney repeated. She lifted her hand in an awkward wave before following her sister.

"Hey—wait a sec," the girl called. "Your name is Whitney, right?"

She paused. "Yeah . . . ?"

"I remember you," the girl said. "From when you volunteered here last summer."

Something in Whitney's stomach hitched. Before she could catch her breath, the girl added, "I'm Alma."

"Alma." Whitney rolled her name around her mouth like a hard candy. She liked the way it melted on her tongue. *Alma.*

Whitney tried to remember if she'd met her before, but she drew a blank. She was pretty sure she would have remembered Alma if she'd met her.

"Whit?" Jude's voice wafted from down the hallway.

"Hi, Alma," Whitney said slowly, her mouth breaking into a grin. "Bye, Alma." And she followed the sound of her sister's voice.

As soon as she disappeared into the hallway, the smile dropped from her lips. Her stomach lurched. *What was that?* Whitney hadn't been that nervous around someone since . . .

Eleanor.

By the time she got to the rec room, Jude's face was fixed in a smirk. "Did you make a new *friend*, Whit?"

Heat crept up Whitney's neck. "What are you talking about?" She said, a little sharper than she'd intended. "Sure, I guess?"

Jude looked at her for a long, horribly uncomfortable minute. "Okay then. I think the rec room is right across the hall."

She followed Jude into the room that had been the epicenter of Cross-Stitch Day, only now each table was covered in a riot of neon paints instead of rainbow embroidery floss. Three massive windows covered almost all of the back wall, washing the already graying residents in even more gray light.

Whitney tried to slow her heartbeat as she scanned the room, looking for Eleanor's grandmother. That was all that this was supposed to be. They'd find Eleanor's last family member still in Bishop, ask her some questions about Eleanor's death, and then maybe she'd finally have the answers to the questions that had been gnawing at her for months.

Not this.

But what was *this*? Alma's soft face and purple lips appeared without invitation in Whitney's mind. She blinked the image away. *This* was nothing.

She was here for Eleanor.

"There," Jude whispered. She nodded toward a lone woman in the back corner. "I think that's her."

As soon as Whitney caught a glimpse of the woman, she knew it was Eleanor's grandmother. Even from this angle, Susannah looked like the kind of woman Eleanor would grow into as she aged. Her wispy white-blond hair was piled on top of her head like a soufflé, just like Eleanor used to do when she was concentrating. The sleeves of her pristine white shirt had been rolled up to the crook of her elbow, and flecks of paint made neon constellations on the backs of her hands.

It made Whitney ache in a way that she hadn't since the day they'd found Eleanor's body on the lawn.

"Ms. Craft?" Jude said softly as she approached the table.

"Who'd like to know?" she answered, not lifting her eyes from the cream-colored canvas in front of her. It was a smear of pinks and greens, like what a field of spring tulips looked like if you were driving by it too fast. It was strange and beautiful.

Whitney sank into the seat across from her. "Hi, Susannah."

At the sound of Whitney's voice, the woman's head snapped up. Her expression softened like melting ice cream. "Oh, Whitney."

Whitney had only met Susannah Craft once, and she almost wished she hadn't. It had been pouring outside when school let out, and Eleanor had suggested that Whitney come back to her place down the street instead of making the long trek to Old Fairview Lane. Whitney could have asked Delilah to take her home in the old sedan after her Spanish club meeting, but the look in Eleanor's eyes made something in her flutter.

They had barely crossed the threshold from the mudroom into the kitchen before Eleanor's lips were on hers. She let out a breathy, feral laugh as she threaded her fingers through Whitney's wet hair, raindrops cascading down her wrist and pooling in the crook of her elbow. They tripped over the laundry basket on their way to Eleanor's room, towels spilling down the stairs like lavender-scented ghosts. As Whitney fumbled for the doorknob, her fingers brushed against something soft and warm.

Eleanor's grandmother stood at the door, a load of towels fresh from the dryer tucked under one arm.

She was positive Susannah remembered that day by the way she looked at Whitney now. There wasn't contempt, or even the whisper of a smirk. She looked utterly, hopelessly broken, like the past six months had shattered something within her and she hadn't been able to find all the pieces again.

She looked like how Whitney felt on the inside.

"I'm so sorry I never reached out," Susannah said, her voice breaking. "I should have."

Whitney shook her head. "No, I could have, too."

They looked at each other for a long moment. All the words Whitney had wanted to say were clotted in her throat.

She'd wanted to apologize for not visiting Susannah after Eleanor died. That she'd never called when she'd heard Susannah had moved into the Nursing Care Center a few months ago. That she'd loved Susannah's granddaughter with the kind of ferocity that made her whisper to weather vanes in the middle of the night. That she still loved her. Her chest tightened, but the words wouldn't come out.

Instead, it was Jude who saved her again. "Hi, Ms. Craft. I'm Jude."

"Whitney's sister," Susannah said. She smiled, her eyes crinkling in the corners. "Eleanor talked about you, too."

Whitney's eyes fluttered. It was a kind thing to say to her sister, but Eleanor talking about Jude? Impossible. They didn't even know each other. In fact, Jude hadn't even realized that Whitney had been dating Eleanor until right before she'd died.

Ms. Craft's assertion seemed to catch Jude off guard, too. "She . . . she did?" Jude said.

"Well, in so many words," she replied. Her smile faded as she looked back at her paint-spattered canvas. "I can never get the wind quite right in these."

Whitney frowned. "The wind?"

"I can't seem to capture it," Susannah said, sweeping her hand over the canvas. "Whenever I paint, it's the flowers or the cornfields that are moving. It's never the *wind*. There's always been something about Bishop that no one can explain." She sighed. "Not even with paint."

Whitney's pulse rocketed. "Out of all the strange things here, why the wind, though?" she asked slowly.

"Your sister knows." Susannah focused her steel blue eyes on Jude. "You can feel it, can't you, Jude?"

Beside her, Jude froze. Her eyes grew wide. "I . . . I don't—"

"Eleanor could, too. Ever since she was a toddler. Whenever that wind kicked up, she would scream like a banshee. She'd scream so hard that her skin would turn as purple as a thunderstorm. At first I thought, you know, it was some sort of trauma from her father leaving her here with me, but when she got older, she told me what was really bothering her." Susannah leaned in and whispered, "The wind traps us here."

A chill coursed down Whitney's spine. She thought of the weather vane in the clearing, the milky green rust settling over the crooked rooster like a layer of film. The way it groaned under the strain of the relentless wind.

The way the wind always seemed to start up as Whitney approached the edge of town.

She closed her eyes, trying to pull her previous conversations with Eleanor to the forefront of her mind. She couldn't remember Eleanor saying anything about the wind. Had Whitney told her about Jude?

My sister's afraid of pretty much everything. She'd laughed into the soft spot near Eleanor's collarbone that last night at the bonfire. *Even the wind.*

Whitney's eyes snapped open. "That can't . . . but there has to be a way out. It's just wind, right? Why stay here?"

Susannah let out a sharp laugh. "Like any of us had a choice. Think about it. When was the last time a woman willingly left this place? Moved away? We can't even get close to the border without the wind pushing us back and punishing us all."

As if on cue, a gust of wind battered the windows, rattling the panes, making all three of them jump. "We can't even *talk* about it," Susannah whispered. "So how are we supposed to leave?"

The wind picked up. The lamp beside them flickered. From the next table over, a man with thick eyebrows yelled, "Stop it with that nonsense, Susannah! You'll scare those kids." He let out a grumble before going back to his painting.

But instead of yelling back, Susannah rolled her eyes. "Shut it, Frank." She sighed heavily. "The thing is, there just aren't many women left here who remember. Who *know*."

Whitney glanced around the dimly lit room. It was true; there was only one other woman in the room, and she was fast asleep pressed up against the corner of the coffee-stained couch. All the other people slapping paint on canvases seemed to be men.

Whitney sat back in her chair, suddenly dizzy. She had always known that there were a lot of accidents in Bishop. A lot of random deaths. But until she *really* looked around this room, let her surroundings soak in, she hadn't realized just how many of them involved women. How many of them never made it to the Nursing Care Center at all.

The wind roared outside, slapping the windows until they groaned. In a matter of minutes, the sky had turned the color of asphalt, the purple underbelly of storm clouds hovering over the swaying sunflowers and distant cornfields.

Whitney looked over at Jude. Her sister's face was lit with the glow of her phone as she frantically tapped the screen. "I've gotta go," she said, snapping her head up to glance at Whitney.

"But it's going to storm."

Jude just shook her head, shoving her phone in her pocket. "I've got to go. See you at home?"

Before Whitney could open her mouth to answer, Jude had already waved an awkward goodbye to Susannah and bolted out the door.

Raindrops began to freckle the windows. The ancient, dusty lamps around the room flickered in unison, like some kind of unheard symphony. Maybe Jude couldn't handle the messed-up energy of this place. Maybe the wind trying to force itself through the cracks and crevices of this place was her breaking point. It was too much to think about.

Whitney got up to leave. "I should go—"

"Wait."

Susannah's voice was so soft that it felt like a breeze against her skin. But the way she looked at Whitney was steady and impenetrable. "I have something for you."

Whitney swallowed. "What is it?"

"Something of Eleanor's. One of the last things she said to me was to make sure you got it . . . if anything ever happened to her."

If anything ever happened to her . . .

Whitney pulled in a breath. Eleanor had been worried she was in danger.

Susannah's face crumpled. "I think it's past time that you see it."

CHAPTER SIXTEEN

Jude stepped out of the Nursing Care Center and into the rain.
Downtown was mostly empty, except for a man holding his toddler's hand as they wove around puddles that had started to form. The wind prickled at her skin, rustling the hair on her arms as she crossed Main Street. It had always rubbed her skin raw, especially at the start of a storm. She'd never thought too much about it; Jude had always been sensitive to everything. The pollen that blanketed Bishop like a golden snow every spring made her eyes sting. She couldn't stand the scent of ketchup fresh from the bottle. She had to cup her palms over her eyes during horror movies.

But what Susannah had said stuck with her.

You can feel it, can't you, Jude?

As soon as Susannah had said those words, Jude knew exactly what she was talking about. It was the erratic pressure changes in the air that thrummed through Jude's veins like her own heartbeat. It was the way the wind moved—deliberately, intentionally— that made her skin crawl. It was how, if she just listened a little bit closer, she knew there was a message waiting for her in the tendrils of the breeze.

That was the *it* Susannah meant. Jude wasn't quite sure what *it* was, though.

Eleanor's grandmother had said something else. *The wind traps us here.*

Something about those words hung heavy in Jude's chest. There was a weight to them, a truth, she couldn't deny. What Jude couldn't figure out was *why*.

She sidestepped a puddle and pulled open the door to Bishop's lone bakery, Butter. Instantly, the scent of burnt coffee flooded her nostrils. She was late. She hurried past the delicate glass displays filled with glossy donuts and crumble-crusted pies to a table near the window.

"I thought you might be standing me up," Bennett said, getting up to greet her as she approached.

Jude stiffened as he wrapped an arm around her back. And then she let herself soften. "I wouldn't stand you up," she said into Bennett's damp T-shirt.

He looked down at her and smiled. "I was really hoping you wouldn't."

Jude let out a breath as she sat at the candy-colored table across from him. Why did he have to be this nice right now? Why did he have to *look* like that? Why did he have to smell like rainwater and pine needles and longing?

Jude shook her head. "So, um, did you bring Whitney's stuff with you?"

"Got it right here." Bennett shoved his hand into his pocket and pulled out a small plastic bag. He pushed it across the table until his fingertips grazed Jude's wrist. "Here."

Jude lifted the bag up to the hanging lantern above them. A single gold hoop shone in the light. "Where's the bracelet?"

Bennett frowned. "What bracelet?"

"The one that was on her wrist. You know, I handed it to you at the hospital before you took her in."

"You didn't hand it to me? I've never had it," Bennett said, his frown deepening. "Is it possible you have it at home?"

Now it was Jude who frowned. "I was pretty sure—"

"I really don't think so," Bennett said quickly, cutting off her thought. "Promise I haven't seen it."

Jude gnawed her lip. She remembered it so clearly—how Whitney's arm had dangled limply against her thigh in the back of the truck. How the tarnished charms had clinked together as the tires rumbled over the gravel. Jude could almost feel the weight of the bracelet as she'd unclipped it, how her hand cupped over Bennett's as she'd placed it in his palm.

"You okay?" Bennett asked. He ran his thumb around the rim of his empty coffee mug. "Your texts sounded like you wanted to talk about something?"

Those texts she'd exchanged with Bennett earlier seemed like a lifetime ago. Had she sounded worried about something then? She'd tried to come off smooth as lake water, unemotional. Like she wasn't trying to pry information out of him. Like she didn't actually *care* if Bennett showed up to Butter to talk to her. Apparently it hadn't worked.

Jude opened her mouth to respond, but a waiter swept into the small space beside them. He set a bubblegum pink plate on the table, along with two spoons. "Enjoy," he said flatly before disappearing.

Her heart hitched as she stared at the buttery yellow dessert in front of her, the powdered sugar layered like a cotton sheet over the top. A lemon bar.

He'd remembered.

Two summers ago, in the middle of July, Bennett had asked Jude to meet him in the sunflower fields. She'd come—because she always came—when Bennett asked her to. When she'd stepped from the clearing into the thicket of flowers, it had felt like she was slipping through a portal into a different world. Suddenly, the sunflowers weren't so scary. Instead of hovering over her like a storm, they hugged her close as she wove through the field. Their velvety petals kissed her skin, whispered the way forward.

She saw the stone gray of his T-shirt before the rest of him took shape in front of her. He materialized in pieces—T-shirt, black sneakers, sun-kissed forearms, hay-bale hair swept across his forehead, freckled nose, and sunburnt lips twisted in a mischievous smile.

Jude had been in love, even though she had never asked for it.

Bennett had spread out the old gingham picnic blanket from his uncle's storm cellar, the frayed edges curling up against flower stems in every direction. *This is for you*, Bennett had said, sinking onto the blanket. *And this, too.*

A lemon bar, glistening on a paper plate in the summer sun.

They'd shared the dessert with a single plastic fork, silence settling between them. When they'd finished, Bennett had looked at Jude with such a softness in his eyes that it made her want to cry. *You have something here*, he'd whispered just before kissing the powdered sugar dusting her upper lip.

We have something here, Jude had thought as they'd sunk into the parched soil together, a chorus of sunflowers pretending to look the other way.

But fate had other plans, and Bennett met Delilah two weeks later.

And now, a single lemon bar sat on a plate between them in this glossy little bakery. But it was so much more than that.

Jude broke right there at that candy-colored table. She pressed her hands to her eyes. "Bennett," she breathed.

There was a long pause. When she slid her palms from her eyes, Bennett was looking at her with the same softness that had cracked open her heart in the sunflower field. "I thought . . . I was trying to do something nice. I'm sorry," he said quietly. His thumb paused on the rim of his coffee mug.

"It's not that," Jude said, her voice wavering. "It's just . . . this is so hard for me, Bennett." She lifted her eyes to his. "Don't you see that? Do you even care?"

"Jude," he said in one breath. His shoulders slumped. "Of course I care."

"Do you ever think about that night?" she whispered. As soon as the words left her lips, she regretted them. They'd been lingering at the edge of her tongue for two years. They'd threatened to jump ship hundreds of times since the night Bennett had met Delilah, the night their mothers vanished and everything—*everything*— had changed. But Jude had always sewn them up tight. If she was honest, she was afraid of Bennett's answer. And more importantly, she'd never wanted to hurt Delilah.

But they'd finally escaped.

Outside, the light drizzle had ramped up into a full-blown storm. It pelted the window beside them, creating a low, melancholy hum that echoed the misery Jude felt as she looked at Bennett from across the untouched lemon bar.

Bennett leaned forward, and his warm hands cupped hers. Jude closed her eyes as she let the feeling of his skin against hers settle into her bones. "Jude, I care about you. I always have."

She opened her eyes, and despite herself, a tear rolled down her cheek. "Then why?" she whispered.

Bennett swallowed, and the muscles in his jaw clenched. "I can't explain it."

Another tear. *Damn it.* "Just . . . please. Help me understand so I can just . . . let this thing go. *Please.*" Jude hated begging. She hated that she had to try to convince people to care as much about something as she did. But she couldn't deal with this anymore, and this conversation was the only way she could see out of this mess.

Jude blinked, and a rush of tears streamed down her cheeks.

"Please just let go," she whispered. She wasn't even sure who she was talking to anymore.

But instead of letting go, Bennett held on tighter. He leaned in so close that his shirt grazed the powdered sugar of the lemon bar. "I wish I could tell you," he whispered. He was so close that Jude could smell the mint on his tongue. "But I literally can't. It's . . . it's not so easy to explain. But I want you to know that it would have been you. It's always *been* you."

And before Jude could understand what was happening, Bennett's lips were on hers, soft and warm and sunburnt, just like they had been two years ago. He kissed her like he meant it. Like they had never stopped.

When the shock had started to fade, and Jude had the sense to figure out what had just happened, she pulled away. Her eyes fluttered open.

But Bennett was no longer looking at her. He stared out the window, eyes wide.

Delilah stood in the pool of light spilling from inside the bakery, cheeks flushed, hair soaked with rainwater. She carried a drenched cloth tote from Rose and Rain over her shoulder. Her other hand was pressed over her mouth.

And she was looking directly at Jude.

CHAPTER SEVENTEEN

The house at the end of Old Fairview Lane was full of ghosts. Delilah was convinced of it.

The ghosts of their mothers haunted every surface of the old home. They watched the girls from their knickknacks and towers of books and unfinished art projects that stared at them from the back of the room. Then there were the other ghosts.

There were the ghosts of the things they'd all refused to look at. The spectral things that hung in the air among the four of them, threatening to tear them apart. The things that had been hidden in plain sight all along.

Delilah hadn't realized what she was looking at. The light from the bakery and the raindrops clinging to the glass had distorted things, so at first it seemed like Jude and Bennett were a single person, a blur of long dark hair and sun-drenched skin. And then she'd blinked, and her whole world became as sharp as a lie.

Even now, a whole day later, Delilah felt as though she'd left part of herself back on Main Street. Maybe she was a ghost now, too.

She lay in her bed early the next morning, not certain if she'd ever slept. The rain had lashed at the house all night, making the roof groan and windowpane behind her dresser rattle. At some point, the girls had come home, one after another, but only one knocked on her closed door. She hadn't answered it. Her phone had buzzed throughout the night, too. Urgent messages from both Bennett and Jude flitted across the screen in a panicked parade.

It's not what it looked like, Bennett said.

Can we talk? Jude texted.

Delilah turned the phone to silent.

The gray of the morning pressed in on the house, smothering the sunflowers in a layer of fog. Delilah pulled on one of her mother's old sweatshirts that said MAKE ART, NOT WAR across the chest and wrangled her curls into a topknot. She poked at the bags under her eyes in the dingy bathroom mirror, trying to remember if she'd looked this disheveled that morning after her mom had disappeared.

The morning after she'd stayed up all night falling in love with Bennett.

Delilah pulled in a breath at the ache that bloomed in her chest. Even two years later, her own sadness still caught her off guard from time to time. She'd woken up that morning in the cellar with her heart tender and longing for her mother. She'd kissed a sleeping Bennett on the cheek before rushing home as the sky bled pink. She'd wanted to wake Indigo to tell her about Bennett, but the only trace she'd found of her was a dying sunflower on the bathroom sink. Delilah hadn't known it then, but her mother had already been gone for hours.

Sometimes Indigo felt more like a dream than someone who had loved her.

What would her mom say now, if she were still here? Would Indigo tell her that it had to have been a misunderstanding, that Jude and Bennett would never do that to her? Or would she tell Delilah that she was worth more than their betrayal?

She tried to picture Indigo waiting for her in the hallway, following her down the stairs and into the kitchen as Delilah filled up her coffee mug, whispering advice that felt like a balm. But when Delilah turned to look, the house was dark and silent.

So she did the thing she did best when things were unbearable: she figured it out.

She slipped out the front door before anyone had even stirred. Outside, the air crackled with energy, wind churning just enough to rustle the sunflower petals. The storm that had started with blustering winds and a clap of thunder yesterday hadn't quite decided overnight what it wanted to do. Instead it just . . . hovered. Sticky and heavy and threatening to pummel them all with the promise of rain.

She walked down Main Street, her coffee mug still hot under her fingertips. When she passed Butter, she glanced in the window. The bakery was the only shop open at this hour, and already another couple had taken up occupancy at the petal-pink table. They leaned toward each other just like Bennett and Jude had only hours ago.

What had happened last night?

She paused in front of the window as the couple stood to leave. Twin pink chairs sat abandoned, but Delilah couldn't stop imagining Bennett in the one to the right, his long torso leaning across the table, his calloused hand cupping Jude's cheek.

It wasn't a secret that Bennett and Caleb Harding were players. Everyone at Bishop High knew it. Delilah knew it even before the party. That hadn't stopped her from falling head over heels in love with him in the storm cellar that night, especially after he'd explained himself.

I know what people say about me, he'd told her, curled on his side in the cellar. *And I'm not going to lie to you; I've made some mistakes with girls. I just . . . Caleb and I don't talk about it much, but it pretty much wrecked us when our parents up and left us a few years back. We love our uncle William, but . . ."* Bennet's eyes fluttered shut. He whispered, *It was just nice to feel wanted is all.*

A spark had flickered in Delilah's heart. She *knew* that feeling. Even though, at the time, she occupied the same space as her mother, Indigo was always just out of reach. A Technicolor ghost that she could never grasp.

But that had been in the Before. Indigo had disappeared for good, and Bennett spent the night curled up on his side, face toward hers, like half of a set of parentheses. When they woke the next morning, he'd kissed the center of her palm and curled her fingers into her hand before telling her that he was, unequivocally, hers.

She'd actually believed him.

Delilah pressed her forehead to the glass. How could she be so *naive*?

The worst part of it was the searing jealousy that had started to creep up her spine. She closed her eyes and the image of Bennett and Jude floated to the surface like foam on a wave. The way Jude's head was cocked to the side so she could lean into Bennett's touch, how her fingers were so easily threaded through his.

Jude had been able to touch her boyfriend as if he were hers.

No lightning. No shocks of pain.

Delilah opened her eyes. A single older man with tufts of white hair around his ears looked up at her from the table. She quickly blinked back tears and gave a half-hearted wave before continuing down the street.

The Gordons' shop was at the very edge of town, and although Delilah had lived here her entire life, she'd never been inside. Honestly, she'd prefer to keep it that way, but given the circumstances, she didn't have another choice.

Delilah glanced up at the sign nailed over the front door. GORDON'S TAXIDERMY, it said, which was about the least inventive name she'd ever heard. She twisted the knob and pushed open the door. The scent of salt and sawdust flooded her nose, making her eyes water. The lobby was painted the color of oatmeal, and a massive stuffed deer stood beside a small desk as if it were tasked with greeting the customers.

Ew. Delilah approached the desk, but there was no one seated behind it. There was no bell on the counter, either. She tipped her head to peer into the back room, but a thick rubber curtain blocked the entryway.

She cleared her throat and set her empty mug down, waiting. Dust floated in front of the single window. After it had settled, she stepped in front of the deer and bent down. It stared back at her with hollow, glassy eyes.

"That's my dad's best work."

Delilah's spine straightened. Evan Gordon stood over her, his dark hair pulled back into a ponytail, sawdust flecking his lips. He smiled. "Nice, isn't it?"

Sure, if you have a thing for dead animals. "Yeah. It's nice," Delilah said.

"Come on, I can talk in the back," Evan said, pulling back the thick curtain.

Delilah froze. "We . . . can't talk out here?"

Evan's eyes shifted to the window then back to her. "I'd rather not, if that's okay."

Delilah followed his gaze. This close to the clearing, and this early in the morning, there wasn't much out there except for the gray. But still, she shrugged and followed Evan into the back of the shop.

As soon as she entered the workroom, Delilah regretted it. Another full-size deer stood beside the door, but this one was only partly constructed. Its hide had been skinned and tanned, but only the back half had been pulled taut over the bulky frame. The front hung like a limp scarf around the neck, the exposed wire skull staring blankly into the distance.

Then there were the waterfowl.

Delilah's eyes widened as she followed Evan to the back of the workroom. What seemed like hundreds of ducks, geese, and pheasants lined the pale wooden shelves, their stiff feathers sticking out at awkward angles. Some seemed to be completely finished, while others were missing essential parts—a pair of wings, a webbed foot, a beak. One mallard Delilah passed had only empty sockets instead of glass eyes.

Evan reached a small workbench tucked into the corner and grabbed something. He turned to face her, a fat bullfrog in his palm. "Isn't this little guy cute?" he said, grinning.

Delilah wrinkled her nose. The truth was, it *was* kind of cute, if you didn't look directly at its eyes. Its throat was the color of a summer squash, and it had been stuffed so it looked as though the frog was mid-ribbit. But the eyes. One was looking just slightly to the left, and the other was too far to the right. Neither of them was looking directly at her.

"Yeah, I know, I'm still working on the eyes," Evan said, setting the frog back on the workbench. "Anyway, what did you want to talk about?"

Delilah scanned the workshop. Fresh hides treated with salt hung from a laundry line through the center of the room. Glassy eyes watched from every angle. Evan's own workbench was stained with copper-colored blood. She flicked her eyes away from the stains. "How did you know my mom?"

Evan fiddled with the frog for a moment. "She was my art teacher. Up at the shop."

The shop had to be Rose and Rain, where Indigo held pop-up classes sometimes. Delilah frowned. "You . . . took art?"

"What do you think this is?" Evan said cheerfully, tapping the frog on the top of its head. "Taxidermy is just another kind of sculpture. Your mom used papier mâché. I use skin." He shrugged. "Not that different."

They could argue about that point later. "So, did you know her well enough to give her your phone number?"

He froze. His voice got low. "How did you know about that?"

Delilah pulled a slip of paper from her pocket and unfolded it. Evan turned to read it. "You wrote it down on her receipt. The day she disappeared."

He snatched the receipt from Delilah's fingers, dark eyes scanning the text. His shoulders slumped when he got to the bottom, and for one strange second, Delilah actually felt something toward Evan Gordon that she couldn't quite place.

His face softened. "We should talk."

"Exactly," she said, folding her arms over her chest.

Outside, a gust of wind threw itself against the window. The whole shop shook as if it had been a boulder instead of the breeze. Delilah's eyes widened. The wind had come out of nowhere. Evan glanced quickly at the window and then back to her. "I don't know how much time we have."

"What—"

"Just listen," Evan said in a tone that she'd only heard him use when he was about to get into a fight with Bo. "I've known the Hardings for a long time, and I overheard Bennett's uncle saying he was spending a lot of time at your mom's house. I'd been trying to figure out a way to warn her."

The wind raged again. It pounded on the shop in angry fits, threatening to strip the whole thing down to its frame. The small lamp on Evan's workbench started to flicker. He reached toward her, eyes wide. "Come with me."

Delilah stared at his open palm for a second too long. In one wrathful fit, the wind lashed against the windows with such force that a spiderweb crack opened up down the middle. Evan didn't wait for her to decide; he grabbed her hand and yanked her back toward the front of the shop.

The windows shattered.

Glass spilled over into the shop, covering birds and bullfrogs in a layer of glittering glass. Delilah bumped her hip on one of the tables, causing a wild rabbit to wobble. Evan grabbed it with his free hand and tucked it under his arm.

He pulled her against the wall closest to the lobby where there were no windows. Together they sank to the cement floor and curled up beneath a workbench as the storm raged.

"Evan, what's going on?" Delilah hated the way the words sounded shaky on their way out, but she had to admit: this was extra strange, even for Bishop. The wind was ever-present, but it came in rolling waves; fits of intensity that ebbed and flowed. But this storm had been pummeling them for days, and it was only getting worse.

"There's something going on with William Harding. He . . . I don't know. I'm still not exactly sure what I saw, but one time I was over there, and I saw him standing in the backyard, like, talking to someone. And the second he stopped, the wind picked up. And not in a normal way." Evan peeked his head out from under the workbench just as another wave of wind slapped against the shop. "It was like this."

Delilah's shoulders relaxed. "Ha, okay. So you think that Bennett's uncle can—what—control the wind?"

"Delilah," he said softly, setting the stuffed rabbit between them. "I'm being serious. Every time I try to talk to someone about it, the wind picks up until I stop or I go back in my house. Like six months ago, I swear to god, I asked Caleb about it when we were drunk and he got all serious. He said, *Soon I'll be able to do it, too.*"

Delilah's stomach lurched. An image of Caleb flitted through her memory, the day of the memorial. How his touch had felt like an electric shock coursing through her veins. How the wind had swallowed them all up as soon as Whitney started to talk about her dead girlfriend. How, even in the past, it didn't slow down until the entire town was tucked away in their houses like well-kept secrets. How they all considered that *normal.*

She listened as the wind continued to protest on the other side of the walls. It wasn't possible—it *couldn't* be. And yet.

There had always been something strange about this place. The sunflowers that hovered around them all like a threat. The way they watched. How they were a little *too* sentient to be just seeds and petals.

How they never seemed to die.

How they seemed to be *watching*.

She had never heard anyone in Bishop talk about the sunflowers, other than to comment on how brilliant they looked under the summer sun's rays. For the most part, she had grown up ignoring them, until she couldn't any longer.

For as long as Delilah could remember, this army of sunflowers had always surrounded Bishop, no matter the season. Even in the coldest winters, they still stood, guarding them all.

From what?

It was a question that had lingered in the back of her mind since she'd found the single sunflower on the bathroom sink, as ludicrous as it sounded. Her mother had plucked it and carried it into their home for a reason. And if Delilah thought there could be something very wrong with the sunflowers, then why not the wind? Strangeness didn't discriminate between flowers and the breeze.

"Why should I believe you?" she said limply. "You hate us. You never even talk to me unless you want to complain about Bo."

Evan closed his eyes and let out a long breath. "I don't hate you. I don't even hate Bo."

"You just like to throw a punch in her direction every once in a while for what—fun?"

He groaned. "First of all, Bo always starts it. I don't know, she just . . . she knows how to push my buttons like no one else can." Evan rubbed his hands over his face. "I'm not exactly proud of it."

Delilah let Evan's words sink in. There was some truth there; Bo *did* know how to push buttons, apparently not just hers. Not that it made the way he treated her okay.

"Second, we've been scrapping like that since we were kids,"

Evan continued. "Remember? She'd always take my Pringles at lunch and then try to kick *my* ass, like I did something wrong." He opened his eyes and looked at her. "Third, she was looking for trouble again with Caleb. I wanted to keep her away, but you know Bo. She doesn't listen."

Delilah paused. "Did you say trouble *again* with Caleb?"

As she said the words, she felt the echo of Caleb's lightning-shock touch vibrate up her arm. How it had seared into her, how she had thought, even then, that those were the hands of someone who understood how power could cause pain.

Evan's dark lashes fluttered. "Listen, that's a conversation for you and Bo." He fiddled with one of the rabbit's ears, tugging at the tufts of fur as if he were pulling weeds. His cheeks turned pink. "But just know, when you do, that I didn't know he was going to do that. And it wasn't okay. It wasn't okay."

They sat in silence. Outside, the wind slapped even harder against the building. Evan turned to her, cheeks even pinker now. "I actually . . . I actually really like you, you know. I just stayed away because of Bennett."

Something that had long been dormant in Delilah stirred. That night at the bonfire, she had watched Evan through the flames, his warm skin aglow in the light, the smoldering look he'd given her over the rim of his plastic cup.

The way that look had made her heart race and her skin flush.

She blinked the thought away. "It doesn't make sense," Delilah said softly. "Then why do you still hang out with them—the Hardings—if they're doing something with the wind? If they creep you out so much?"

"There are a lot of strange things in this town," Evan said slowly. "It's best to keep the strangest one close to be safe."

Delilah followed the rhythm of his long fingers. The rabbit was gross, but Evan's olive skin and long fingers danced delicately along the thicket of fur. There was a freckle in the shape of a crescent moon just above his wristbone.

"I learned a lot from your mom," he said softly, interrupting Delilah's thoughts. "She taught me how some artists leave little pieces of themselves in their work. Like this one artist, he used to crush up rose petals and put them in his paint, or other artists write little messages in spaces people can't see unless they're really paying attention. I started doing it, too."

Gently, he tilted the rabbit so the tail was visible. His fingers parted the fur, exposing a single white thread the color of heavy cream. It was so thin that even this close up, it was barely noticeable. "This is from a blanket I used to sleep with all the time when I was a kid." He cleared his throat. "My mom made it."

Delilah's heart lurched. Cecilia Gordon had died only a few years ago. Cancer, they said. She'd gone quickly.

Evan looked up at her from under his dark lashes and Delilah felt parts of herself falling away like an avalanche.

Responsible. *Crumbling into dust.*

Thoughtful. *Slipping away.*

Committed. *Gone.*

Delilah wrapped her hand around the back of his neck and pulled him closer. When she kissed Evan, he didn't pull away. And his lips, his touch, his body didn't hurt.

But the wind wouldn't let up. The wall behind them groaned so loudly that they both jumped, splitting apart like land struck by lightning.

There was a loud, mournful groan. And then the whole shop shuddered before the roof came crashing in.

Chapter Eighteen

Bo was going to have to confront William Harding herself.

She'd barely seen Whitney in the past day or so, and Jude was a nonissue. It wasn't like she'd help with this kind of thing. And Delilah? Well, it was probably for the best that she never found out anything about it.

But Bo was starting to get antsy. Something was happening here that made her stomach knot with dread. They had to do something—anything—and quickly.

Bo yanked open the junk drawer in the kitchen. She pawed through the contents. Ink pens with bite marks (Whitney's doing, for sure), a riot of wrinkled receipts, bent-up bookmarks, and a random screwdriver.

No pepper spray.

She shut the door and tapped her fingers on the countertop. She could have sworn there was pepper spray there. She could remember the way Delilah had hitched both eyebrows before saying, *This isn't for everyday use, Bo,* before dropping the cannister into the drawer.

But maybe she hadn't been completely paying attention, either. Delilah's endless rules felt like sandpaper against her skin if she listened for too long.

It had to be around here somewhere.

Bo pulled open cupboard after cupboard, searching. She wasn't even exactly sure if she needed the pepper spray, but having a weapon of some sort in this situation could only help. Actually, having a weapon in *most* situations could help.

She closed one cupboard and opened the next. It was completely possible that she would bring up the recent surge in deaths with Mr. Harding. That she'd talk about the bloodstained knife in the clearing, and he would give her a completely logical explanation for it. Something that Bo couldn't quite puzzle together. Or he wouldn't.

Finally, she found it.

Delilah had tucked it into the back corner of the cabinet with all the pots and pans, probably because she knew Bo would never go in there.

Bo held the small black container in the center of her palm. Something in her felt irrevocably . . . *sad* as she looked at it. When Delilah had first brought the pepper spray home a few weeks after the disappearance, Bo had laughed. *Like we'll ever need it,* she had scoffed.

You never know, Delilah had said, her tone somber. *We're on our own now.*

She'd never thought that she'd *really* need to bring a cannister of pepper spray with her, no matter where she went in town. Her fists had always been enough.

Something was happening in Bishop that made Bo's skin prickle. She'd spent the afternoon searching for any information she could find about their mothers' disappearance on the internet. Nothing turned up. But dozens of women dead or missing in a town as small as this one was surely newsworthy, at least.

And then there were the other things.

The way the wind seemed to push back harder lately. All those deaths stacking up, closer and closer together. The way the sunflowers hovered so close that Bo swore she could hear the echo of warnings on their petals. The one that had leaned in through the window and whispered, *Look.*

And she couldn't stop thinking about that knife.

When Bo had told the rest of the girls about the bloodstained knife she'd found in the clearing, she'd left out one important fact.

She'd brought it home with her.

She still wasn't sure why she'd done it; it was almost like she couldn't stop her hands from gripping the handle, slipping it into her pocket, and carrying it home. All she knew was that she didn't want that knife to get buried again. That she needed to keep it safe.

And to Bo, there was nowhere safer than the kitchen at Old Fairview Lane. It was where her mother had curled pillowy dough into cinnamon rolls, where she scrubbed garden dirt from her fingernails while steam wafted from the sink. Where she listened to Delilah, up before everyone else, opening cupboards and clinking glasses together as she put away the dishes from the night before.

Bo took a breath and opened the drawer closest to the oven. A pile of worn kitchen cloths sat inside, just like they had since Bo and Cori had moved in here. She pulled out the top one and set it on the counter, revealing the knife.

She chewed her lip. It was the first time she'd really looked at it since that night. The rust color still stained the blade, and in the light she noticed a few splatters on the handle.

This knife had been used for something dark and ugly, that much she knew. But she couldn't allow herself to think too much about it, because the thoughts would lead her down the rabbit hole of wondering if she was standing on her mother's bones each time she went to the clearing.

"Oh, I didn't know you were home."

Bo jumped, slamming the drawer shut and spinning to find

Jude hovering at the entrance to the kitchen. "I didn't know you were home, either."

Jude's eyes fluttered. "Have you seen Delilah?"

"No. I heard her leave early this morning." Bo shifted so Jude couldn't see the pepper spray still in her hand. She tucked it into her back pocket. "What do you need her for?"

Jude glanced at the floor. "I just. Um . . ."

"It's no big deal," Bo said quickly. "You don't have to tell me. I've got to get going anyway." She squeezed past Jude, careful to conceal the lump in her pocket. Sometimes it was just easier to cut Jude a break from trying to explain her thoughts than putting her on the spot when she wasn't ready to share.

As Bo marched through the living room, her heart started to race. What was she *doing*? Did she really think she'd show up at town hall and, what, force Mr. Harding to tell her what he knew about those dead women?

Bo let out a strangled little laugh. Like a can of pepper spray was going to convince her old history teacher to tell her Bishop's secrets. He could have known where those files were hidden because he was always helping out at the town hall anyway.

But she had to try.

She pulled open the front door, just a little bit, but the wind did the rest of the work for her. The door slammed into the side of the house, shaking the entire porch and making Bo sway on her feet. In just a few short hours the sky had transformed from cornflower blue to a slab of asphalt gray, and the wind was so fierce that even the sunflowers shriveled under its roar.

The storm sirens started.

They wailed through town, the edges just touching the last house on Old Fairview Lane.

Delilah. Whitney.

Bo should call them, just to make sure they were okay. She spun around. Jude's bare feet crested the porch, her phone already to her ear. Even with the wind and sirens, Bo could hear Whitney's raspy voice telling the caller to leave a message.

Jude's hand dropped. "I have no idea where she is. She wasn't here when I woke up."

"Delilah's still out there . . ." Bo looked back out into the storm. It could be a tornado. It definitely wouldn't be strange for a tornado to touch down in the middle of Kansas. But how many times had the sirens warned them of impending doom, only for everyone in town to scurry home and spend all afternoon boarding up the windows while the wind dissipated around them?

Bo started down the steps.

"Wait, you can't go out there," Jude said, her shoulders tensing. "What am I supposed to do here by myself?"

Bo paused, her hair whipping over her face. "I've gotta go. I have something that I have to do."

For a long moment, there was nothing but the roar of the wind and the waning sirens. "This one's different," Jude said. "This storm is more dangerous."

Bo turned around. For once, Jude didn't look scared. She stared back at Bo with a fierceness that she'd never witnessed before.

"There's something I need to tell you," she said.

CHAPTER NINETEEN

Whitney stood in front of the Bishop Nursing Care Center, trying to talk herself into going inside. But the second she built up enough courage to walk in the lights flickered once, twice, then snapped off. The sirens roared as she stood alone in the lobby, the faded green notebook Eleanor's grandmother had given her poking out of her messenger bag like a spindly weed.

The door to the rest of the center swung open and Alma marched through, a flashlight tucked under her arm. Her mouth opened when she saw Whitney. This time her lips were painted a soft coral. "Oh. Hey. What are you doing back here?"

Whitney's cheeks flooded with heat, though she wasn't sure why. She pulled out the notebook from her bag. "I have to return this to Susannah." It was a half-truth, really. Eleanor's grandmother hadn't asked for the notebook back when she gave it to Whitney yesterday, but she hadn't *not* asked for it back. Besides, Whitney still had a lot of questions about what she'd found inside the notebook, and she needed answers.

"Oh, right," Alma said, squeezing behind the office chair to reach an electrical box. She positioned the flashlight under her chin as she opened the panel. "Can you hold this for me really quick?"

Whitney squeezed behind the chair to grab the flashlight. She shone it into a labyrinth of colored wires and meaningless switches as Alma poked and prodded. She mumbled something to herself as she snapped one of the switches on and off. Nothing happened. "Welp," she said, shutting the door and turning to Whitney. "Looks like the storm did a number on the power grid."

She was so close that Whitney could see a tiny smudge of coral in the corner of her mouth. Whitney swallowed. "Oh, okay," she said with a shaky breath.

Alma slid out behind the desk first, her warm hand brushing against Whitney's, making the hair on the back of her arm stand up. Whitney followed, one hand still tightly gripping the notebook. "So, can I go back there?"

"No, I'm sorry," Alma said, shaking her head. "It's a security issue without any power. No lights, no cameras. It's not safe for any of the residents."

Whitney almost laughed. As if she'd go back there and, what, hurt someone? But the look on Alma's face told her that she wasn't about to budge. "Got it. Well, can you give this to her then? Whenever the lights turn back on?" She set the notebook on the desk and tentatively slid it toward Alma.

Alma laughed and pushed it back. "Where do you think you're going?"

". . . Back home?"

"In that storm? No way." Alma looked out the window and winced. "That rain is coming down pretty hard, and the wind? Oof. Why don't you just wait it out for a bit?"

Whitney followed Alma's gaze. Even in the short time she'd been in the lobby, the sky had already turned a threatening slate gray. And the wind was particularly awful, banging against the door and howling like a banshee. She turned back to Alma. "Okay. Just until it calms down."

Something flitted across Alma's face that Whitney didn't recognize. "Come on. Come sit." She walked over to the faded plaid couch in the corner and sat on one side, tucking her legs beneath her. Whitney grabbed the notebook and followed.

She sank into the other seat, careful to sit so her sore shoulder didn't bump up against the back of the sofa. She ran her charcoal-colored fingernails nervously over the edges of the notebook.

"So what's with that?" Alma asked, eyes flicking to Whitney's fingers, then back up to her eyes.

Shit. Whitney glanced down at the notebook—*Eleanor's* notebook. After Jude had left the Nursing Care Center yesterday, Susannah had retrieved this notebook from her bedroom. *Eleanor wrote in it a lot before she died*, Susannah had explained. *But I can't understand it. Maybe you can?*

Whitney had flipped through the pages, slowly at first, absorbing every loop of Eleanor's cursive. She had run her thumb across the pencil markings, desperate to understand Eleanor's half sentences and random sketches. Nothing had been dated, so she couldn't tell how long Eleanor had been writing in it before she died. There was something about the wind, with a pencil-drawn diagram of arrows circling what looked like Bishop in the center. And there was a list of dates stacked in the corner of another page, with names Whitney didn't recognize.

Then there was the weirdest part of all. On the last written page, somewhere in the middle of the notebook, there was a name at the very top: *Edward Dingal.* It was circled, and beneath it Eleanor had taped a newspaper article as delicate as lace.

Bishop Township Celebrates 100 Years
Descendants of Edward J. Dingal, the official founder of Bishop, who passed away in 1901, gathered in front of the newly constructed

community center to celebrate 100 years since Dingal signed the deed. Robert J. Dingal stands center front with his children.

There was a black-and-white photo that Eleanor had cut out with painstaking precision. A tall, lanky man in a dress coat stood in front of the community center, bowler hat on his head. He cradled a baby with chunky thighs in one arm and held the tiny hand of a towheaded toddler with his other.

Then there was the part that made Whitney's stomach lurch.

There were two words written below the article in Eleanor's handwriting.

THEY KNOW.

Whitney assumed Eleanor had been talking about Edward Dingal, but who else was included in "they"?

And more importantly: What was it that "they" knew?

She had quickly scanned the rest of the page. Eleanor's prim cursive became wilder, more erratic as she wrote. *Dingal was a founder,* she wrote. History Obscura *says the first official landmark built in Bishop was a cemetery on the westernmost border in the 1800s. Out of all things, why a cemetery? Did he kill people to obtain the land? As a sacrifice of some kind? Does the land need to be ruined—flooded, burnt?—to stop the curse?*

And then, at the very bottom of the page:

His descendants must still live here.

Whitney felt Alma's dark eyes watching her as she clutched the notebook. She couldn't tell her about this. Not only because she couldn't explain what Eleanor's thoughts meant, but because it felt like a betrayal of the darkest kind.

Eleanor hadn't shared this with her when she was alive. Whitney was sure she wouldn't want her to share it with Alma now.

"It's . . . it was my girlfriend's." Whitney shifted to tuck it back into her bag. "Susannah gave it to me to look at and I was trying to give it back to her. She was her—my girlfriend's—grandmother."

Alma's eyes fluttered. "Eleanor?"

"Yeah," Whitney said slowly. "Did you know her?"

"Only from what Susannah says about her," Alma said softly. "I'm sorry for your loss."

There was something about the way Alma said those words that made Whitney crumble right there on that shitty sofa in the Nursing Care Center lobby. Between Eleanor and her mom, she'd heard them a million times in the past two years. And they'd always felt like nothing, like a scrape that was supposed to sting but had hardened instead. But the way the words rolled over Alma's tongue, how she couldn't quite look at Whitney when she said them. How Whitney couldn't stop staring at the tiny divot at the top of her lips.

She wanted to know what it was like to kiss those lips.

Whitney let out a breath as soon as the thought flitted across her mind. *No,* she was confused. She just missed Eleanor, and seeing Susannah, and reading her notebook, had dredged up all that heartache like silt from a river. That was all it was.

"We could try to talk to her, you know," Alma said, lifting an eyebrow. "Have you ever tried before?"

An icy chill crawled down Whitney's spine. Alma couldn't possibly know about the weather vane. "What did you say?"

"Tried to talk to her?" Alma hopped up from the sofa and began riffling through a shelf below the desk. "Aha, here they are." She lifted the deck to show Whitney. "My cards."

Even with the storm continuing to brew outside, Whitney's whole body relaxed as Alma bounded back over to the sofa, a deck of faded oracle cards in her hand.

"We could try it with these. My mom taught me to read them." Alma curled her long legs beneath her as she shuffled the cards. "Is there anything you want to ask her?" she asked, not looking up.

Whitney swallowed the knot forming in her throat. She'd dreamed of this moment a hundred million times in the past six months. She'd woken up in a tangle of blankets more nights than she could count, her lashes still damp with tears, begging god or the universe or even the empty, dust-filled space around her for relief. Just one more conversation. One more chance to hold Eleanor's hand tight and ask her to stay. Please. Just stay.

She knew that whatever these cards were wouldn't give her that. But, more than anything, Whitney was tired of talking to the creaking weather vane and hoping the wind responded. She was tired of talking to *herself* and pretending that was enough.

There was only one question she had left. And she wanted a real answer.

"How did you really die, Eleanor?" Whitney whispered.

The question clung to the air like smoke. It pressed on Whitney's lungs, clotted up her throat as she watched Alma's fingers pick through the cards.

Alma set them out, facedown—one, two, three—then tucked the rest of the deck into the corner of the sofa. She glanced up at Whitney. "Are you sure you want to know?"

Whitney paused. "Yeah," she said. "I do."

Alma nodded once, then flipped over the first card. A woman with amber hair stood at the center of the image holding a black, swollen orb. *Dark Moon*, the words read at the top.

"Oh," Alma said. She pressed her lips into a tight line.

Whitney glanced between her and the card. "What does it mean?"

"It's the card of knowledge. See that moon the person's holding? It represents a secret—a big one. And the person's holding it alone." Alma's fingers tapped the card. "Is it possible Eleanor had a secret?"

If you only knew, Whitney's thoughts trailed back to the notebook. She nodded. "Yeah, it's possible."

Alma flipped over the next card. This one had a person in the center, her long hair snaking between mounds of dirt. She lay in an awkward position between makeshift graves, her neck bent at an angle that made Whitney's stomach curdle. There was an open ditch beside her, and behind her, a wall of flowers pressed in from all sides. A single word flitted across the top: *Graveyard*.

Alma cleared her throat. "It kind of looks like . . ."

". . . the clearing," Whitney finished.

She couldn't stop staring at how much the graveyard in the image looked like the dusty patch of earth where there had been bonfires and first kisses, disappearances and . . .

Murder?

Eleanor had mentioned something about a cemetery in her notes: it was Bishop's first landmark and had been placed on the town's western edge.

But that wasn't where the cemetery was now.

Bishop Cemetery—the only one that Whitney knew of, at least—was only a few blocks from the town center. Something had happened to this one, the original, but what?

An image creeped into the back of Whitney's mind like fog rolling in over the lake. Jude's open palm in their dimly lit bedroom, the tarnished acorn charm glinting in the buttery lamplight. The bloodstain on the cap.

The knife Bo had found in the clearing.

She pinched her eyes shut. *No.* The pain of losing Eleanor in some kind of freak incident had just started to settle into her bones, all these months later. She wasn't sure she could take the idea of Eleanor being swept away from her by violence. Whitney felt like she was splintering from the inside out.

"Let's see if there's anything else," Alma added quickly. And then, in an almost whisper, "Eleanor, what do you want to tell us?"

She flipped the final card.

It was *The Veil*. This time, there were no people on the card. There was only a crumbling stone archway, a gauzy veil draped over it and blowing in the breeze. Just behind the veil was a single oak tree drenched in summer sunlight, almost as if the archway led to somewhere much sweeter. And clustered at the roots were dozens of glossy acorns.

Acorns.

Whitney's heartbeat skyrocketed. Her hand flew to her mouth. "Oh. Oh shit."

Alma's eyes grew wide. "What is it?"

"I don't know," Whitney said slowly, and it was true. Her mind felt like it had been infested, ideas skittering out from dark places too fast for her to catch any of them. She didn't know what the cards meant. She just knew she wanted to throw up. "I have to go," she said, standing. "I have to go somewhere."

"But it's still storming." Alma stood, causing the cards to slide into the crease of the sofa. "I'm so sorry. Did I do something wrong?"

That was the thing—Alma had done everything *right*. She'd been sitting at the front desk, just minding her business and living her life, and Whitney had shown up at the door. And as much as Whitney had tried to convince herself she was only coming back to the Nursing Care Center to return the notebook, even though Susannah hadn't asked for it back, she knew the truth.

She had come to see Alma again.

Alma had made Whitney feel, for one precious second, like she could be someone new. She could be someone outside of this relentless grief.

But she'd forgotten that her pain wasn't a wall—it was a black hole. It sucked people in. She'd let it pull Alma closer, and there was nothing at the core for Whitney to offer her. Just . . . emptiness that felt like it would go on forever.

Outside, the storm had only grown angrier. Rain pelted the siding, and the windows had started to fog, turning the world a depressing gray pockmarked with sunflower yellow. A siren wailed, but it wasn't the storm siren.

"The ambulance?" Alma said, squinting out the window.

The ambulance. As in the only one Bishop had, used only for real emergencies.

"I'm so sorry, Alma." Whitney swallowed. "I've gotta go."

The look on Alma's face made something in Whitney unravel. And before she could say anything, Alma pulled Whitney into a hug.

She smelled like vanilla and hand sanitizer and a regret so deep that it actually hurt. "It's okay to want to be happy again," she whispered. "You're not betraying her."

Whitney pulled away. Her mouth was only inches from Alma's. It would be so easy, but it was so, so hard.

She pressed her lips into a smile. "Then why does it feel like it?"

They untangled from each other. When Whitney looked back before she stepped into the storm, Alma wasn't watching. She'd gone back to the sofa and collected her cards. She cupped them in her hands like they were fragile, delicate things.

Like the future was something that could be easily shattered.

She was right.

CHAPTER TWENTY

There's something I need to tell you.

Jude regretted the words the second they left her mouth. She hadn't even planned to say them; they slipped through her lips like rainwater between her fingers, and Bo responded with a feral "Fine" and stormed back toward the house.

"Wait," Jude said, sticking out her palm. "We should go somewhere safer."

This storm was different. Jude could feel it in her bones. It hurt in the same way that bumping her elbow on a door hinge hurt, like a reverberation that flashed through her entire body and rattled her teeth.

Bo threw her arms up. "Like where, Jude?" she yelled over the wind. "Where are we going to go right now?"

The storm answered before Jude could. A fierce gale slammed against the old house, rocking it to its frame. The old ash tree in the side yard groaned.

And then it snapped.

A limb splintered from the trunk so fast that by the time Jude blinked, the limb was already swinging toward the house.

"Run!" Jude screamed. She grabbed Bo's wrist and yanked her off the porch before the limb connected. The branches smashed into the spindly pillar beside them, and the entire house shook. Jude didn't wait around to see the damage. Every nerve in her body pulled her toward the abandoned storm cellar around back.

"No," Bo said. She jerked back. "*No.*"

"Bo, we have to!" Jude pleaded. The storm hovered so close to them that Jude could taste the rain and malice on her tongue. "Come on. Please."

Bo gritted her teeth. And then she took off running.

Jude chased after her to the backyard as what was left of the ash tree limb pinwheeled above them. She dropped to her knees and dug through the cracked pots in Cori's abandoned vegetable garden until she found the cellar key jangling at the bottom of the last one. She poured it into her hand and turned.

Bo wasn't behind her. Her heart climbed into her throat.

Bo emerged from the sunflower field behind the cellar like a ghost, petals swirling behind her. She held a single flower clutched in her fist.

"Come on!" Jude said. She met Bo at the cellar, hands shaking as she jammed the key into the lock. Together they pulled on the metal doors until they creaked open. Must and darkness greeted them. Jude grabbed Bo's hand before she could change her mind.

Jude's sneakers kicked up a cloud of dust as she descended, knuckles white as she squeezed Bo's fingers. "One sec," Bo said. She jabbed the sunflower upward like a soft-petaled sword, then carefully closed the doors around it, leaving the head exposed to the storm. "So Lilah and Whit know where we are."

Jude tried to push the panic from her lungs as the slab gray sky waned into a sliver of light. It had been years since she'd last been in a storm cellar, and the Hardings' was a million times nicer than this. It was the same shape and size as this one, but it had less of an "underground crypt" vibe. There was electricity. And cushioned chairs. There were delicate string lights and a bookshelf and a soft, gingham picnic blanket that Jude knew all too well.

This cellar? It wasn't the kind of place you wanted to hang out in.

But as soon as Bo had closed the doors and turned on the battery-powered lantern in the corner, drenching them both in a tangerine glow, Jude's pulse began to slow. The wind was out there. It couldn't hurt them while they hid underground.

"Tell me." Bo turned toward her. While Jude felt calm, Bo looked positively wild. Her honey blond hair was windswept across her face, the flyaways clinging to her chapped lips. She pushed her hair out of her eyes. "You said you needed to tell me something."

Oh no. She'd convinced Bo not to trek out into the storm by promising her something. She could lie. Tell her something about Susannah, or the Nursing Care Center, or some other perfectly safe piece of information. But if Jude could feel the wind, Bo could feel the truth. Trying to lie to her was like building a cage for a tiger out of toothpicks. She'd claw her way out, and it wouldn't even be a struggle.

Jude closed her eyes, and for a second, she imagined the soft glow of string lights above her, Bennett's warm hands around her waist, the frayed edges of the snowmelt blue blanket beneath her. "I . . . I was with Bennett yesterday."

Bo lifted her eyebrows. "Oh yeah?"

Jude opened her eyes. "He kissed me. At Butter. And I think . . . I *know* Delilah saw us." Heat crept up her neck, making her cheeks hot with shame. She stared at her sneakers in the dim light.

"Did you want him to?"

She looked up. "What do you mean, he's Delilah's—"

"Jude." Bo's voice was gentle when she said her name. "Did you want him to?"

Jude let out a breath. "Yes," she whispered.

Bo didn't say anything for a long moment. She leaned her head against the cement wall and closed her eyes. "I know what that's like. To get swept away by a Harding."

Jude's spine straightened. She opened her mouth to say something but decided against it. The other thing about toothpicks was that they could snap with just a tiny amount of pressure. Instead, she waited, listening to her heart beat in time with Bo's shallow breaths and the echo of the storm outside. After a moment, Bo cleared her throat. "Something bad happened that night. When our moms went missing."

"Yeah?"

The skin between Bo's eyebrows wrinkled. "It's, um. I was at the party. And Caleb was there with everyone. And I just . . . I don't know. Maybe I had too much to drink, but I really liked talking to him. This is going to sound weird, but just looking up at him . . . he *felt* different than the other guys in this town. Like, when he told me to follow him into the cellar, I almost felt like I couldn't say no . . . that he was pulling me by invisible strings, if that makes sense."

Jude swallowed the knot forming in her throat. Every time she blinked, she saw Bennett's fingers entwined with hers, the shaky sound of her breath echoing off cement walls as she followed him into the very same cellar Bo was talking about now.

Jude understood how to long for someone. She knew the intricacies of the invisible string that kept you tangled up tight in the promise of something more. "I know that feeling," she said softly.

"And then he opened the door to his uncle's cellar." Bo's voice cracked. At the word *cellar*, Jude's whole body stilled.

"And I just remember seeing all these sunflowers staring at me before I climbed down the steps. They were so still, Jude, and they were all turned in my direction, like they were waiting for me to ruin my own life." Bo swallowed, and even in the dark, Jude could see the tear roll down her cheek. "Like they were warning me."

Jude felt her own throat clotting up with tears. She set her hand on top of Bo's sweaty palm. "What happened down there?"

It was those four words whispered in the dark that finally broke her. Bo's chest heaved as she sobbed into her hands. "It happened so fast. We were talking, and then we weren't. I told him no—I *screamed* it. But we were in the cellar and no one heard us except for those stupid fucking flowers." She dragged her hands down her face and looked at Jude. "He took everything from me."

Jude wrapped her arms around Bo for the first time in two years. Bo softened into her embrace as Jude cradled her, rocked her. She set her chin on top of Bo's damp hair and listened to the wind trying to break down the doors.

It wasn't just the wind.

Someone was banging on the doors.

Bo unraveled from Jude. "What the . . ."

Bang. Bang. BANG.

Jude slowly crept up the stairs toward the doors. When she pushed them open, a cloud of petals wafted into the cellar, followed by a rain-soaked Whitney.

She pounded down the steps, the storm still clinging to her shoes. "Thanks for the flower," she said. "I was freaking out when I saw the porch and you weren't in the house." She slid onto the bench across from Bo and dropped her messenger bag onto the floor with a soggy *plop*. "Where's Delilah?"

Jude glanced at Bo. "You haven't seen her, either?"

"No," Whitney said, wringing out her hair. "She wasn't home when I left this morning."

The air in the cellar grew still. Outside, the storm still raged.

And no one knew where to find Delilah.

CHAPTER TWENTY-ONE

The first thing Delilah heard was the siren. The second was Bennett's voice.

"You're okay, Lilah," he said. "You're okay."

But Delilah felt anything but okay. She winced as she sat up. Her head felt like it was filled with bricks, and spots danced around the edges of her vision when she tried to keep her eyes open for too long. She squinted, taking in the scene around her.

Firefighters, police, and other people rushed around the shop like a swarm of gnats, their footsteps slapping the pavement, voices sharp and urgent. It was still raining, but the wind had dulled to an irritated breeze, and Bishop's lone fire truck stood in front of Gordon's Taxidermy, the top lights still flashing intermittently.

"Where's Evan?" she asked. The words felt thick on her tongue.

"Shh, you're okay," Bennett's voice wafted in. He wasn't there, and all of a sudden he was standing next to her, his calloused hand on top of hers.

She blinked. Beneath her was the soft padding of a gurney that had been wheeled into the lot next to the shop. Beside her, a nurse secured a scratchy Velcro band to her forearm. "Hold still, love."

Her heartbeat thrummed in her ears as the nurse pressed her stethoscope to the soft skin in the crook of her arm. More people shuffled past her as a van rolled through the lot. Her spine straightened. "Where is Evan?"

The only response was the hiss of the pump as the nurse listened to Delilah's heartbeat ping-pong through her veins. She glanced over her shoulder. "Bennett?"

But Bennett just shook his head, his lips pressed into a thin line.

The nurse piped up. "Try to calm down, love. I can't get a good read."

"I can't—" She scooted up the gurney she had been lying on. "I have to—"

The ambulance door flung open. Two EMTs pushed a second gurney toward the ramp leading into the back.

Evan was on it.

But he barely looked like the person Delilah had kissed only minutes ago. His face had already started to swell, his skin stretched taut over welts and bruises. There was a slash so deep over his left eye that the socket looked more like a bruised plum than skin.

And he wasn't moving.

Delilah scrambled to her feet. "You can't just get up and go! You hit your head!" the nurse yelled. She reached for Delilah's wrist, but before the nurse could touch her, Delilah ripped off the cuff and tossed it onto the gurney. She started toward the ambulance.

Bennett stepped in front of her. She tried to move around him, but he caught her in his arms and pulled her into his chest. "It's okay. He'll be okay. They'll take care of him at the hospital," he whispered into her hair.

Whatever had hit Delilah in the head must have dulled her senses, because for the first time in months, she didn't hurt when her boyfriend touched her. There was still something there, though.

It hovered in the back of her mind like a nightmare, waiting for her to wake up again. It felt like the echo of pain, like she was remembering the bone-shattering lightning zipping through her instead of actually feeling it.

Bennett's heartbeat drummed methodically in his chest. The solidness of his body next to hers and the lilt of his words made her soften. Delilah's head throbbed as she pressed her forehead to his shirt.

There was one bang and then another as the ambulance doors slammed shut. The engine roared to life, and just as quickly as it came, the ambulance was gone, kicking up fresh mud behind it.

Bennett squeezed her tighter. She felt her lungs press in on each other, forcing her to pull in deeper breaths. The pain lingered around the edges of her breaths, poking, prodding, begging her to wake. But Delilah ignored it.

All she wanted to do was stay here, in Bennett's arms, for a little bit longer. Her cheek warmed against his petal-soft shirt, and her entire body unwound. *Why was I upset again?* She couldn't remember. It must not have been important.

Another engine kicked on, this one louder and older. Delilah peeked from beneath Bennett's arm. Bishop's ancient fire truck pulled out of the muddy parking lot and swung back around toward the station. What was left of Gordon's Taxidermy jutted up from the ground like a broken tooth. Part of the roof had completely caved in, and shattered glass covered the ground like confetti.

Delilah pulled away. "Oh my god. I was *in there*?"

Bennett grabbed her hand and pulled her close again. "Apparently so."

"Bennett . . ." she said softly. She looked up, but he just stared at the space between their feet. He couldn't know what had happened inside the taxidermy shop—it was impossible.

Delilah squeezed her eyes shut and winced as the knot on her forehead started to throb. Everything was so murky. She remembered the scent of sweat and sawdust, the hundreds of beady glass eyes watching her as she curled up under the workbench with Evan and . . .

The kiss.

Something raced through her. It was the dip in her stomach whenever she rode her bike down the hill on Freemont, the electricity in the air before another inevitable storm. The possibility of it all.

And it didn't hurt at all.

Maybe it was never supposed to.

"I need to talk to you," Delilah said softly. "It's about—"

"You know what? It doesn't really matter," Bennett said quickly. Finally, he looked at her from under long, blond lashes, and Delilah started to feel fuzzy around the edges all over again. He leaned in so close that the tip of his nose brushed against hers. "You and me, we have to be together, okay?"

Have to.

Not *want to.* Or even *are going to. Have to.*

Delilah slowly shook her head, trying to clear the fog. "Wait, how did you even know I was here?"

Bennett's eyes grew wide, just for a second, then his face relaxed into a grin. "Oh, you know, the wind told me." He hooked his arm around her shoulder and laughed. "Come on, Lilah. I live right down the street. Saw the whole shop go down so we came to check on Evan."

"We?"

He nodded toward the dilapidated taxidermy shop. Delilah followed his gaze. Caleb was standing in the spot where the lobby used to be, waving his hands as he talked animatedly to his uncle. William Harding stood next to the rubble, raking a hand through his hair.

He dropped his hand and glanced up at them.

Every nerve in Delilah's body twinged as both William and Caleb turned to look at her, their expressions stony. Some deep-seated instinct clawed at her.

Bennett squeezed her shoulder just a little too tightly. "You're going to be okay. *We're* going to be okay." He pressed his lips to her temple and whispered, "Why don't you come back to my place and I'll take care of you?"

Delilah let the words settle inside her like glitter in a snow globe. She could imagine lying on Bennett's worn-in sofa, her body fitting into the grooves of the cushion beside his, wrapped in his mom's old afghan. All she would have to do is sleep—not worry about making sure there were enough vegetables for Jude, that Whitney hadn't given herself another tattoo, that Bo . . . well, that Bo hadn't hurt anyone enough to land her in prison.

Plus, she could touch him.

She could *actually touch him* without pretending it didn't hurt.

Tears of relief pricked the corners of her eyes. "Okay," Delilah said, leaning into him. "Let's go to your house."

They were halfway to Bennett's truck when she noticed Caleb behind them. She turned. "Are you coming back with us, too?"

Caleb's eyes snapped to Bennett's. There was something there, communicated between them, but Delilah's head was too foggy to understand. "Yeah," he said, not looking at her. "I'm gonna go with you."

He walked beside them through the lot, which had already be-gun to clear. Bennett guided her to the passenger side of his truck, which was flush against a wall of sunflowers. They tickled the back of her neck as she reached for the door.

Run.

Delilah froze. The fog in her head cleared.

Run.

It wasn't exactly that she *heard* the word; it was more like she felt the shape of it just at the edge of her consciousness. But it was there, the echo of a warning. Her entire body snapped on like a light switch.

Run.

"You getting in?"

Delilah turned. Caleb hovered over her, his jaw clenched, with one hand on the open door. The engine kicked on as Bennett started the truck from the driver's side. She watched the silhouette of him waiting, one hand resting on top of the steering wheel.

"I don't . . . I don't think I can?" she said slowly. She only realized it was true once the words were out of her mouth.

Caleb's eyebrows knitted together. "Why not?"

Delilah swallowed. She didn't like how close he was, the way his body curved over hers, pressing her into the truck. She could smell sweat and mint gum on him, and the combination made her woozy. She needed air.

She needed out.

"I have to go." She didn't wait for Caleb to give her permission.

Delilah slipped out beneath his arm and started to run. Behind her, she heard them yell, "Hey! Hey, come back here!"

She ran straight into the sunflower fields, praying she'd come out on the other side alive.

CHAPTER TWENTY-TWO

Come home.

Those were the words Bo chanted in her head as she shoved open the cellar doors and grabbed the sunflower stem she had stuck into the metal clasp. It didn't matter how fierce the wind was, or how hard the rain pelted her skin as she marched back to the house. She had to do *something*.

And she couldn't sit in that cellar for one second longer.

Come home.

Bo chanted the words again, trying to calm the tightness in her stomach. The wind swept away the last petals still clinging to the sunflower in her hand. They twisted and writhed as they wafted into the sunflower field. She tossed the limp stem into the field after them.

"Bo!" Jude yelled.

She didn't turn around. She had to find Delilah.

Bo couldn't explain the clenching sensation in her gut—like something with sharp claws had started to squeeze. All she knew was it told her something wasn't right. That Delilah wasn't okay.

"BO!"

Jude jogged up beside her, the wind turning her cheeks raw and pink. "Come back to the cellar."

Whitney marched up behind them. "Come *on*," she gasped. "Don't be stubborn."

Bo gritted her teeth. "I'm not *stubborn*. I'm worried." She glanced out at the oppressive sky, the sunflowers curled in on themselves. "She wouldn't just leave us."

Even before the words left her lips, Bo knew they were true. Just like she knew they were true every time she said them about her own mother. Cori Wagner would never leave them, not on purpose. And neither would Delilah Cortez.

Her stomach clenched tighter. "Something's wrong."

"Yeah, you're out here in this storm," Whitney said, frowning. She hooked her arm around Bo's and pulled. "We've got to get back inside."

"No." Bo pulled her arm free. "I'm not going back in there." And before Whitney could grab her again, or Jude could look at her with those sad, watery eyes, she started to run. Her sneakers sank into gray-brown puddles, kicking up muddy water behind her as she rounded the front of the house.

Bo slowed as the porch came into view. The old ash tree hung limp, its top branches poking through what was left of their roof. The east half of the porch was completely smashed, spiderweb cracks crawling across the cement slab. More pots—gem-colored things that Indigo had made and Cori had filled with spindly basil plants— lay in the rubble, potting soil oozing out of them like intestines.

She felt Whitney and Jude beside her before she saw them. Whitney let out a low breath. "Oh shit."

"It's worse than I thought," Jude said softly. She turned to them. "What are we gonna do?"

Bo didn't know. The house—*their* house—would have to be repaired. It probably wasn't safe for them to go inside.

But where were they supposed to go?

They had no one here.

Bo closed her eyes. *Delilah, where are you?*

"I'm here."

Bo spun around. Delilah stood in front of a row of sunflowers, petals clinging to her wet hair. Her fingers shook as she plucked a petal from her bottom lip and let it waft to the earth. It took everything in Bo not to burst into tears right there on the front lawn.

"Lilah," she whispered. And then she threw herself toward her.

"Wait." Delilah went rigid as Bo reached for her. When she pulled away, Delilah had placed her palm over her forehead. She winced as Bo gently peeled her fingers away.

There was a knot the size of an orange on Delilah's forehead. It was an aggressive purple that throbbed, and the slash through the center hadn't scabbed up yet. Fresh blood creased her eyelid when she tried to smile at Bo. "I'm fine, really."

Bo swallowed the lump in her throat. "You're not fine," she whispered.

"Delilah." Jude gasped. "We've got to get you to the doctor or—"

"*No*," Delilah said firmly. "I can't. We can't. I . . ." She trailed off as the wind whipped her hair across her face. She carefully peeled it away from her wound and said, "We've got to get in the house."

Jude frowned. "But you should—"

"*Now*. Right now. It won't stop until we're inside."

She didn't wait for the rest of the girls to follow. Delilah marched toward the dilapidated porch and climbed what was left of the steps. Bo only waited a second before following her into the house. Even though it looked like it was on the verge of collapse from the outside, the damage hadn't seeped very far inside. A section of wallpaper in the kitchen had ripped at the seam from the impact, revealing the innards of the drywall and coating the tile with flecks of insulation foam. The rest of the place looked like it had when

Bo had woken up. Except, when she flicked the switch, the lights didn't turn on.

Whitney stumbled into the house, followed quickly by Jude. As soon as Jude closed the door behind her, the wind softened, until it sputtered out. Bo watched out the front window as the hunched-over sunflowers slowly began to lift their heads. They peeked under their halo of petals, then tentatively looked toward the calming sky.

"Delilah." Bo turned to her. "What the hell is going on?"

"Where *were* you?" Whitney asked, crossing her arms over her chest.

"We were worried," Jude added.

Delilah hobbled to the kitchen and pulled a bag of frozen carrots from the fridge. She winced as she pressed it to her forehead. "You first. What happened to the house?"

"The wind blew. The tree took out the porch. Now there's a hole in the kitchen," Bo said, matter-of-fact. "Your turn."

"We'll have to call someone—"

"*Delilah*," Bo snapped.

"Okay, fine." She leaned on the counter, still holding the bag to her forehead. "I don't know how to explain this, but . . . I think William Harding can control the wind." She squeezed her eyes shut.

But no one laughed.

The room grew silent as all four of them stilled. Jude picked at her nails. Whitney poked at the crack in the wall in the kitchen. And Bo could barely breathe. "What do you mean?" she asked.

"I went to Gordon's Taxidermy this morning," Delilah said, running her fingers along the cracked countertop. "Evan knew my mom, I guess. He'd been trying to tell her something before she disappeared. He thought that—I don't know how to say this—that Bennett's uncle actually *talks to the wind*. Like he saw him do it. And Evan said that every time he tries to talk about what he saw happen with the wind, or about the Hardings, the wind gets more violent until he stops or goes back home."

"It's like an enforcer," Jude said slowly. "Like it's trying to keep us from knowing something."

"Keep us trapped in our houses," Whitney said, joining Delilah at the counter.

"Evan told me all this, and then the windows shattered and the whole shop came down. I woke up, and Bennett, Caleb, and Mr. Harding were there, and I"—Delilah swallowed—"I didn't want to be there. I don't know. I wanted to crawl out of my skin. I ran into the sunflower field, and then . . . I heard you."

Delilah looked at Bo with glassy eyes. "I heard you calling for me."

Whitney and Jude turned to her. She suddenly felt woozy.

Come home.

How many times had she chanted those words, pleading with Bishop to let Delilah come home? But they'd been in her head; Bo had never so much as whispered them into the wind.

The sunflower.

She'd been holding it in her fist while she ran and chanted, its petals wafting into the field. And Delilah had been waiting on the other side.

"The Hardings know something." Bo started to pace. "When I was at the town hall earlier, I snuck into the mayor's office—"

"Bo!" Delilah said.

But Bo just waved her hand. "I was looking for records. With so many women dead and missing, I knew there had to be some kind of record of that. But they weren't where they should have been, so I went to look in the office and, here's the thing: Mr. Harding caught me in there. *And he knew about the hidden files.*"

"What did the files say?" Whitney asked, gnawing on her lip.

Bo stopped moving. "A woman has died every six months for the past two years."

Whitney's face crumbled. "Eleanor."

"Eleanor," Bo confirmed. "According to those files, we're right on schedule for someone else to bite it soon."

"Come on, Bo," Delilah said softly. "Do you have to say it like that? It's not funny."

"That's the thing; it's *not* funny," Bo said, white-hot anger searing through her. "The Hardings are a part of this. I know it."

The room grew quiet again. Bo glanced at Jude, whose face was wound into a complicated expression. "It might not be in their control, though. Maybe there's a reason why they're acting like this," Jude added.

Bo felt her knees buckle as the entire world tilted on its axis. She stared at Jude. "Maybe there's a *reason they're acting like this*?"

Jude shook her head. "No, I didn't mean—"

"Was there a good reason why Caleb raped me?"

The question hung over them all like a thunderstorm. Bo's whole body began to shake. She'd finally said the word out loud. She'd finally told them—and herself—the truth.

Jude's face blossomed pink. Delilah dropped the bag of carrots on the floor. Whitney marched into the living room and wrapped Bo in a fierce hug.

"There's *no* reason for that," Whitney whispered in her ear.

"Bo," Delilah said, gently placing her hand on her shoulder. "I had no idea."

Bo closed her eyes. "No one did." She untethered herself from Whitney and began to pace again. There was so much anger inside her that it felt like it would burst through her veins at any second. She curled her hands into fists and squeezed. "We're trapped in this town. How are we going to get out of here?"

Whitney cleared her throat. "I know someone who might have an idea."

Bo turned to her. "Who?"

"Eleanor."

Chapter Twenty-Three

Whitney told them everything.

She told them about her visit with Susannah Craft. She showed them Eleanor's notebook, watched their eyes scan the pages as they read through her notes and took in the photo of Robert Dingal taped inside. She told them about the gaping hole that had resided where her heart used to be since Eleanor had died, how sometimes she felt more like a black hole than a person. How she'd never stopped waiting for Eleanor to come back, to come home, even though she knew Eleanor was buried six feet underground.

She told them about the old weather vane in the clearing, and how she could hear the whisper of Eleanor's voice when the wind blew past it, and how the echo of that word was the only thing Whitney had been clinging to for the past six months.

They all listened, carefully and quietly, even when Whitney explained that Eleanor seemed convinced Bishop was built on cursed land, and that its founder had somehow started it all. After a moment, Bo was the first to respond. "Edward Dingal," she said slowly, as if trying out the sound of the syllables on her tongue. "I saw his name on a document in the town hall. Eleanor was right; he *was* the founder."

Jude swallowed. "Edward Dingal died a long time ago, though. Maybe the curse died with him?"

Delilah let out a shaky breath. "No, remember the last line Eleanor wrote? *His descendants must still live here*? They're . . . still here."

They're still here. The words burrowed into Whitney's mind as she stood in the damaged kitchen with the other girls. The wind had destroyed their home. The wind that, apparently, William Harding could control. The records of dead and missing women stacked up in a desk drawer. Which William Harding was hiding.

And Eleanor's death, which, Whitney was almost certain, now more than ever, wasn't an accident.

"The Hardings. They're the common denominator," Whitney said, her voice breaking. She glanced up. "Eleanor's notebook said the curse needed *a sacrifice of some kind*. What if *women* are the sacrifice? And the Hardings have a part in it?"

Delilah let out a long, low breath and walked into the kitchen, while Bo followed behind her with the thawing bag of carrots. Jude choked out a quiet sob. Whitney had pulled her sister into a hug, but the second she did, she understood that Jude's tears weren't only from shock. The way her sister folded in on herself when Whitney touched her told her that Jude was crying about something—or someone—else, too.

She felt herself stiffen as she held Jude. She wanted to believe her sister was crying over the revelation, or what had happened to Delilah, or maybe even her own guilt over not going into the hospital with Whitney, instead leaving her alone in a strange building with the Hardings. But something told her Jude wasn't crying over any of that.

Whitney didn't have a chance to talk to her sister about it then. Bo bustled into the room, her hands now empty of the bag of carrots. "We should go up to the weather vane," she said. "We don't know if that wind is really Eleanor or not, but that may be our only chance to ask her about what she found."

Delilah appeared in the doorway. "Okay," she agreed. "But we should go soon."

Whitney's stomach sank. *The weather vane.* It *had* to be Eleanor. Whitney had spent the past six months of her life curled up beside the rusted metal, hooking Eleanor's bracelet to the dented rooster tail, crying until the earth softened beneath her cheek. It was the only direct connection to Eleanor she had left.

She'd get Eleanor to talk more. To talk to them all.

"Okay, let's do it," Whitney said. Jude nodded solemnly beside her. Before they could say anything else, Delilah was out the door, Bo trailing closely behind her. Whitney untangled herself from Jude, careful to avoid her injured shoulder, and together they followed.

The girls took the dirt path closest to the sunflower fields, even though they were mostly flooded. "Maybe this way it won't notice we're going to the clearing," Delilah said, stumbling over a puddle. Whitney didn't know if she meant the wind or Bishop, but either way, she was more than okay with the idea of staying out of sight.

She couldn't help thinking about Alma as they snaked through the outskirts of town. What would she think if she saw Whitney, soaked to the bone and traipsing across town to talk to her dead girlfriend after she'd run out on Alma at the Nursing Care Center?

Why do I even care?

Her heartbeat hitched when she thought about the way the watery gray light from the windows highlighted the curve of Alma's jaw, the small nick in her chin. Whitney wanted to know the story behind that scar. She wanted to plant a petal-soft kiss on it.

Whitney knew why she cared what Alma thought. But she couldn't think too hard about it or else she would fall apart. And now was not the time for falling apart.

They came up to the clearing, and Whitney almost didn't recognize it at first. The dirt was a thick, sludgy brown instead of the dusty taupe it usually was, and huge puddles pockmarked it like they'd torn open the earth from the bottom up. What had been left of their mothers' statues had been completely cleared out except for a few cracked stones. Even the plywood board that had protected the knife and bloody charm beneath it was gone.

It was like her mom had never existed at all.

Jealousy washed over Whitney as she watched Bo kick through the dirt and Delilah rake her fingers through her damp hair. Their mothers had disappeared, too, but at least they'd *had* them at one point.

Ava Montgomery had been a lot of things to a lot of people, so much so that she hadn't been able to give very much to Whitney and Jude near the end. She was Bishop High's most popular teacher; the waitlist for her literature classes was astronomical. She stayed late and arrived early, inviting students into her classroom to talk about Shakespeare or social justice or the wishes and dreams they could never tell their parents. Every time Whitney had gone into her mother's classroom, there'd been no room for her.

Her mom had been so busy in the months leading up to her disappearance that she hadn't gotten to meet Eleanor. *Invite her over for dinner,* Ava had said as she hauled another load of books into the trunk of the sedan. *I want to meet her.*

But she'd never gotten the chance.

She'd come home late that entire week, well past dinnertime, until Whitney finally walked up to the high school to beg her mom to come home. But Ava had been busy kissing Mr. Harding in the shadowy parking lot. And then, just like that, she was gone the next day.

They were all gone.

Whitney's hands shook as she approached the weather vane. She felt Jude's fingers caress her good shoulder as she inched forward. As soon as she got close enough to touch it, the wind picked up. The rusted metal pole was slightly bent in the middle after the storm, but it was still upright, for the most part. When Whitney touched it, it wasn't Eleanor she thought of. It was Alma.

Her face floated into Whitney's mind. *Have you tried talking to her?*

Whitney hadn't answered the question; she wasn't sure *how* to without sounding like she was completely unhinged. But Alma's cards had told her what she'd known in her heart all along—Eleanor was somehow still around.

Whitney could feel her. Maybe it was in the wind, the weather vane. Maybe it was in the knotty oak tree on Alma's card, or the parade of acorns clinging to the grass beneath it. All Whitney knew was that she was here, and this was how she could talk to her.

"Eleanor," she whispered, her fingers grazing the metal. "Are you there?"

A gust of wind jetted across the clearing, pushing Whitney's hair over her face. Around her, the sunflowers swayed and shuddered to the sound of a symphony that Whitney couldn't hear. The weather vane groaned beneath her fingers. And then it started to spin.

But this time, instead of doing this alone, Delilah, Jude, and Bo joined her. Jude grabbed her hand and squeezed as the wind picked up in intensity. Whitney pressed her fingers into the pole harder. "What do you know about Bishop and the Hardings?"

More.

"More *what*?" Her eyes pricked with tears. She had had enough. Whatever this ghostly Eleanor craved, Whitney didn't seem to have enough of it. "I don't understand!" she yelled.

The wind lashed so hard at her that she stumbled, but Jude quickly pulled her upright while Delilah and Bo steadied her. Whitney stared at the crooked old rooster free-spinning on its axis. *More,* it hissed.

"I don't know what you want more of!" Whitney yelled. A feral scream ripped through her. "I can't do this anymore, Eleanor!"

She screamed again, and the wind screamed with her. It blazed through the clearing with such force that all four girls stumbled and fell, a series of gasps and groans echoing through the clearing. Whitney skidded to her knees, her injured shoulder colliding with Bo's back, sending a white-hot current of pain coursing through her. When she tried to get up, the wind pushed her down again. And again.

It took her breath away, drying her tears before they had the chance to roll down her cheeks. She felt Jude's arm around hers as she pulled Whitney to her feet.

She stared at the frantically spinning rooster. *You have to listen to me, too, Eleanor.* She gritted her teeth. *Listen to me!*

"Eleanor!" Whitney yelled.

The weather vane shrieked in pain. And then it snapped in half.

It happened so fast and so slow at the same time. Whitney watched as the rust-speckled rooster, her only line to the love of her life, fell to the earth.

Whitney screamed.

CHAPTER TWENTY-FOUR

A shock of pain coursed through Jude, and it didn't belong to her.

When her sister dropped to her knees, Jude had a second to catch her breath before Whitney let out another low, guttural scream, and the pain seared through her all over again.

Jude had never had that twin thing with Whitney. She'd never been able to read her sister's thoughts, and they'd never looked at each other from across a room and said *ice cream* or *cartwheels* or whatever word they'd both been thinking of at the same time. For a while after their mom disappeared, Jude had convinced herself that she couldn't connect with her sister when she was almost always out of the house at one party or another. But as she felt Whitney's pain as if it were her own, as it rattled Jude's bones and made her want to crumple into the mud beside her, she finally understood.

Sometimes there just weren't words for that kind of ache.

"Whit, we can fix it. We can fix it," Jude said, wrapping her arms around Whitney as the wind threaded between them. She squeezed. "I'm going to fix it."

Jude stood and rounded on what was left of the rooster. It was in bad shape. It must have hit a piece of stone when it snapped, and now it sat, mangled, in the mud. Bo joined her, digging through the mud with her bare hands to loosen it, and Delilah helped her hoist it back onto the pole. Together they held it in place as the wind roared across the clearing.

Whitney wiped her hand across her face, leaving behind a gash of mud. She looked up. "Eleanor?"

Jude squeezed her eyes closed. *Come on.*

Whitney just shook her head. "I can't hear her anymore."

"Come on," Jude whispered. But even she knew that whatever spell Whitney had been under had splintered when the weather vane had. Whatever connection she had to Eleanor had been broken. Jude closed her eyes. Looking at the hope on Whitney's face was unbearable.

Whitney stood and let out a breath. Jude let the rooster drop back into the mud with a *thwick* while Bo and Delilah watched. "Maybe it wasn't the weather vane, Whit. You could still talk to her, you know? You don't need some old rusty piece of metal to do that."

"I can't." Whitney's voice shook. "I've never heard her anywhere else, except . . ." She trailed off, pinching the bridge of her nose. "It doesn't matter." She kicked what was left of the weather vane toward the sunflower fields surrounding them.

Bo raked her hands through her hair. "What are we supposed to do now?" she yelled over the wind. "That was our only lead."

"We go back home," Delilah said. "This storm is going to rip the whole town apart if we don't get away from the clearing. Let's get out of here and regroup." She turned to leave.

Whitney rubbed the mud-stained knees of her jeans. "Yeah," she said. "I'm ready."

Jude took one last look at the sunflowers swaying in the wind before turning to follow. Something she couldn't describe pulled at her, begging her to stay in the clearing. She paused to scan it, just for a second, and the wind softened. It caressed her cheek, threaded itself through her tangle of curls. And then she heard it, as clear as day: *The Harding house.*

She stilled.

Harding, it whispered again.

Her heart picked up speed. *Harding house.* They needed to go to the Harding house.

"Wait," Jude called. One by one, the girls turned around. "Something . . . I can hear something."

Whitney let out a breath as Jude cocked her head to the side to listen again. She frowned. "I think the wind is telling us to . . . go to the Harding house?"

Delilah scoffed. "Yeah, I'm sure it is, Jude," she said, turning back toward the path out of the clearing. "Come on, let's go home."

Jude's mouth dropped open. "Delilah . . ."

Delilah spun around, her long hair swinging across her face. "You wanna talk about this now?"

"I—"

"Are we going to talk about the fact that I *saw you* kissing my boyfriend in Butter?"

Jude closed her eyes. "I can explain that."

Delilah marched toward her until she was so close that Jude could smell her coconut shampoo. Her face softened. "Would you have told me if I hadn't seen it, Jude?" Her voice cracked around the words.

Tears pricked at the corners of Jude's eyes. "It's more complicated than—"

"What's so complicated! You kissed him—"

"He kissed me!" Jude pulled in a breath. "*He kissed me.* And that wasn't the first time, Lilah."

Delilah stumbled back as if Jude had slapped her. "What did you say?"

Jude swallowed. Tears rolled thick and hot down her cheeks. "Before you and Bennett got together . . . we were together. Sort of. That whole summer before everything happened, Bennett and I were . . ."

"Oh my god," Delilah said.

Jude's face grew hot. "I *really* liked him. *Like* him. But he fell in love with you. And that was that, until I met him at Butter to get Whitney's bracelet back, and he kissed me."

"My bracelet?" Whitney tucked her hair behind her ears to keep it from blowing in her face. "Where is it now?"

"He said he didn't have it," Jude said, her voice trembling. "But I could have sworn I gave it to him at the . . . the hospital."

The hospital. The word hung heavy in the air between them. Jude hadn't brought it up since Whitney had come home with her shoulder haphazardly patched. The truth was, she still wasn't sure why she hadn't fought harder to follow her sister into the hospital, especially when she saw that the building seemed . . . odd. Not like a regular hospital. She hadn't wanted to be difficult. But then there was the way Bennett had looked at her when he told her to stay in the truck.

His eyes had said, *Don't question it.*

It sent a chill up her spine.

Delilah pressed her hand to her lips. "Oh my god," she said again.

A gust of wind roared in Jude's ears. *The Harding house.*

"Lilah," Jude said softly, pulling Delilah's hand away from her mouth. She glanced up at the swollen knot on Delilah's forehead, the fear tucked away in the corners of her eyes from running away from Bennett and Caleb through the fields. "I don't know why, but I think this wind is trying to tell us to go to Bennett's. It has nothing to do with what I want. I promise."

Delilah swallowed. "What *do* you want, Jude?"

"I . . . I don't know." Jude chewed her lip. It was the truth, but only a sliver of it. The rest of it was something she couldn't explain, to Delilah or even to herself. More than anything, Jude wanted to tumble into the kind of head-over-heels love that Whitney and Eleanor had had. She'd thought she had that with Bennett; a part of her *still* wanted that with him. But then she'd seen her sister writhing in pain on the mud-soaked earth. She'd felt Whitney's pain as if it were her own, and that was when she knew.

Bennett Harding would never cry like that over her.

As much as Jude wished she could just forget about Bennett, she still loved him. Even though she wished she didn't.

Whitney's eyebrows knitted together as she stepped in front of Jude and squeezed her shoulders. "Are you telling the truth, Jude? About the wind?"

Jude blinked back tears. "Yeah," she said, nodding. "I keep hearing it: *the Harding house.*"

"Okay, then." Whitney turned to Delilah and Bo. "We've got to go there."

Delilah let out a long breath. "What are we going to do? We can't just show up there and ask them if they have anything to do with a bunch of dead girls or if they can control the wind."

"What else are we supposed to do?" Bo interjected. "Our house is messed up, the storm's still hanging around, we have no way to talk to Eleanor. The only thing we know is that the Hardings have something to do with all of it. So why not?"

Delilah stared down the path for a long moment. "Okay." She turned to Jude. "But I'm the one who talks to Bennett."

Bo glanced at her. "Are you sure you want to do that—"

"Yes," Delilah said, lifting her chin. "I can do it."

She didn't wait for a response before taking off toward the other side of the clearing. Bo and Whitney followed, careful to avoid the web of murky puddles, with Jude stepping in the footprints they'd already left behind.

Together they walked down Main, passing the boarded-up shops while stepping over roof shingles that had been yanked free during the worst of the storm. They hadn't gotten very far before Jude saw the flashes of red and blue.

Two cop cars were parked in front of the Hardings' house.

Freddy Gordon, Evan's dad, stood in front of the navy house, the skin under his eyes swollen and purple. William Harding stood next to him, hand clasping his shoulder, as they both talked to the cops.

Caleb stood on the front porch, watching.

"What's going on?" Delilah asked slowly. She approached the house, with Whitney and Bo close behind.

"Jude." Bennett's voice wafted in from behind her. When she turned, Jude didn't find the Bennett she'd fallen in love with over time. Instead she found a little boy, skin pale and eyes heavy with dark circles. He let out a shaky breath, and before she could open her mouth to ask him what was wrong, he scooped her up in a hug so fierce that it took her breath away. "I'm scared," he whispered, burying his head in her neck.

Jude should have pulled away; she knew that.

She should have told Bennett to let her go, finally and completely, so he could be with Delilah and stop stringing her heart along by chains. But his warm breath on her neck made her thaw and the way he shook in her arms made her break. He might not love her like Whitney loved Eleanor, not yet. But Jude could feel the possibility in his embrace.

"What's wrong?" she whispered.

Bennett lifted his head, tears rolling down his cheeks.

"Evan's dead."

CHAPTER TWENTY-FIVE

Evan Gordon is dead.

The words echoed through Delilah's head, trying to find purchase, but they kept slipping and sliding across her mind. They just wouldn't stick.

It wasn't possible.

Delilah's lips had been on his only hours ago, and now he was gone.

Caleb leaned against the porch railing, his arms crossed over his chest. After what Bo had told them, just looking at him now made Delilah feel ill. Instinctively, she moved in front of the steps to block him from getting any closer to Bo.

"The wind was just too much, I guess," Caleb said, staring out across the porch. "It got so wild out there that the whole ambulance flipped on the way to the hospital. No one survived."

No one survived.

Tears rolled down her cheeks. If she closed her eyes, she could still taste Evan's lips, still smell the salt and sweat between them, the way his fingertips gently grazed her stomach. It was the first time she'd kissed someone other than Bennett, and the wind had taken him from her only minutes later. This fucking *town* had taken someone from her again.

When Delilah opened her eyes, Caleb was watching her carefully. "I didn't know you and Evan were so close," he said.

"I didn't know you and Evan weren't," she snapped, brushing a tear from her top lip. "Your best friend just *died*. Why aren't you upset?"

Caleb's eyelashes fluttered. He looked out at the front lawn, where his uncle and Evan's dad still stood, talking to the cops. The wind was only a tepid breeze now, lightly tousling their hair. "I am," he said softly.

"Delilah!" William Harding separated from the dozen or so people standing near the sidewalk and started to climb the porch steps. "I haven't seen you around here lately." When he reached the landing, he gave her a small, sad smile. "Really bad news about Evan. Really bad."

From behind her, Bo let out a huff. "Yeah, I'd say so."

Delilah didn't turn to look at her. Instead, she kept her eyes on Caleb. As soon as his uncle's shoes crested the porch, Caleb's shoulders stiffened. It was so slight that Delilah had almost missed it, until she noticed how Caleb refused to look in their direction. He lifted his head. "Bo, you don't have any right to talk about Evan."

This time, Delilah turned. Bo's jaw was clenched so tight that Delilah was positive she'd ground her teeth into dust. "I can say whatever I want," Bo replied, but the words weren't nearly as menacing as the expression on her face.

Caleb said something back, but all Delilah could hear was the *whoosh* of her heartbeat thrumming in her ears. Just over Mr. Harding's shoulder, Jude and Bennett were huddled together at the edge of the driveway.

Bennett stood so close to Jude that his chin almost grazed the top of her head. His face was pink and splotchy, and he held her hand. Both of his hands were cupped around hers so carefully, like he was holding something precious.

And the way he looked at her: Delilah knew that expression.

It was the way he'd looked at her that night in the cellar, when he told her he was falling in love with her.

She started to run.

"Wait, where are you going?" Bo yelled.

Delilah hopped off the steps, past the cop cars, and back toward downtown. Despite the throbbing in her head, she ran as if standing there at the Harding house for one more second would crack her open from the inside out.

Tears blurred her vision as she crossed downtown and circled back to Old Fairview Lane. The wind blew after her, but it only pushed her forward, away from the center of town and toward her house, slamming the front door behind her.

She climbed the creaky old stairs to her bedroom. When she pushed open the door, her heart sank. Bennett was everywhere in here: faded photographs stuck onto corkboard, one of his heather-gray hoodies hanging from her headboard. The air even smelled like the echo of him, all sun-kissed skin and bonfire smoke.

She shut the door and sank to the floor on the landing.

Delilah hadn't lain in this spot since the night after she'd reported her mom as a missing person. On that night, she'd curled into a tight ball, her cheek flush with the floor, and stared into Indigo's empty studio. Her mother's last words echoed through her mind.

Go have a good time, Indigo had said with a smile, pressing her cool hand to her daughter's cheek. *Nothing here is permanent.*

But what had Delilah done? She had shown up at that party and fallen head over heels in love by the time the sun had crested the horizon the next morning. Once she'd seen Bennett Harding cross the clearing toward her, it was all over.

But there had been that moment before.

That night at the party. That second where she'd looked through the smoke of the bonfire and seen Evan. His dark eyes sparkled in the firelight, hair pulled back tight, with one loose curl cupping his cheek. Something in her chest fluttered as his gaze connected with hers.

The moment was interrupted by Bennett sidling up to her, teeth glinting, eyes intense. Delilah fell under a new kind of spell, and this one, she was realizing, felt like less of a choice.

There had always been something about Bennett that kept her bound, in a way. That had infected her heart like a virus, made her feel a little less like, well, *herself*. And like she was all Bennett's.

It might have been different. Delilah could have crossed to the other side of the fire, looked into Evan's sparkling eyes, and said hi. But she hadn't gotten the chance. Bennett had shown up and soaked her to the bone with his unwavering attention, and that had been it. Delilah had barely talked to Evan again until a few hours ago.

And now he was gone forever.

Delilah curled her knees into her chest and looked into her mom's studio. She hadn't been in there since she'd found the receipt and the balm for Bo's scraped-up knee. Scrapes she'd gotten from fighting with Evan. When her mom first disappeared, Delilah spent almost every day in the studio, tracing her fingers over Indigo's unfinished papier mâché pieces, wondering what they would have looked like wearing lemony yellow and forest green hues. But as time passed, and the pieces never got finished, Delilah couldn't stand to spend more than a few minutes in there. Time pressed on, and Indigo's art remained stagnant and covered in dust.

Evan had known that side of her mom, a side that Delilah would never get to know. And it was a side of Evan that Delilah would never get to explore, either. It was too much to bear.

She pulled herself to her feet and tiptoed into the studio, even though no one else was home. When she pushed open the door, dust fluttered through the air. Everything was the same as the day she'd found the paints from Rose and Rain. Even the desk drawer was slightly ajar, as she'd left it. This time, though, Delilah didn't dig through the desk. She headed toward the unfinished papier mâché.

They were propped up in a row, some rounder than others, but all four of Indigo's creations looked like unfinished mannequin heads. Delilah could see where her mother had started to shape noses and lips and eye sockets, where earlobes and chins protruded. She pulled up her mother's old desk chair and sat down so she was at eye level with them all.

She tried to imagine Indigo in her studio, paisley skirt swirling at her ankles as she smoothed the silky paper over Styrofoam. The soft, dulcet tones of her singing voice as she dipped long strips of paper in glue over and over again. Indigo had still been working on these pieces the day before she vanished, and by the paint that Delilah had found, she'd planned on finishing them. Even still, there was no urgency here. No curdled glue or lumpy slivers of paper; the work hadn't been rushed. Her mother couldn't have known what was about to happen to her.

Delilah stood and examined the last piece. There was a spiderweb crack just below the right earlobe. She poked it, and a bit of papier mâché crumbled, opening the hole wider.

There was something inside.

Her pulse picked up as she pushed on the mannequin's neck and the hole widened. She jabbed her entire fist inside, tearing open Indigo's carefully placed paper strips. Her fingers brushed against something feather-light and brittle.

Delilah pulled the slip of paper from the hole and held it in her palm.

It was an obituary.

But this wasn't something Indigo had cut out of the *Bishop Bugle*. It was written on a slip of lined paper in black ink. Her mother's curlicue handwriting flitted across the page.

Mary Beth Jacobson, Indigo had written at the top. *Taken too soon. Cursed by gender. Murdered without consequence.*

Delilah gasped. The paper fluttered out of her hand and onto the rug at her feet.

She leaned closer to the art piece and peeked in the hole. There was nothing else inside besides the makeshift wire frame that Indigo had assembled to prop up the Styrofoam head. She glanced down at the paper staring up at her from the floor.

Cursed by gender.

Murdered without consequence.

She had known Mary Beth. Even though she'd been a grade below Delilah, they'd still ended up in one of Mr. Harding's history classes together. Delilah had taken History of Midwestern America as an elective to help shore up her transcripts for college, but Mary Beth had taken it to get her history requirements out of the way. They'd sat next to each other in the front row, and although Delilah had liked her, there had always been an unspoken competition between the two of them to impress Mr. Harding the most.

Two months later, Mary Beth had dropped dead walking home from soccer practice.

A heart attack, the official obituary in the *Bugle* had said. But Mary Beth had been captain of the track team. She was the kind of person who woke up before the sun just to feel her heart pumping through her veins while she ran around the perimeter of town.

Delilah bent down to scoop up the paper. She'd always thought the circumstances were weird, but she hadn't thought much of it at the time. Just another Bishop tragedy.

Indigo, though, had thought a lot about it.

Delilah ran her fingers over what was left of the papier mâché bust. She could almost imagine her mother's delicate hands as she painted the lips ballet pink. Maybe those painted-on lips had belonged to Mary Beth Jacobson.

Maybe all of these unfinished pieces were really unfinished *women.*

One by one, Delilah placed the pieces on the old rug. She pulled open her mother's desk drawer and pulled out a razor blade. She poked and cut and tore at the remaining three busts until she reached the secrets her mother had stored inside. More paper. More self-made obituaries.

Natalie Hart
Tatiana Sellers
Vivian Cho
Cursed by gender.
Murdered without consequence.

In two of the busts, her mother had included cut-out pictures of the dead women. One looked as if it had been snipped from the *Bugle.* A blurry version of Tatiana smiled brilliantly from the sepia-toned paper. Beneath it, a few sentences from the article were still visible.

> *Tatiana Sellers (left) with the chess club she coached at Bishop Middle School. Sellers was found dead several hundred yards outside Bishop, in the sunflower fields, on Sunday.*

Delilah held the picture next to her mother's handwriting. Like all the others, it read *Cursed by gender.* But Delilah had known Tati—she'd taken a few chess lessons from her when she was in middle school. Tati's sex had been labeled "male" at birth, but she had been a woman for most of her life. It seemed that whoever—or whatever—Delilah's mother thought was killing these people only cared that they were women.

Delilah picked up the image of Vivian Cho. Vivian's luminous face grinned up at her from the photograph. A small child with dark, wavy hair stood beside her, and next to each of them was a finished canvas painting propped up on an easel.

The girl was her mother.

She flipped the photo over. *Mrs. Cho and Indigo at the art fair,* the note on the back read.

Something clawed up Delilah's throat as she sat in the middle of the studio, staring at the graveyard of art and paper splayed out around her. At first it felt like a knot, as though if she opened her mouth too quickly she'd burst into tears. But instead she wanted to scream.

Her mother had known. She'd *known* there was something dangerous about this town, something wrong about all these lost and missing women.

Eleanor's loopy handwriting appeared in Delilah's mind.

Did he kill people to obtain the land? A sacrifice of some kind?

All of these women. *Murdered without consequence.*

Indigo Cortez had known all of this, and she hadn't told Delilah any of it.

She'd left her here to defend herself.

Heat roared through her veins. There was one thing her mother had gotten wrong, though. These women weren't "cursed by gender." Their gender was never the curse.

The land—and the men who tended to it—were the real curse.

Delilah stumbled to her feet and clomped down the stairs, then searched the piles of misfit items stored in the breezeway. She pawed through broken mesh screens and table lamps that never stood upright until she found what she was looking for.

A baseball bat.

Bo had played baseball for only one season, but she'd never gotten rid of the bat. Now Delilah swung it over her shoulder and carried it back into Indigo's studio with gritted teeth. She flung open the door and stood before the mess she'd made on her mother's latch-hook rug.

She loved Indigo, probably more than she'd ever love anyone

in her entire life. But this? It was too much. Indigo had betrayed them all.

Delilah wondered how much of her life could have been different if her mother had told her about her suspicions. If, instead of touching her cheek and telling her to have fun on that last day, she'd told her to *stay*.

Stay home.

Stay with me.

Delilah wouldn't hurt so much when she should be in love. Evan might even still be alive.

Delilah lifted the bat over her head. She swung hard and fast.

It made a *thwuck* sound as it smashed into the first bust. A cloud of dried glue exploded into the air, speckling Delilah's skin with plaster snow. She swung again. And again.

Delilah swung until her muscles ached, but her heart hurt less.

She didn't hear the door downstairs open. Footsteps padded up the stairs, light and urgent.

It wasn't until the studio door opened that Delilah realized she wasn't alone in the house on Old Fairview Lane.

As soon as she saw Bo, she dropped the bat at her side. Bo ran to her and without a word, pulled Delilah to her chest.

Indigo's last words to her were *Nothing here is permanent.* But maybe she had been wrong.

Maybe the things that mattered most were.

CHAPTER TWENTY-SIX

Y ou're gonna be okay," Bo said as Delilah melted into her
arms. *I'll make sure of it.*

Delilah untangled herself from Bo's arms and wiped her eyes. "I
made a huge mess."

Bo kicked her sneaker through the aftermath of Delilah's rage,
unearthing a riot of papers and photos. Delilah had smashed Indigo's art with such force that the plaster had ground down into the
old rug. When Bo pushed her shoe across the wool, little clouds of
dust puffed in the air.

She knelt and sorted through the cryptic messages. They were
strange at best, but that was kind of how Indigo rolled. She was an
artiste, as her mom had said with an eye roll more than once. She
liked to push boundaries.

Bo paused on one of the images. She lifted the clip of Tatiana
Sellers closer to her face to inspect it. She hadn't known Tati, except for what Delilah had said about her, but she recognized her
smiling face from this same newspaper article. Bo had read it over
a bowl of Honey Nut Cheerios the day after it was published.

Tati's newly formed chess club had been featured in the *Bugle*. The image showed her in the front lobby of town hall with two gangly preteens next to her. But there was a plaque hanging directly over her head that Bo hadn't paid any attention to years ago.

There was an image pasted onto the plaque that looked vaguely familiar. Bo leaned in so close that the tip of her nose almost grazed the paper. It was blurry, but she could just make out a photograph of an older white man with a baby in one arm and a toddler standing beside him.

"Those are Edward Dingal's descendants," she said, her stomach sinking. "Behind Tatiana, on that plaque."

Bo closed her eyes trying to remember the layout of the lobby. Oatmeal-colored walls, dusty carpet, a hulking wooden desk front and center. Other than a faded Kansas state flag hanging in the corner, Bo was almost certain the walls had been bare. The plaque was no longer there.

Delilah sank down onto the carpet beside Bo. "Yeah, I guess that does look like the photo from Eleanor's notebook."

Bo set down the paper and looked at Delilah. "I swear, that plaque isn't hanging up in town hall anymore, but that's Dingal's son in the photo. Why have we never heard of him?"

"And his kids," Delilah said, frowning. "What happened to the kids in the photo?"

It was a good question, one Bo hadn't considered before. If Edward Dingal had died in 1901 like Bo had read in the town records, then his grandkids could even still be around, technically. They'd be old, but it was possible.

"I don't know," Bo said slowly. She glanced at Delilah out of the corner of her eye. "Do you think your mom knew?"

Delilah sat for a long moment. "I'm not sure, but I think . . . I think she was trying to figure it out." As soon as the words left her mouth her bottom lip quivered. "I just wish she'd told us about it."

Bo looked out the dingy window. Even from here she could see the storm hovering on the horizon, just past the sunflower fields and the rows of ripe corn baking in the summer heat. She felt as though she had been looking up at the purple underbellies of clouds her entire life, that there was always the threat of gale-force winds pushing up against the town's boundaries. And then there were the sunflowers, a butter-colored army always standing at attention. Always watching.

But what are they waiting for?

"Maybe it wasn't safe," Bo said slowly.

"What?" Delilah said, blinking back tears.

"Maybe your mom was, I don't know, *scared*. Like, she hid these pictures of dead women inside those busts. Maybe it wasn't really about making some kind of statement. Maybe she was hiding information until she could figure out what to do about it."

Delilah's eyebrows knitted together. "That doesn't . . ." But she didn't finish the sentence. Instead, she hopped off the rug and marched over to the old desk in the corner. She yanked open the drawer and unearthed the wooden crescent moon from inside.

Bo joined her at the desk. Delilah's fingers shook as she turned the moon over in her hands. "My mom was acting really strange those last couple of days," she said. "I saw this piece and she got weird about it. Told me to leave her alone." She swallowed. "But maybe she was just trying to hide something here, too."

Bo saw the tiny catch before Delilah did. Carefully, she guided Delilah's fingers to it, and together they slid the lid off the top. There wasn't much space inside, and there was only a single, tightly folded piece of paper inside.

"I don't know if I can do it." Delilah looked at Bo, her face crumpling.

"I'll do it," Bo said softly. She pulled the paper from inside the wooden crevice and gently unfolded it. Her eyes quickly scanned the blocky handwriting.

It was a letter.

Indigo,
Please, we need to talk. I promise, what you saw wasn't
what you think. Meet me in the clearing after dusk this
evening and I'll explain.

> *All my love,*
> *William*

Bo's mouth dropped open. She handed the letter to Delilah, who scanned it. By the time she finished, her face was as pale as a winter morning. "My mom . . . and William Harding?"

Bo's stomach clenched. "But how? How did anyone not know about this?"

The door downstairs groaned.

There was a solemn *click* as the door closed. Heavy footsteps paced through the living room.

Delilah's eyes snapped to Bo's. "What do we do?" she whispered.

Bo swallowed as she soaked in the terror streaking across Delilah's face. She didn't know what to do.

No. She knew what she had to do. Some part of her had always known. It was the same part of her that had nudged her toward the knife in the clearing, that had told her to bring it home. It was the part of her that had urged her to find the pepper spray, to grab a weapon. Any weapon.

Bo scanned the room. Her eyes landed on the baseball bat laying on the floor. She grabbed it and swung it over her shoulder.

She only got to the landing before she came face-to-face with the man standing on the stairs.

William Harding stood in front of her, his face twisted with rage. He lunged.

Bo swung.

CHAPTER TWENTY-SEVEN

Whitney started to go after Delilah, but Bo held up her hand. "I'll go," she said with the kind of tone that meant it wasn't up for debate, before leaping off the porch and running back toward the house.

When Whitney turned around, she saw what had made Delilah run in the first place: Jude snuggled up a little too close to her boyfriend. She grimaced. "Jude!"

Jude looked back at her with her big doe eyes, and that made Whitney want to rage even more. She marched down the Hardings' porch steps. "What do you think you're doing?"

Jude pulled away from Bennett. Her eyelashes fluttered. "We were just talking."

Whitney glanced between them. Neither would look her in the eye. "Oh yeah? It really looks like this is just 'talking.'"

"I went to her first," Bennett said, holding up his hands defensively. "Jude was just here for me."

"So was *your girlfriend,* Bennett!" Whitney waved back toward the porch. "She was less than ten feet away and you went to Jude instead. What is wrong with you? Why are you doing this?"

Jude opened her mouth to say something, but Whitney held up a finger. "No. I don't want to hear whatever it is you're about to say. And I don't care that he came to you. Delilah should come first." She jabbed her finger into her sister's chest. "*We* come first."

"Whitney, I—"

But Whitney didn't stick around to listen to her sister's excuses. She spun around and marched away from the Harding house, back toward Main Street. Whatever happened at the hospital had opened up a crack between them, but what Jude was doing with Bennett had shattered what was left of their relationship. Whitney had never been this furious at Jude in her entire life. She'd never been so ashamed to call Jude her sister.

As she walked, her boots slapping the pavement, tendrils of guilt poked through the fury. When did this whole thing between Jude and Bennett start? From the way they looked at each other, it seemed like they'd fallen for each other some time ago. Whitney knew the way Jude loved; she put her whole heart into it.

And Whitney had been too grief-stricken to notice.

She shook her head. *No.* This wasn't her fault. This was Jude's fault for betraying Delilah. For betraying them all. Whitney would talk to Delilah when she got back to the house, apologize for Jude. Hopefully it would be enough.

She turned the corner and was greeted by a web of yellow tape.

It stretched across the front of Bishop Nursing Care Center, blocking off the walkway leading to the front door. From here, the building looked mostly intact besides a couple of shattered windows.

Even so, panic pressed on Whitney's lungs. She lifted the tape and ran straight into the Nursing Care Center. "Alma!" she yelled. "Are you in here?"

There was no answer. The lobby looked the same as it had when Whitney had left in a hurry. Same plaid sofa, same dishwater gray carpet, same Formica counter in the corner.

But Alma wasn't sitting behind it. No one was.

"Alma!" she yelled again. She wrung her hands until they were raw. Alma had to be okay. Nothing could happen to her. She opened her mouth to yell again when the door to the rest of the center swung open. Alma entered, face glistening and shirt damp with sweat. She jerked to a stop. "Whitney?"

"Oh, thank god," Whitney let out in one breath. "I saw the yellow tape and—"

Alma's face softened. "You thought something happened to me?"

Whitney swallowed. She took a tentative step forward until she was close enough to see the beads of sweat dotting Alma's collarbone. "Yeah. I was . . . I got really worried."

Alma glanced at Whitney's lips and then back to her eyes. "It's just the power grid," she said slowly. "The storm knocked it out, and we've got medics parked around back trying to help the patients on oxygen. Plus, it's so freaking hot in here without air conditioning."

Whitney scanned the lobby, the wall of aggressive yellow tape and flowers pressing in on the cracked windows. The last thread she had to Eleanor had been completely taken from her when the weather vane snapped. This place, and the notebook tucked into her bag, were all she had left.

"Is Susannah okay?" Whitney asked, squeezing her hands together so tightly that her knuckles turned white. *Please let her be okay.*

"She's okay," Alma said, shifting toward the desk. She pulled open the bottom drawer and began to thumb through files. "I just have to contact their families to let them know what happened, and the computer's pretty much fried."

Alma's fingers skimmed through the manila folders until they found purchase on the one she was looking for. She slid the folder out and began to flip through it.

Whitney glanced into the drawer. The top edge of one of the folders was visible.

Robert J. Dingal

Everything in Whitney went completely still. She stared at the penciled-in name. The name of the man from Eleanor's notebook.

"Alma," said Whitney carefully, "does Robert Dingal stay here?"

"What?" Alma looked at the file and then back to Whitney. "Oh, no. Those are files of past residents. Deceased."

Whitney bit her lip. "Listen, I know you're not supposed to do this, but I really need to see what's in that file."

Alma's eyes narrowed. "I want to keep my job, Whitney."

"I know, I know. But please, just hear me out." She took a breath, then reached for Alma's hand. Heat radiated through her fingertips all the way to her cheeks. "This place . . . it's weird, right? Haven't you ever thought about how it feels kind of like . . . like we're trapped in here?"

To Whitney's surprise, Alma didn't pull her hand away. Instead she looked Whitney in the eye and said, "Yes."

"I think . . . well, I'm trying to find out where it all started—the weird windstorms, the sunflowers, all of it. And I think it starts right here, with the Dingal family." Whitney threaded her fingers through Alma's before she could say anything. "I need to see what's in there so we have even a chance of getting out of here."

"Before we end up like Eleanor," Alma said softly.

Whitney swallowed. "Yeah. Before we end up like Eleanor."

Alma stilled, listening, but the only footsteps were outside the building. "Okay. But we have to hurry before anyone sees us." She gently untangled her fingers from Whitney's and pulled out Robert Dingal's file.

Together, they flipped through the contents. It was mostly just patient notes, scribbled half thoughts about medications, bedtimes, and recreation activities. Apparently knitting hadn't been one of Robert Dingal's preferred activities. He'd throw the plastic knitting needles every time someone placed them in his fragile hands.

Alma stopped at his birth certificate. She pushed it toward Whitney. "Look at the birth parents."

Whitney's eyes slid across the delicate handwriting on the old certificate, the cloudy gray photocopied edges.

Mother's name: Mary Katherine Dewey
Father's name: Edward James Dingal

"Edward was his father," she said slowly. "This confirms it."

It wasn't that the information surprised Whitney, but feeling the weight of the words on her tongue made her pause. It was real. Eleanor had known something about the connection between the Dingal family and how this town came to be, and Whitney had it right here, in front of her. And even more than that: the Dingals had still been here up until very recently.

Alma flipped to the next page and held the faded, yellowing paper close to her face. Whitney leaned closer. It was almost impossible to read the penciled-in markings in the dim light of the lobby, but she could just barely make out the typed font at the top of the page.

Visitor's Log.

Something fierce and shaky pumped through Whitney's veins as she scanned the page. This was it. There had to be something here. The people who'd visited Robert Dingal had to have some kind of familial connection to him, or at least be *like* family.

"Whoa," Alma whispered, her long fingers sweeping down the list.

It was a short log, really. There were only three people who came to visit Robert Dingal.

The first was his wife, Eloise. She only came to visit a handful of times, in the very beginning, her handwriting careful and poised as she signed her name on the whisper-thin lines. After a few visits, she never came back.

The rest of the list was filled with a name that Whitney recognized. That made her blood run cold.

"Harding," Alma said softly.

Harding.

Phillip Harding and William Harding. Bennett's dad and uncle.

Whitney ran her finger along the list beside Alma's. She felt the heat radiating from Alma's skin as they stood side by side, so close that Whitney could smell the undertones of her grassy body wash. She quickly blinked the thought away.

The brothers took turns visiting their father in the Nursing Care Center for years, until his name stopped appearing on the log. That must have been around the time Phillip decided to pack up and leave town. It was only William after that.

William Harding.

William Harding.

William Harding.

Somewhere stamped in history, the center began asking for the relationship between the visitor and patient. And that was where Whitney first saw the words that connected this entire web of secrets. The one that Eleanor had been trying to stitch together before she died.

William Harding.

Relationship: son.

Whitney's chest tightened. She felt like crying. It was right here, the familial connection to this land and the curse Eleanor had sworn was baked into the soil. She'd found what Eleanor couldn't.

"Mr. Harding is Robert Dingal's son. He's a blood relative of the founders," Whitney whispered. She grabbed her messenger bag and pulled out the green notebook, still heavy with rain. The pages crinkled as she flipped to the last section Eleanor had written in.

The sepia-toned photo of Robert Dingal in front of town hall was still taped inside, although it looked a lot worse for the wear after the storm Whitney had dragged it through. Water rings speckled Robert's face, but she could still make out the image of the two children beside him.

Phillip and William Harding.

"But how?" Whitney asked. "Why do they have a different last name than their ancestors?"

Alma shrugged beside her. "It's not all that uncommon, really. I see it a lot working here. A lot of times there's a generation that decides to take a piece of their ancestors' names and make it into a new one going forward, especially if they're part of a generation that was a part of the American West migration."

"Like they want a fresh start—a new name—to start over?"

"Or they want to wash the blood of Indigenous people murdered for land off their hands." Alma lifted an eyebrow. "Something like that."

Wash the blood off their hands.

The words sang through Whitney like a ballad. If the Dingals had blood on their hands, so much so that Phillip and William had changed their last name, then it must be the kind of blood that sticks around. The kind of atrocities that marinate in the soil like rust-colored fossils, waiting to be uncovered. Like rust-colored acorn charms.

"Look." Alma pointed to the bottom of the visitor's log. Hovering just below her fingertip was another name.

Bennett Harding.

Relationship: grandson

Caleb's name was there, too. They had to have been only kids when they visited their grandfather. Whitney wondered if their uncle had dragged them here, or if they'd come on their own. Would old grandpa Dingal tell them stories about the bloodstains on his hands, the lies their family told to keep this land? Or did he tell them more?

Did they know what their great-grandfather Edward had done to acquire this cursed land, and more importantly, did they know how to stop it?

Alma opened her mouth to say something, but she seemed to think better of it and gently pressed her lips together. After a moment, she gazed at Whitney. "What *is* weird about the Dingals changing their name is that they're responsible for this town. There's usually some pride associated with that. Makes me think there's an awful, dark reason why the original founders of this place would have changed their last name."

"Like they didn't want anyone to know."

Alma nodded. She was close. So, so close. All it would take was one push, one feral gust of wind to blow Whitney's lips right into hers.

Alma leaned in closer. Whitney's pulse raced.

Her breath smelled like the echo of cinnamon, and her skin smelled like summer grass and sweat, and her face was so close to her that she could feel Alma's petal-soft hair cradling Whitney's cheek like a leafy tendril. She could feel the aura of Alma's Chap-Stick brushing against her lips.

The door was flung open. Alma jumped.

"Miss Thompson," a man in a camel-colored hat said to Alma. He turned to Whitney and said nothing at all. "We're checking in to make sure everything's all right up here."

"Everything's fine, Sheriff Ableman." She cleared her throat. "I was just checking the electrical box again."

"Ah." Jeff Ableman nodded, never taking his eyes off Whitney. Whitney lifted her chin and stared right back. "Well, it looks like the power should be back up soon. And we've got the patients as comfortable as we can until then, so why don't you head on back home, Miss Montgomery?"

Whitney blinked at the sound of her own name. She'd had plenty of encounters with Jeff Ableman in her past life. In the

Before. More than a few times the sheriff and his cronies had driven her across town as she stumbled over her words in the back seat of his beat-up sedan, telling him that he could fuck right off. One time he even told her he'd lock her up in Bishop's single, lonely jail cell for the night if she didn't *show a little respect around here.*

Whitney had nodded solemnly until he turned back to the road. And then she'd flipped him off in the rearview mirror.

Her mother would never let him lock her up. She'd never let this mediocre white man hold her hostage just because of a few cuss words and a lot of attitude. And maybe a little drinking.

But now he looked at her as if he'd just realized she existed, like she had been a curly-haired, tattooed nightmare that had haunted him for a while, but the thought had dissipated. His eyes drifted to the notebook splayed open on the counter. "Is that something that belongs to you, Miss Montgomery?"

His eyes didn't leave the photo of Robert Dingal. The page full of Eleanor's scribbles.

THEY KNOW.

Whitney's blood ran cold.

"It's mine," she said, flipping the notebook closed.

"Ah," he said again, pulling his hat tighter around his eyes. "Well, I better have a look." He reached for the notebook.

Whitney opened her mouth to say something, but Alma was faster. "Wait! You can't take her notebook!" She shouldered herself closer to the counter. Her hand slapped the waterlogged cover before the sheriff could grab it.

"Miss Thompson, are you defying an officer of the law right now?" Indignant rage flared in Jeff Ableman's eyes like liquid smoke. It was the kind of rage that men kept nestled deep beneath their ribs, the kind that rose between the bones whenever someone didn't automatically hang on their words like laundry drying on the line. It was the kind of rage that killed for disobedience, even when you never belonged to that man in the first place.

Alma let out a small, shaky breath. She lifted her chin as she slid the notebook closer to herself. "If that officer of the law is trying to take personal property without a warrant and no good reason whatsoever, then yeah, I am. You can't just take it because you want it."

Whitney's pulse hummed under her skin. This wasn't just about the notebook anymore; this was about how deep the secrets ran through this town. How the police were never really there to protect *her*—they only cared about protecting the Hardings. They would lock Whitney up in a dust-laden cell for this transgression, she was sure of it. And for Alma, a Black girl, the consequences were much worse.

Jeff Ableman grew unnaturally still. "Well, Miss Thompson, as an officer of the law, I can confiscate anything I damn well please. Now hand it over."

"No," Alma snapped. She held the notebook to her heart. "It's not yours."

"Really?" His voice lowered. "You really want to do this?"

Whitney stepped in. "No, it's fine. She's just—"

"He can't do this to you, Whitney," Alma whispered. She turned back to the sheriff. "Do *you* really want to do this?"

At that, Ableman let out a barking laugh. "Alma Thompson, you're under arrest for resisting a reasonable request from an officer."

Whitney's mouth dropped open. "*WHAT?* You can't do that—"

"I sure can. Now, Miss Thompson, are you going to make this hard or easy?"

Alma looked at Whitney for a long moment, still clinging to the notebook. "It's okay, I promise. I'll be fine." As she said the words, her face crumpled. Even she wasn't sure she believed it.

"Alma, *please.* This is nuts! He's being—"

But Alma gave her a sharp look, as if to say *Stop before he takes you, too.* Ableman smirked. "That's what I thought. Come on, you can call your family from the station." He hooked his hand so tightly around Alma's arm that Whitney could already see where his fingerprints would leave bruises. He still made it a point to rip Eleanor's notebook from her hands and tuck it under his arm before heading to the door.

"Stay out of trouble, Miss Montgomery," he said, tipping his hat.

Alma turned around, her lip quivering. "Come back for me, okay?" she said as the sheriff yanked her forward. "Come find me."

The door swung shut behind them.

The last piece of Whitney's old love was gone, and the possibility of a new love had been stolen.

CHAPTER TWENTY-EIGHT

Jude stood on the creaking porch of the Harding house, waiting for everything to come crumbling down around her.

Maybe it already had.

Delilah had seen her with Bennett at Butter only two days ago, and their lives had burned to the ground in the hours since. Jude had been the one to light the match.

She knew in her heart that Delilah would find out how she felt about Bennett eventually—she *had* to. That part was inevitable. But the way it had happened . . . Jude hadn't wanted it to happen like that. She'd wanted to tell Delilah on her own.

Jude hadn't had any idea that Bennett would look at her like that, kiss her like that, the scent of powdered sugar wafting in the space between them. She hadn't known that she'd let herself fall for him over a batch of lemon bars. Again.

God, what was it about Bennett Harding that made everything in her melt like butter sitting out on the counter? Every time she considered letting him go—really letting go this time—he always swooped in. Bits of him at a time, like an apparition. First his subtle scent, the echo of him still lingering outside Delilah's bed-room. Then, parts of him appeared around the house. A grass-stained hoodie slung over the back of the sofa. His dad's barn-red toolbox, just as scarred as he was, sitting next to the toilet in the half bath. The empty condom wrapper Jude had found when she emptied the trash one blisteringly hot afternoon. And then, all of a sudden, he appeared at the front door like a surefooted storm, eyes the color of rain, threatening to drown her all over again.

Even though Delilah had marched off, Bo quick on her heels, and Whitney had followed shortly after, Jude had stayed. She'd *stayed*. The cops had hopped back into their vehicles, shutting their doors on Evan Gordon's life—*slam, slam*—after Mr. Hard-ing left. Even Caleb had wandered off, mumbling something about checking a leak around back, though he was in a designer polo shirt and there were no tools in sight.

"Jude?" Bennett's voice cut through her thoughts. He'd been on the porch beside her since everyone else had dispersed, but she had been swept up in her own thoughts. "You want to go inside for a minute?" he asked.

She looked up at him. She did want to go inside for a minute. She really, really did. And that was the problem. But even if she wanted to go back to the house on Old Fairview Lane, she couldn't. Delilah and Bo had to hate her at this point, and Whitney . . . well she couldn't think too hard about her sister's words or she was cer-tain her heart would split open in her chest, right there on the porch.

"Sure."

He held the screen door for her, and because his uncle wasn't there, he didn't ask her to take off her shoes. Instead, he reached for her hand and led her up the freshly polished staircase. Jude glanced down as they climbed the stairs. The entire house gleamed—hardwood floors, marble countertops, full-length windows. It was all pristine. Controlled. Meanwhile, the scene just outside the window was a chaotic mash-up of wind-strewn petals and flooding fields.

Bennet pulled her toward the room on the left. He didn't even ask if she wanted to go into his bedroom. He must have smelled it on her like summer-sweet berries on the vine.

Bennett had barely closed the door before he leaned in to kiss her. His body was pressed up against hers so hard that Jude's lungs screamed for air. She tried to pull away, but he swallowed her whole.

"Wait," she said. She pushed against his chest, but he didn't budge. "*Wait*," she tried again.

This time, Bennett released her, breath heavy. He wiped his mouth. "What's wrong? I thought you wanted this, too?"

"I do . . ." *But I don't. Not like this.*

He lifted an eyebrow. "Then what's the problem?"

Jude sank onto the corner of his bed, her knees bumping up against the heavy dresser. Something on its surface glinted in the waning sunlight.

Whitney's bracelet.

Jude's whole body stilled. Her heart climbed into her throat.

Bennett saw it the same time she did. He dove for it, but Jude was faster. She snatched it in her fist and held it behind her back. "You lied," she said, breathless. And then: "*Why?*"

Bennett made a half-hearted attempt to grab the bracelet, then gave up and rolled over onto his back, red splotches blooming on his cheeks. "I don't know what to say."

Jude gritted her teeth. "Try me."

The air hung heavy around them as specks of dust wafted through the air like desolate confetti. "This town . . . it's not okay." A single speck of dust landed on his upper lip.

Jude stiffened. "Yeah, well, you're not the only one who noticed."

"But I'm one of the only ones who can do something about it." He flipped over onto his stomach and looked up at her. "My uncle,

Caleb, me—we're direct descendants of the man who founded this place. The legend goes that the land would only let my great-great-grandfather build on it as long as we kept feeding it. And if we ever stop, the winds will come and tear it all down."

Jude's heartbeat picked up speed. "Feed it *what*?"

Slowly, he reached for her arm. His calloused hand braceleted her wrist. "Blood."

Jude stared at his hand wrapped tightly around her wrist. It wasn't a gentle touch.

He was holding her to keep her from running.

She opened her mouth to scream, but Bennett's free hand clamped tightly over her mouth before she'd even finished the thought. What was she going to scream, anyway? *The guy I'm in love with wants to feed me to a bloodthirsty town*?

And if she was really being honest, no one was coming for her anyway.

"Jude! Listen to me. Listen." Bennett's face was so close to hers that she could see the tiny golden flecks in his eyes. "I would never hurt you. Just let me talk for a second, okay?"

Jude nodded slowly, and Bennett released his hand from her mouth. Jude's heartbeat roared in her ears. She suddenly felt dizzy as she glanced out the window at the brewing storm.

The wind. It had whispered in her ear back at the clearing: *Harding house.* And she had been naive enough to listen.

It had been a trap.

"I'm telling you this so you understand," he said, his eyes pleading with her. "Please."

Jude let out a shaky breath. "Tell me."

Bennett nodded. "This town—the land beneath it—needs blood. Not all the time, but every so often. It has to have the blood to stop the storms. It's our job to keep it happy so we can all stay safe. And it tells us when it's . . . hungry."

"Who's *us*?" Jude could feel the answer humming through her veins. But she wanted Bennett to say it, to confirm the truth that had been nestled between her ribs all along.

He lowered his eyes. "My family. My uncle, Caleb—"

"And you?"

Bennett's eyes snapped up to meet hers. "*No.* No. I haven't . . . I haven't had to do anything about . . . *that.*"

"But your brother and your uncle have . . ." She let the implication hang heavy in the space between them. *Your brother and your uncle have killed people.*

No.

You've killed women.

"Your dad . . ."

"That's why he left," Bennett said, gritting his teeth. "He didn't want to do this anymore."

Anymore. The word rolled around Jude's mind like a marble. She squeezed her fist tighter around Whitney's stolen bracelet. *Eleanor's* bracelet. "Eleanor Craft. Your family killed her." It wasn't a question; it was the truth.

Did they kill our mothers then, too?

Jude had heard the whisper of something malicious on the wind every time she approached the clearing. She had heard it in the echo of the storms that hovered over their house, in the recesses of the nightmares she'd had since she was a child. She'd always chalked it up to being sensitive, intuitive, a raw nerve exposed to the cold. But some part of her must have sensed an evil here all along. She just hadn't wanted to believe it.

Bennett sighed heavily. "I didn't want to—we didn't want to. But the town tells us who it wants next. It's kind of like, I don't know, a feeling. My uncle says it starts by his ribs, but Caleb's is in his fingertips. It's like a magnet. Draws you to the person and gets stronger and stronger until you . . . you know."

"Kill them," Jude whispered.

He nodded slowly, his eyes lingering on the soft underside of her wrist. Her heart thrummed through her veins like a wild rabbit's, so quick she was sure Bennett could hear panicked thumping just beneath her skin.

It all happened so fast. Jude bolted off the bed, but Bennett knew. He'd anticipated this. As soon as he'd seen the fear in her eyes, his face twisted into anger. He lunged.

"Shh," he said, clamping his hand over her mouth again. "Jude, it's not you. I'm not going to kill you. *No one's* going to kill you."

But Jude's racing heart whispered, *Don't believe him.* Even if what he said—he hadn't killed anyone—was true, his family had. And while Bennett might not have done the deed himself, he had known about Eleanor. He'd kept her bracelet tucked away.

He'd hidden the evidence.

Bennett's face softened, and for a second, it almost looked like he was going to cry. "It's always been you," he whispered. "I've wanted to be with you since the first time we kissed in the sunflower fields. But this *thing*, it's kept me hostage. Jude, look at me."

Jude's eyes slid to his. He pressed his forehead to hers, but he didn't take his hand from her mouth. "I need you to know I'm doing this so we can be together."

An image of Delilah's face bloomed in her mind. The knot on her forehead, the dark circles beneath her eyes. How she had been inseparable from Bennett the second they locked eyes at the bonfire.

Delilah. It was Delilah.

A scream ripped through the air.

Bennett. Jude mouthed the syllables of his name behind his calloused hand. *Screw you.*

And then she bit down. Hard.

Bennett yanked his hand back. Jude scrambled off the bed, toward the door, toward the half-open window.

William Harding's truck was back in the driveway, both doors flung open. He stood beside the passenger door, face covered in a curtain of blood.

Jude saw light brown curls first. And she knew for sure. She knew.

I'm doing this so we can be together.

William pulled Delilah from the passenger side of the truck. She stumbled forward, but he caught her before she could fall.

Her hands were zip-tied behind her back.

"DELILAH!" Jude screamed. She slapped the window with open palms.

Delilah didn't turn around.

"I'm so sorry." Bennett's voice, hovering right behind her. "So, so sorry."

She spun around just in time for him to grab her wrists. Jude heard the *click* of zip ties, the pinch of her veins beneath the plastic. He dragged her back to the bed while she kicked and screamed. For a second Bennett's grip loosened, but only just enough so she could slither to the floor beside the bed. He quickly regained hold of her. There was another *click*. Another pinch.

Bennett finished the work of tying Jude to the bedpost, then stood in front of her. He looked almost heartbroken about it, and if Jude had seen him like this in any other situation, she would have swept him up in her arms like she had in front of his house. That was probably how she'd gotten into this situation in the first place.

"I'll come back. It'll be okay when I get back."

Jude said nothing. Bennett bent down and planted a whisper-soft kiss on her forehead.

And then he locked her in his bedroom with one last *click*.

CHAPTER TWENTY-NINE

Click, click, click.

The dial on the storm cellar turned, millimeter by millimeter, as William Harding unlocked the door. *Was there always a lock on the cellar doors?* Delilah couldn't remember. She was certain she would have remembered it that first night. She was certain she wouldn't have followed Bennett down, down, down into this underground prison if she'd seen it.

But then again, there had been a lot Delilah hadn't seen.

Click.

William grunted as he pulled open the cellar doors. "Go on," he said to her, not unkindly. And that made it even worse.

She still wasn't sure exactly what had happened back at the house on Old Fairview Lane. The last thing she remembered for sure, that felt as solid as the cement walls around her, was the baseball bat in her hands. The way she could slide her fingers along the glossy finish. How she had to dig her toes into her mother's rug for purchase before she swung. The way the air filled with specks of plaster and betrayal.

And delicate, pink hands gripping the handle. The guttural sound Bo made before she swung. Delilah could still picture the shape of her shoulder blades jutting out from under her T-shirt like broken wings.

And then . . . nothing.

There had been a rush of sound from the stairwell. Bo's rage screams and then her fear screams. And then just a whimper before the house finally fell silent.

The rest had been a blur. As soon as William stumbled the rest of the way up the stairs, his face full of blood and vengeance, Delilah had felt the dull roar of pain echoing in the space behind her jaw. When he touched her, every nerve in her body caught fire.

William Harding's touch made her feel powerless, like just the light graze of his fingers on her arm soaked up all of her grit and resilience—all of her determination to stay alive, at least for the other girls—like a sponge. There was physical pain, for sure, but even more than that was the sense of being drained until there was nothing left.

"Here," William said, guiding her to a soft spot on the floor. She sat, woozy, as he cut her zip-ties with a soft snip. Her fingers grabbed the blue gingham blanket beneath her.

The picnic blanket.

Her and Bennett's blanket.

"Where's Bennett?" she asked, but it came out more like *Where Bent?* She was so dizzy. Her whole body screamed in pain.

"Don't worry about him right now. Caleb?" William grunted as he pushed open the metal door and a sliver of gray light streaked in. One of his eyes was completely swollen shut, and the other looked like it was on its way. Both eyes were as puffy and purple as ripe plums.

A shadow fell over the room as Caleb entered the cellar. He handed his uncle an old dish towel without even glancing in Delilah's direction.

William mumbled something that sounded like *Thank you* as he mopped his face. It was too late; the blood had dried in the wrinkles on his forehead, the crinkles in the corners of his eyes that all the older women in town swooned over.

"That little bitch," he snarled.

Bo.

Where was she? Delilah had to find her.

Bo had to be okay.

With both of them so close in this small, dank room, Delilah thought her heart would simply stop beating any second. It was too much pain. She clutched her chest and whimpered. After a moment, she closed her eyes and tried to focus, tried to listen.

"She won't be a problem anymore," William said, matter-of-fact, tossing the towel onto a bench. "She went down pretty easily, actually."

Something about the way he said the last part made Caleb stiffen. "I mean, yeah," he said slowly. "I suspected as much."

"Then you should have taken care of it a while ago," William snapped. "There have been too many missteps this time."

"Sorry," Caleb mumbled. He took a step closer to where Delilah was sitting. Her chest began to burn.

William sighed. "I know this work isn't . . . glamorous. But it's what we've been tasked with. Your father couldn't hack it. He left you to get away from—"

"That's not me," Caleb interrupted. "I'm not scared like he was."

There was a long pause. Delilah could only just make out their shapes in the dark, but she was sure William was considering whether Caleb was telling the truth. He'd always had a way, even when he was just her docile history teacher, of melting the walls around safely kept lies with just one look.

Finally, he said, "You'll have to prove it."

There was the scraping sound of a chair moving closer. Delilah's pulse quickened.

"There's nothing to be afraid of," William said, his voice as soft as a lullaby. His shadow sat on the edge of a metal folding chair. There was a *click* as he turned on a lantern.

They stood over her, these sick men who looked like hungry wolves in the shadows. Caleb swallowed, and the muscles in his neck flickered in the light. An ivy leaf identical to Bennett's danced on his skin.

Caleb's was just below his earlobe; she'd seen it a hundred times over the years. And when she'd asked the brothers about their matching birthmarks, they'd simply shrugged and said, *Runs in our family.*

"The ivy leaf," Delilah said, staring at William. "Where's yours?"

He gazed at her with that wall-melting look until she wanted to crawl out of her own skin. And then he smiled. "Nowhere you'd be able to see it, but your mother did."

She gritted her teeth at the mention of her mother. *Was this the last thing she saw before she died?*

"Indigo knew, too," he said, leaning closer. "About all of this. Well, most of it. She was a Bloom, like you."

The image of that wilted-sunflower goodbye staining their bathroom sink flitted through her mind. *A Bloom.*

"There's always a consequence for spilling blood on cursed land," William continued. "It took us quite a while to figure out what was happening. We knew more sunflowers cropped up whenever blood had been shed, but we didn't realize the town had evolved. That there were women—*alive,* still—who could feel the curse in our bloodline."

Delilah closed her eyes. She tried to focus on her own heartbeat, but its panicked thrum was muffled by the pain coursing through her. The pain that told her that these men were dangerous, that they had done something unfathomable to the girls' mothers. That they had killed before. That they wanted to kill her now.

But Bennett. There had to be goodness there . . . didn't there?

She had lain with him right here on this blanket, each of them curled onto their sides. He hadn't hurt her. Bennett had whispered that he was falling in love while her cheek was pressed to the cold, damp floor beneath them.

Bang, bang, bang.

Delilah jumped. Caleb and William looked at each other with raised eyebrows. "Nice of him to finally show up," Caleb grumbled, pushing open the cellar doors.

Delilah knew it was him before she saw the shape of his shadow. Bennett sauntered slowly down the cement steps, pausing on the last one. She couldn't see his face in the dark, but she knew he was looking at her. And it terrified her.

"Lilah," he said softly, stepping around his brother. He sank to his knees beside her. For a second, Delilah wished he would lie beside her, and they could go back to being parentheses instead of . . . whatever they were now.

Gently, he tucked a strand of her hair behind her ear.

Delilah screamed.

Bennett's touch felt like a million razor blades on her skin, scraping away at her layer by layer. While William and Caleb's touches were painful, they felt more like an echo, a deep-seated memory of pain that always lingered, like joints that always ached when it rained. Bennett felt like a fresh wound. A fatal one.

"Hey, you're okay." He touched her again, this time by cupping her chin in his hand.

It was unbearable. Pain rocketed through every inch of Delilah as if she were being electrocuted and drained of all energy at the same time. Her eyes watered. Fat tears made rivulets down her cheeks.

She saw her mother.

Indigo Cortez stood behind the three men like a vengeful ghost. Her wild curls that matched Delilah's hung loose around her shoulders, and her gauzy white dress ruffled in the nonexistent breeze. She wore a crown of sunflowers in her hair. Her mouth made a rose-colored circle as she leaned over them all.

"Mom," Delilah whispered.

Her mother's O-shaped lips whispered a single word. It hung in the air between them, as potent as a secret.

"Bo," Delilah repeated. *Bo.*

Her mother disappeared, leaving behind a cloud of petals.

Everything went dark.

CHAPTER THIRTY

If there was one thing Bo knew how to do, it was die.

She'd done it a hundred times before. She'd died when she fell out of the old ash tree beside their house, her ribs snapping like matchsticks all the way down. She'd died when Evan Gordon pulled down her underwear on the chalk-stained playground in kindergarten, and she died that night in the cellar, Caleb's breath hot and sharp on her neck. Bo had even died before she was born—she came out a blue-tinted lump who couldn't catch her breath without a quick slap on the back from her mother's midwife.

And now she was doing it all over again.

Bo sank into the mud like a stone in the sea. The field was waterlogged from the ongoing storm, and it pulled her under with its muddy fists. And she let it.

More than anything, Bo was tired.

Things had always seemed easier for the other girls—for everyone, really. Whitney had always been the prettiest one, the one who made everyone's head turn. Jude had always been the soft one, the one who stray barn cats trotted up to and people trusted with their secrets—with their whole selves. And Delilah. Delilah was everything Bo could never be. She was smarter than anyone Bo had ever met, but it was a quiet, unassuming smartness. She didn't need to throw it in your face. There was just the deep understanding that she would use her brains to get out of this wretched place, and that would be the last anyone would see of Delilah Jane Cortez again.

She winced as she closed her eyes. There was a knot forming in the corner of her eye that had already started to balloon. And then there was the metallic taste of blood still lingering in the corners of her mouth. She vaguely remembered the crack of the bat as William swung, how she'd ducked just in time to avoid the full impact of his rage. She hadn't missed it completely, though. The edge had caught her temple.

Bo couldn't remember what had happened after that.

All she knew was that every last bone in her body ached. Whenever she tried to open her eyes, the predawn light forced them closed. She couldn't even lift her head to see how much she had bled, if she was still bleeding. And she had no idea where William was. For all she knew, he could be standing just out of view, watching her slowly gain consciousness from behind a wall of sunflowers.

So she just lay there.

This would be the last time she died.

It seemed like hours, or maybe it had only been seconds, when she heard the first whisper.

Bo opened her eyes.

It was almost like the echo of a whisper, so faint she wasn't sure she hadn't said it in her own head. It lingered at the edge of consciousness like a dream she couldn't quite remember.

And then she heard it.

Bo.

She winced as she tried to lift her head. There was a blur of aggressive yellow all around her, hovering over her. She squinted at the sky, but she could only see ribbons of gray-blue through the thicket of sunflowers.

Bo.

Her name, clearer this time. She rolled to her side and tried to sit, but her hands wouldn't budge. She pulled, but the rope around her wrists burned against her skin, leaving it raw and pink.

Bo's hands shook as she fiddled with the fraying rope. *Breathe,* she told herself. *You're not in the cellar.* She threaded her fingers together and squeezed until her knuckles turned white. *You're not trapped in the cellar with him.*

"Ropes," she whispered to herself, as if this situation were any better than Caleb's strong hands clamped around her wrists as he held them over her head, the cracked cement floor of the cellar kissing sweaty skin, leaving behind scrapes and scars. When she was sure her fear wouldn't betray her, she loosened her fingers. "You can get out of ropes."

Help me.

The whisper was just as close, but it felt different. It *was* different.

Bo didn't know how, or who it belonged to. The sunflower beside her dipped closer, caressing her shoulder with its buttery petals. A seed of hope bloomed within her.

Get up.

Her eyes filled with tears. "I'm trying," she whispered. The sunflower was so close that Bo's breath made its petals shudder. As if on cue, it curled in on itself, giving Bo space to rise up from the mud. She plunged both hands deep and dragged herself to her knees. A second rope cut into her ankles as she wriggled into a sitting position. She paused to catch her breath.

The storm seemed to have passed, for now, and while the sky looked hazy, there wasn't the threat of wind or rain lingering above the field. That was a plus; it'd be easier to see exactly where William had dragged her.

William. Even just thinking his name made the hair on the back of Bo's neck rise. Bits of memory were starting to come back to her now. The crack of the bat, then the blur of pastel wallpaper as Bo's head smashed against it. The drop of her stomach as she started to fall, the wooden stairs reaching up to greet her like a row of coffee-stained teeth. Hitting a solid mass, but not the stairs. Not the floor. The sensation of being dragged across the gravel driveway, pebbles pockmarking her skin.

Even as she'd lain semiconscious in the fields, her body utterly ravaged, some part of Bo had asked, *How is he doing this?* in the dark recesses of her mind. William Harding had to be in his fifties. Tall and lanky like Caleb and Bennett, but without the muscle from summer jobs on the farm. Some part of Bo had been trying to work out the raw power in that swing of the bat. How he'd carried her down those stairs as quick as a heartbeat, dragged her body deep into this field. As she sat here, staring at the miles of yellow surrounding her, she couldn't help feeling like it *hadn't* been only William Harding's brute strength. Someone—or something—had to have been helping him.

Bo shook her head. That must have been a harder hit than she'd thought. She was starting to think like Whitney now, with all of her makeshift séances at the old weather vane, trying to channel the supernatural between gusts of wind. Bo was going to have to figure this out on her own.

She inched toward a sunflower with a particularly thick stalk. She reached for it, but her weight was too much, and the flower snapped in half in her hand.

Bo's shoulder hit the mud. She rolled onto her back. Her heartbeat crawled up her throat and panic rose within her like bile. She clawed at ropes tied so tightly that her freckled skin was starting to purple.

She had clawed at Caleb's sweat-speckled shirt, grasped at the bulging muscles of his back as he pressed all of his weight into her. She'd gritted her teeth and tried to yell and tried to scream and when she finally realized no one would hear her this far beneath the earth, she'd just tried to breathe until it was over.

Be safe, her mother had said before Bo left for the party. Bo had thought it was a joke.

She'd spent the last two years longing for five more minutes that day. Just five more minutes. Everything could have been different if Bo had grabbed the pepper spray from the kitchen drawer, and if she'd gone into her mom's office, wrapped her in a hug, and whispered, *You be safe, too,* in her ear.

It was too late. For all of it.

Bo started to cry.

It was the ugly kind of cry that she never let anyone else see, the kind she only participated in on long, sunbaked runs when she could claim the tears were sweat. She sobbed and screamed until her throat was raw, until her head ached, until she'd made a puddle in the soil under her cheek. She cried until her face was streaked with mud and salt. She only hoped that when someone eventually found her body out here—if anyone ever found her—they wouldn't judge her for lying down and giving up.

Bo felt the whispers before she heard them.

They felt like rough hands gently cupping her chin, like the heavy handle of her mother's rake while Bo helped her wrangle the vegetable garden, like the impact of her tiny fist against Evan's chest when she'd started another fight in the school parking lot. They whispered to her in hurried, hushed voices, breaking into a crescendo as she wiped her tears away with the back of her hand.

Bo, they said. *Look.*

The sunflowers swiveled to her left. She lifted her head.

Just at the edge of her fingertips was a knife.

Bo's heart picked up speed. She reached for it, wrapping her fingers around the handle and pulling it closer. This was it, the same knife she'd found buried in the clearing, the same knife she'd hidden away in the kitchen drawer. Somehow, miraculously, it was here in this field beside her, and the sunflowers had shown her where to find it.

Thank you, thank you, thank you, Bo thought as she pressed the handle between her palms to keep it steady. She started with the ropes around her ankles. When the last thread had snapped and the rope drooped, she finally stood. Bo maneuvered the blade so the edge caressed the rope around her wrists. And then she pressed her hands, the rope, the knife against a heavy stalk. The added pressure was just enough for the knife to slide through, freeing her.

Bo. Get up.

"Who are you?" she said, shaking free of the ropes.

A pause. And then: *the Blooms.*

"The Blooms," Bo repeated softly, rolling the word over her tongue.

The dead.

The missing.

The sacrifices.

As Bo stood, surrounded by yellow in every direction, the whispers swelled. The flowers bent their heads, their petals stretching to her like wiggling fingers. Their voices—they each had a distinct voice—begged to be heard.

Drowned me in my bathtub.

Cut my wrists in the clearing.

Buried me alive.

She closed her eyes, trying to fight down the nausea rolling through her so she could sort through the voices. Some seemed vaguely familiar, like she might have heard them in a previous lifetime, saying "Hello" to her on the street or telling her not to forget her receipt at the corner store. Most she didn't recognize at all.

And none of them belonged to her mother.

But the dead and the lonely still called to her. Their pleas, their stories hummed through her veins as she stood farther into the field than she'd ever been. They told her about how they'd been slain, how the cops had covered it up. About the babies they'd left behind while their blood marinated in Bishop's soil, feeding it. They told Bo their secrets and dreams in whispery sobs that made everything inside her ache.

"What do you want me to do?" she asked, turning her palms to the inky sky. Her eyes pricked with fresh tears.

The flowers grew quiet. One whispered: *Harding.*

And then another. *Harding.*

They began to chant-whisper together, their voices rippling through the field in every direction.

Harding.

Harding.

Harding.

Bo looked at the knife still in her hand. A bloody secret that was meant to stay buried. But she hadn't left it there; she'd dug it up. She'd brought it home. And now it was here, in her hand, a curse turned into a second chance.

She tightened her fingers around the knife and started forward. The sunflowers slowly parted, showing her the way, as their petals trembled with excitement.

Bo wouldn't die again, alone in this sunflower graveyard.

She was finally going to live.

CHAPTER THIRTY-ONE

When the sheriff pulled Alma out the door, he took all the air in the room with him.

Whitney still stood behind the counter, Robert Dingal's birth certificate hanging limply from her hand. From somewhere in the bowels of the building, a drill hummed. Probably someone messing with the circuits, trying to get the electricity on again. She turned to the blank computer screen in front of her and numbly tapped the mouse. Nothing happened. Alma's words echoed in her mind. *It's just the power grid. The storm knocked it out.*

Whitney slumped into Alma's desk chair. If she concentrated hard enough, she could almost feel Alma's fingers brushing against hers, smell the echo of her grassy soap lingering in the air.

She was gone. Sheriff Ableman had taken her—and Eleanor's notebook—away, leaving Whitney with nothing but a birth certificate that proved how utterly, irrevocably fucked this town was.

And what was she supposed to do with that anyway? It wasn't like anyone would listen to, let alone believe her. She didn't even have the notebook anymore—all she had were a few photocopied documents and a strong suspicion. Alma couldn't back her up. And the cops . . . the cops weren't safe, either.

Whitney had had her issues with Bishop's three-person police force, including the sheriff, but this was different. This was tampering with evidence, pushing what they didn't want to see under the rug. This was about protecting the Hardings and, honestly, all the other men of this town. As long as they kept all the deaths under wraps, these men could keep on living their happy little lives without interruption. Without facing consequences.

They'd never give her the notebook back. They'd already taken Eleanor from her; they'd never let Alma out, even if Whitney showed up at the station and rattled the door like a banshee.

"Fuck," she said, sliding her hands from her eyes. She glanced down at the dishwater-colored carpet beneath her.

Alma's backpack sat against the cabinets, half unzipped. Even from here, Whitney could see the indigo laminate of an oracle card. She knew it was silly, that it wouldn't do anything to help her free Alma. But something about the way the card peeked out of the pocket beckoned to her.

Whitney reached for the cards. "Eleanor, if you're really a spirit or whatever, I could really use your help right now." She started to shuffle, trying to remember the way Alma's delicate brown hands had sorted through them so gracefully. What was she supposed to ask? She couldn't be doing this right.

Have you tried talking to her? Alma's voice whispered in her mind.

Whitney's hands stilled. She took a deep breath. "Eleanor, I'm lost," she said, her voice cracking. "I need help. What should I do? How do I get out of this?"

She started to shuffle through the cards again. As she did, a single card jumped from the deck and wafted to the ground, landing faceup.

It was *The Veil*.

Cold washed over her. This was the same card Alma had pulled for her while they were sitting on the lumpy sofa, pretending their knees weren't touching. Whitney bent down to pick it up, her eyes searching for something—anything—Eleanor might have to tell her. The crumbling stone archway, the gauzy veil, the oak tree, and the acorns. None of it stood out. None of it *said* anything.

Whitney could feel the last bits of her heart fraying around the edges. She swallowed down the knot in her throat. She desperately wanted to let go of this, of Eleanor, but at the same time she was afraid to, and the thought of either was tearing her apart.

Whitney started to toss the card onto the desk when something beneath the oak tree caught her eye. She grabbed her phone and held its flashlight up to the image to examine it.

There was a cluster of acorns beneath the shade of the oak tree; Whitney had noticed them the first time. But the whole thing had freaked her out so much that she hadn't stuck around long enough to really look at it.

The acorns were in the shape of an *E.*

Whitney gasped, throwing the card onto the desk. She rubbed her eyes. She couldn't be seeing this right now.

Whitney.

She jerked at the sound of her own name and glanced around the room. There was no one else here.

Follow me.

"Who is this?" Whitney asked, but the whisper was silent. The only sound was a soft *tap, tap, tap* on the window. Slowly, she slid off the chair and tiptoed to the window.

The lot was empty. All of the staff had gone home, except for the night-shift nurses taking care of the patients in the back. There was no one outside.

Whitney pressed her forehead to the glass, but all she saw was the flashing lights of the fire truck parked down the street and a row of sunflowers poking up from a grassy patch on the other side of the window. They leaned closer.

Tap, tap, tap.

She backed away, but the sunflowers didn't. They tapped their blank faces against the glass, petals filtering out the inky sky. Whitney curled her fingers under the window frame and lifted. Storm-heavy air seeped into the room, followed by a burst of petals. They floated around her like dust in an attic.

Follow me, the whisper said again, and this time, Whitney could hear the lilt of Eleanor's voice within it.

She flung herself out the front door. A single petal twirled on an invisible breeze just beyond the entrance to the Nursing Care Center. In wonder, Whitney walked toward it.

She followed it around the corner and into the small cul-de-sac behind Main Street. Whitney knew where the petal was taking her before she reached the third house on the left. Some part of her had known she'd end up here eventually, one way or another.

As she approached Eleanor's old house, the petal floated gently into the empty flower bed next to the porch. Another family lived here now—the Jacobsons. Instead of puffy peonies, the beds were pocked with toy cars, an air pump, and a deflated football. But the oak tree still stood.

There were no acorns nestled beneath it like there had been in the card. But Whitney remembered the exact spot where the cops had found Eleanor's body. She'd been walking home in the middle of the day, they'd said. She'd just dropped dead ten feet from her porch steps, right beneath the oak tree. Her grandmother had found her facedown in the grass the next morning. Whitney had rode by the house on her bike more than a dozen times in the week after. Sometimes she even stopped across the street and watched the police tape flicker in the wind.

Whitney stood in that same spot now. There was no police tape marking off the area, but she knew. She could feel Eleanor's last breaths in the air, her body rigid in the soil beneath her feet. The police tape, the "investigation" afterward—it was all a joke. Whitney was sure no one had tried to figure out how Eleanor died. They just pretended in order to appease Susannah.

Whitney glanced up at the dark house. She dropped to her knees and ran her palm over the parched grass. *Okay, Eleanor,* she thought. *What do you want me to see?*

Whitney started to dig. She clawed at the grass with her bare hands, yanking up fistfuls of dirt and tossing them to the side. She dug until her palms ached and black crescent moons were caked under her fingernails. Moonlight stained the dark earth. Beads of sweat slid down her forehead and clung to her eyelashes like gnats in a web.

Her fingers bumped up against something solid.

She glanced up at the house. The windows were still dark, the shadows inside unflinching. She plunged both hands into the earth and pulled.

The dirt fell away as she lifted the object out of the ground. It was rectangular, thick, heavy. Whitney blew away the last of the debris.

It was a book. Not just any book, but the one her mother always assigned her ninth-grade advanced English class: *The Handmaid's Tale.*

Her mom always got shit for it, to which she explained to the PTA that advanced English was *optional* and students could choose another, thematically similar book if they wanted. But most didn't—not the girls, anyway. Whitney opened the cover and read the inside flap.

Eleanor Craft

9th—advanced English

Ms. Montgomery

She let out a breath. Eleanor had been in her mom's class. Had Eleanor ever mentioned it before? All those fever-pitched conversations in the peachy glow of the bonfire had blurred with time. Whitney tried to flip through the pages.

But there *were* no pages in the center.

Eleanor had glued the center of the pages together before cutting a big hole through thousands and thousands of Margaret Atwood's words. Tucked in the center was a lighter and a plastic bottle. Whitney carefully finessed the bottle out of the hole and read the faded label.

Lighter fluid.

Tires squealed as a car rolled up beside her. A man with bushy eyebrows and a splotchy red face rolled down his window. *Mr. Jacobson.* "Hey, what are you doing to my lawn?"

Whitney shoved the bottle back into the book. "I—" Whitney started to respond, but it was too late. He'd already thrown the car in park and started to open the door.

Run.

Whitney didn't know if that voice came from Eleanor, or the sunflowers, or something else entirely, but she didn't care. She shoved the book under her arm and ran, leaving a trail of dirt behind her.

"HEY!" Footsteps pattered behind her. She picked up speed as she turned the corner. They started to fade.

She slowed for a second to catch her breath. If she kept going straight, she'd wind up on Main Street, and she could take it down a couple blocks to the station. And then she could . . .

What?

Whitney opened the book. The lighter and plastic bottle winked up at her. Eleanor had been saving these for something, hiding them away in her old English book so no one would catch on. Maybe she even had this book with her the night she died.

Or she'd been trying to get to it.

Whitney's stomach hitched as she thought of Eleanor walking home in the dark from the bonfire, her clothes still smoky and her lips raw and pink from their kisses. Someone following her in the dark. Eleanor's heart thrumming in her veins as she hid beneath the oak, digging up the book she'd hidden—the plan she'd made—with her bare hands. Maybe she had even planned to tell Whitney about it the next day when they met in the clearing.

Not getting very far before someone had come back to finish the job.

Tires squealed as Mr. Jacobson's car swung around the corner. Whitney snapped the book shut and bolted toward the street. *Shit, shit, shit.* The engine growled as the car picked up speed. "Hey! What did you take from my yard?"

When she reached Main Street, she headed toward town hall. The police station was right next door. Alma had to be in there somewhere. She had to be.

People had just begun to poke their heads out of the shops and restaurants they had been trapped in during the storm. Roof shingles littered the street like oversized dinner plates, and the tendrils of errant branches draped over sidewalks and lampposts. Whitney hopped over the debris and kept running. She only had a minute before Mr. Jacobson would be able to turn and follow her.

The station loomed just up ahead. Whitney slowed long enough to pull out the lighter and fluid from inside the book. She pulled in a deep breath.

And pictured Eleanor.

That last night together, knees touching, fingers threaded together behind a wall of smoke at the bonfire. The tiny silver flame charm that Whitney had slipped onto her bracelet. The night she'd decided that she was in love with Eleanor Craft.

Burn it all down, a voice whispered.

Tires caressed the cement as Mr. Jacobson's car turned down the street. Whitney's hands shook as she doused *The Handmaid's Tale* in clear fluid. She tossed the empty bottle onto the street and ran.

The lobby was mostly empty except for two cops sitting at small wooden desks, and Alma, who was slumped over in a plastic folding chair in the corner.

All three snapped their heads up. The tallest one stood. "Miss, what are you—"

Whitney flicked the lighter and touched it to the book. It burst into flames. She tossed the book at the desk in front of her.

The cops yelled something at her, but her heart was roaring too loud in her ears to hear. This was it. She'd never be able to come back from this. She was a felon. There was no way Sheriff Ableman wouldn't press charges and drop her at the county jail to rot.

She'd have to make this worth it.

"Alma, let's go!" she yelled. Alma hopped out of the chair, eyes wild with panic, and ran toward her. Whitney grabbed her hand and pulled her through the front door.

The fire alarm had started to wail, but the truck wasn't ready. It was still parked back at the Nursing Care Center, trying to deal with sick patients and downed power lines. They might actually make it out of here.

"Where to?" Alma asked, breathless.

Whitney paused, trying to think. They could go back to the house, start up her mom's old sedan, try to get out of this place before the car broke down on the highway. They could—

Something slammed into Whitney with such force that it felt like a hammer to the chest. She stumbled back, her arms pin-wheeling, grasping for Alma. Someone grabbed her wrists and wrenched them behind her back. Pain streaked across her injured shoulder. Cold metal snapped onto her wrists in quick succession. *Snap, snap.*

"We've got them," Sheriff Ableman said breathlessly into the phone tucked against his ear. "We're bringing them to you now."

The wind started to pick up, howling with disapproval.

Whitney's heart sank.

They were trapped.

CHAPTER THIRTY-TWO

Jude pulled at the zip ties around her wrists until her skin bled.

Outside of Bennett's room, the rest of the world was quiet. The wind had softened into a tepid breeze, and Delilah's screams had all but vanished behind the cellar doors. Bile rose into her throat at the thought of Delilah, trapped behind those steel doors. But as much as she tried, she couldn't free herself. After a while, she stopped fighting and pressed her forehead against the bedpost.

"I messed up," she whispered to the empty room.

Her mother had always told her that mistakes could be fixed. *Jude, baby, you don't have to be so hard on yourself,* she'd say, lifting Jude's chin until she looked her mother in the eye. *There's always another way.*

Jude looked at the bedpost in front of her. Bennett had tied her wrists so tightly around it that her nose was almost brushing against the nicks and notches in the wood. If there was another way out of this, she couldn't see past the post in front of her to find it. She half-heartedly pulled at the zip ties. They didn't budge.

She closed her eyes. As much as she tried to push it down, there was a tiny part of her that whispered in her head. *This is just the way it is,* the voice said. *This is the best you'll ever get.*

She knew it wasn't her mother's voice, but it didn't feel like it totally belonged to herself, either. It felt a bit like a curse, something that had latched onto her that night when she'd been born during a vicious storm. Maybe if she hadn't screamed so much, it would have passed her by, carried away like petals in the wind.

But she had, and it was still there, pressing on her throat, choking her voice. Reminding her that of all the girls, she was the least important. She wasn't gorgeous like Whitney or brave like Bo or confident like Delilah. She was just soft—too soft. Too quiet. Too plain. Outside Bishop, there was zero chance that someone like Bennett would notice her, fall in love with her. Want her to stay.

Jude gritted her teeth. *No.*

Her eyes snapped open. There had to be a way.

She slid her wrists down to the floor, her cheek pressing hard against the bedpost. If she could just adjust herself, tilt her neck a bit so she could wedge the post against her shoulder, she might be able to lift it and—

The post groaned as Jude lifted it, barely an inch, off the floor. She yanked her wrists out from beneath it and let the bed drop with a *thud.*

She sat back, trying to catch her breath. She'd done it. At least she could move around Bennett's room now, even if she was locked in.

"Get *off* her!" a voice screamed from outside.

Whitney. Jude crawled to the window and peeked out. One of the storm cellar doors had been opened, but all she could see was a black pit beneath it. No sign of Delilah.

Her sister stumbled into view first, followed by another girl. Jude squinted. It was the girl from the front desk at the Nursing Care Center—Alma? She watched as the girl grabbed Whitney's arm to keep her upright.

"Don't touch her!" Whitney yelled again as another person

came into view. It was Sheriff Ableman wearing his camel-colored button-up as he marched behind them. Something glinted in his hand.

A pistol.

Jude let out a guttural scream. Ableman pushed them toward the open cellar, knocking over a watering can and an old shovel propped against the brick. From the side of the house, all three Hardings, including Bennett, ran toward them. The wind kicked up as if it had been summoned, blowing Whitney's wild curls over her eyes. She stumbled.

"I can't. I have to . . ." Jude didn't finish her thought. She pulled herself up, careful to avoid the window, and snuck toward Bennett's desk. There had to be something that could break her free.

The desk was mostly empty except for a Rubik's Cube and a stack of worn notebooks from last year's classes. Jude glanced at the shelf hovering above it. A few books, a pile of track and field medals Bennett had never bothered to hang up, and a single picture frame. She stood on her tiptoes to look.

Jude remembered when this photo had been taken. It was the last day of school in late May, and the weather had already turned oppressively hot. Bennett stood on his front porch steps, sunburnt, one arm wrapped around his brother and the other around Delilah. Whitney had been there, too, just to the side of the porch, and so had Jude. They'd all decided to meet up at the Harding house before heading to the clearing for an end-of-the-year bonfire.

Jude's face was half hidden by the shade of the porch, but even from here she could see now how clear it was. Her body language said everything she'd tried so hard to keep concealed. Her head tilted in Bennett's direction, almost as if he were a magnet and she couldn't help being drawn to him. Her eyes looked at the camera, but not really. She had one eye on Bennett at all times, as if she couldn't stand waiting one more second to jump back into his orbit after the camera went *snap*.

Jude's cheeks flushed with heat. She couldn't believe how naive she had been. She couldn't believe she'd done that to Delilah—to them all, really.

A burst of wind rattled the house. Outside, the screaming had started up again, this time laced with panic instead of rage. Alma was yelling now, too, but Jude couldn't make out the words.

She reached both hands over her head and smacked the frame from the shelf. It tumbled onto the desk with a loud *crack,* and then to the floor, where the glass shattered. Jude bent down and grabbed the largest shard of glass. Her fingers shook as she inched it between her palms, careful not to cut herself.

Another scream, this time slightly muffled. If Whitney and Alma weren't already in the cellar, they were close.

Pressing her palms together like a prayer with the glass between them, Jude pushed her hands into the floor. It was just enough pressure for the glass to cut through the zip tie, freeing her wrists. She set the glass down and raced for the door. It was locked.

Jude let go of the doorknob. *Think, think, think.* She scanned the room.

The extra key. Bennett might have clicked the lock shut on his way out, but he hadn't taken the spare key with him. Jude knew there was another. He'd shown it to her one night when he'd snuck her into his house after his uncle had gone to bed. *In case you ever want to surprise me when I'm not here,* he'd said, delivering his best farm-boy grin before tucking it in a small box inside his desk. *Maybe get under the covers and wait for me?*

Ugh. The thought made her stomach lurch because she knew that Past Jude would have actually *done* it. She would have shown up and waited for him for hours, with the door locked in case his brother or uncle tried to come in. But he met Delilah only three days later, and that had been the end of that.

She opened the desk drawers and fumbled through their contents until she found the box. She cracked it open. The key stared back at her.

"Thank god," she whispered, jamming it into the door. With a quick *click*, she was finally free. She raced down the stairs, her pulse running wild in her veins. Jude reached the back door and flung herself onto the grass.

Whitney and Alma were gone.

But Bo was standing in their place.

Jude's heart climbed up her throat as she watched Bo, circling the storm cellar like a rabid wolf. She was covered in blood—so much blood—and one eye was swollen completely shut. "Let them *go,*" she growled.

William stood on the other side of the cellar, watching as Bo slowly reached toward her pocket. He let out a laugh. "I wouldn't try it if I were you. What do you have there—a Taser? Pepper spray? A knife? That won't get you very far here, little girl."

William calmly lifted his arm, palm open to the sky. As if it had been waiting for his signal, the wind roared on cue. He smirked. "This whole town only listens to *me*. You're just like your pathetic mother, trying to fight against something ancient, so much bigger than you. This is the way we've always done it. This is the way it's going to be." He flicked his hand toward Bo, and the wind followed.

It raged, lashing Bo from every direction. She wobbled before hitting the ground—hard. Jude saw something glint as it fell out of her pocket.

The weapon. It must have been something Bo planned to use.

She gasped. *It was the knife.*

The one Bo had tucked into the kitchen drawer beside the oven when she thought Jude wasn't paying attention. Bo had saved it just in case.

Of something like this.

Jude crouched down and crawled toward the sunflower fields

pressing against the edge of the yard. If she could just slip between the stalks, she could loop around closer to the cellar, help Bo, and grab the knife.

As soon as she reached the fields, she stood and ran, weaving through the stalks toward the cellar. Beyond the flowers, Bo was yelling, but the words were lost on the wind. Jude slowed as she got closer.

William's enormous hands were wrapped around Bo's bare ankles as he dragged her through the grass. She was barely moving anymore. Her hands hung limp above her head as a trail of fresh blood followed her to the open cellar doors.

BO! Jude thought it, but when she opened her mouth to scream, her throat closed up like a river dam. She crouched near the ground and reached for the knife still nestled in the grass.

You won't use it, a voice hissed. The wind lashed her skin. *You're not strong enough.*

"Yes, I *am*," Jude whispered, gritting her teeth. Her fingers grazed the handle. She wrapped her hand around it and slid it toward her. *I can do this.*

Bo let out a groan as William easily lifted her onto his shoulder. She dangled like a limp dishrag as he carried her down the cellar stairs.

Caleb and Bennett were still outside, the wind raking through their hair and rippling their shirts. They were so close, no more than a few feet from her. She could inch just a little closer, steady the knife. Catch them off guard.

She slowly stood, keeping her eyes trained on Caleb as he waved his arms animatedly, talking to Bennett about something she couldn't quite hear. She gripped the knife until her knuckles turned white. With William in the cellar, the wind started to calm.

". . . The other one?" Caleb asked with a sneer.

Jude paused. It was so much easier to hear every snap in the fields without the wind to distract them.

Bennett turned toward his brother and scoffed. "Jude? Nah, we don't have to worry about her. She's on our side."

Caleb slapped his brother on the back. "Okay. We're trusting you."

"Trust me," Bennett said, as they both walked toward the stairs. "Jude would never betray me."

Jude watched it all happen in slow motion. Her heartbeat roared in her ears as she watched the Harding brothers walk in the opposite direction of her hiding place. *Wait!* she wanted to scream. *You should be worried about me.*

But the words got knotted up in her throat, just like they always did.

Caleb went down the cellar stairs first, his blond hair disappearing as he descended. Bennett paused. He glanced up at his bedroom window, then turned back toward the cellar. A small smile played on his lips as he kept going, shutting the doors behind him.

Jude swallowed. "You should be worried about me," she whispered to the deserted yard.

No one answered.

CHAPTER THIRTY-THREE

Delilah felt them enter the cellar.

Even though everything in her still screamed with pain, she'd had a few moments of relief when William's cellphone had started to vibrate the moment he got close enough to the stairs to get service. Then he'd flung open the doors and headed out into the daylight, followed closely by Caleb and Bennett.

She wasn't sure if she'd fallen asleep, but time seemed to move differently down here. It was slower and faster at the same time. Eventually, the pain had subsided enough that Delilah could sit up with her back against the wall. Her throat was so dry. She didn't know if it had been minutes or days since they'd dragged her here.

Then the doors started to open. First for Whitney and a girl she recognized from school. And then a second time for Bo, who looked about as bad as Delilah felt. Jude was nowhere to be found.

Together the four of them sat huddled in this dank, dusty prison, Whitney pressed beside her and Bo's head on Delilah's shoulder. "You're bleeding," Delilah had whispered when she saw the cut at Bo's temple.

But Bo had only responded with "He's a bastard" before her eyes fluttered shut.

The door creaked open again. Footsteps descended the stairs as three silhouettes entered. The doors groaned as they slammed shut, drowning them all in darkness except for the watery light from a single lantern in the corner of the room.

"Okay," William said, as if he were gathering their attention to start a meeting. The edges of his shadow reached overhead and pulled a chain. A lightbulb turned on with a *click*. "Let's just lay things out as they are now, okay? That way, this will go smoother."

Beside her, Bo's eyes fluttered open. She winced as she tried to lift her head. Delilah propped her upright, her head still on Delilah's shoulder.

"From what my nephews have told me, it seems like you all have become . . . aware of what's been happening here." William smiled at them, the corners of his eyes crinkling. "Which, really, shouldn't be much of a surprise, considering your mothers caught on as well."

Delilah stilled. Images of Indigo's handwritten obituaries poking out from the plaster like ghostly weeds flitted through her mind. The secret letter from William to her mother.

I promise, what you saw wasn't what you think.

Meet me in the clearing after dusk this evening and I'll explain.

"What did you do to them?" Delilah croaked.

William smiled at her like she was a toddler. "What did *I* do? Ha. The question you should be asking is what did *they* do. I tried to get them to stop. I warned Cori not to dig too deep, but when Ava started going off the rails in our faculty meetings, talking about how we needed to 'protect our girls,' I knew they were questioning. They were never going to stop," he said with a chuckle. "They were warned, and they just did it anyway."

Whitney shook beside Delilah. "Fuck you."

"Ah. Ava always talked about how much of a pistol you were."

William smiled. "It's a bit of a shame you weren't the one chosen this time. Maybe next time."

He turned to Delilah now. "Honestly, you all wouldn't be in this mess if your mothers had just done what they were supposed to. Indigo *knew*. She was one of the ones who could feel the curse in her blood. She *knew* she was supposed to be the next sacrifice. If she had met me in the clearing that night instead of running off—or whatever she did—then I could have done what I needed to do so the land could feed. It would have been satiated for much longer." He sighed. "But now look where we're at. The land never got fed the blood of the one it wanted, and we've had to supplement wherever we could since then. But it's not the same; it's constantly starving. It's getting angrier. Can't you feel it?"

His words rang in the dead space around Delilah. She could feel it; some ancient part of her had known Bishop was furious. Maybe that was why she had worked so hard to build up her walls, to shore up the house on Old Fairview Lane with limp cardboard boxes, to make sure she knew where each of the girls was every second of the day. She had known, in her heart and in her blood, that they had always been in danger.

"Why would you want to kill her?" Delilah asked softly. "I thought you were in love with her."

Beside his uncle, Bennett cleared his throat. William's face softened, just for a second. "None of that matters. I don't get to pick who the land chooses; I just follow orders to deliver."

"But you never did it," Delilah pushed. "You never killed her."

William turned toward a shelf in the cellar, reaching to the very top. "No," he said firmly. "She never showed up to the clearing. By the time I went to find her, she and Cori and Ava were gone."

Gone.

Alive.

Our mothers are alive, Delilah thought. The words felt like a hurricane and a drizzle all at once. Some part of her had always hung on to hope in the back of her mind, clung to the thought like rain on the wind. But hearing someone else confirm it felt like the rumbling of a storm, taking her breath away.

"Then why the memorial?" Bo's voice cracked around the words. "You knew they weren't dead. Why put on a big show?"

Metal scraped against wood as William pulled down a rust-speckled box and handed it to Caleb. "A lot has happened in that clearing. A lot." He lifted the box's lid. "But the worst was that Eleanor girl. Caleb, do you remember what a bloody mess that was? She just would *not* stop fighting us. It was a good thing we did it in the clearing and then set her in front of her house. Looked a lot cleaner all around that way."

Caleb's eyes gazed somewhere in the distance, as if he were remembering. William nudged him, and he blinked. "She just kept coming back," he said quietly. "I still see her everywhere."

Whitney stiffened. "You're the one who did it." It was a statement, not a question.

Caleb didn't look at her, at any of them.

"It was his turn," William said, shrugging. "We all have to learn at some point. But it was a bit . . . rough for a first go, I'd say, and with the storms getting worse and worse, that earth just kept getting churned up. We found everything in that clearing—ripped fabric, clumps of hair, you name it. So we thought we'd put something in its place, some kind of statue. And the people here, they loved your moms. They'd never argue about some nice statues of them up in the clearing. Plus, your moms wouldn't dare show their faces around here again if everyone thought they were dead."

William plunged his hand into the metal box and pulled out a hunting knife. Delilah pulled in a breath. "None of this matters, really. Delilah, you know, and I know, that you're the one this land craves. It's time to fulfill that promise, and finally feed it the blood it deserves."

The girl beside Whitney screamed, but William didn't move.

Instead, he turned and handed the knife to Bennett. "It's your turn now."

Spots danced around Delilah's eyes as he approached. Bo yelled, but it came out more like a whimper. William grabbed her and clamped his massive hands around her wrists to hold her still. Delilah yelped.

Bennett sank to his knees in front of her. Even in the dim light of the cellar, his skin looked pale and clammy. His uncle pushed the hunting knife into Bennett's hands. "Do it."

Delilah looked him in the eyes. She lifted her chin. *Do it.*

Bennett's hand shook as he pressed the tip of the knife to the soft spot beneath her chin. Her heart pounded so fiercely, she was sure he could hear it, too.

He stared at her for a long moment before dropping the knife, nicking her skin. She felt a drop of blood roll down her neck.

Bennett closed his eyes. "I can't."

William's face darkened. He ripped the knife from Bennett's hand and pushed the edge of the blade to Delilah's skin. Beside her, the girls yelled. Bo lifted her head. "Fuck you!" she said, her voice cracking.

Every nerve in Delilah's body seared with pain. William leaned in so close, she could smell the sourness on his breath. "I waited too long for your mother," he snarled. "I won't make the same mistake twice."

The blade was hot and quick. She gasped, bringing her fingers to touch her neck.

Blood poured down the backs of her hands, her arms.

It puddled on the floor, drowning her, pulling her under.

CHAPTER THIRTY-FOUR

What about the others?" Caleb asked, averting his eyes from the mess on the floor.

William wiped the knife, and blood splattered at Bo's feet. "We won't kill them, not until the land asks us to." He carefully set the knife back in the box and tucked it under his arm. "But we *will* leave them here for a bit. So they can learn a lesson."

He turned to Bo. This time, there was no smile. "Especially this one."

Bo spat, but her mouth was so parched that nothing came out except flecks of dried blood. William lifted an eyebrow before turning back toward the stairs. "Let's go," he said, waving to his nephews.

Caleb quickly followed, but Bennett didn't budge. He stood under the peach glow of the single dangling lightbulb, his eyes wild with panic. "I . . . I . . ."

"Let's *go*," William said, gruff this time. He clamped his hand around Bennett's shoulder and pulled him toward the stairs. The doors groaned open, and the Hardings filed out one by one before locking them all in the dark.

No one made a sound.

"Delilah?" Whitney whispered. But there was only a soft gurgle.

Bo crawled toward the shelves in the corner. Her hands slid through Delilah's blood as she made her way toward the patch of peachy light illuminating part of the room. She gritted her teeth as she pulled herself up and felt her way around the shelves.

William had taken the box with the knife. Bo's hands shook as she searched around for something—*anything*—that could help Delilah. There were old books and crusty paintbrushes, a couple of half-empty cardboard boxes, and an electric lantern. Her fingers slid against the metal of the lantern as she searched for the switch.

Click. Light flooded the cellar. Bo swung the lantern toward the girls.

It was so much worse than she could have imagined.

There was blood everywhere. Whitney and Alma had scrambled to their feet and were holding each other. Delilah sat slumped against the wall, the bottom of her curls soaked in her blood. She wasn't moving.

Bo's stomach lurched. "Lilah!" Bo raced toward her and dropped the lantern with a *clang*. She shook Delilah's shoulders. "Lilah, wake up. Wake up. *Please.*"

Delilah moaned. Her head lolled back, exposing her neck. The cut was a fierce, angry red, but from what Bo could see, it wasn't as deep as she'd thought. If she could just figure out how to stanch the bleeding, maybe Delilah could still make it.

She *had* to make it.

"Our shirts," Whitney said, as if she'd been reading Bo's mind. "Maybe we can make a bandage?"

Alma nodded. She started to pull at her shirt. "I can help."

Bo glanced down at her own worn tank top, soaked through

with sweat and blood. They'd need something heavier to stop this kind of bleeding.

The blanket. The blue gingham blanket was still spread out on the floor, as if the Hardings had purposely left it there as a reminder of all the damage they'd inflicted on top of that blanket, in this underground prison. She looked up at Whitney and Alma. "We'll need something denser. Help me with this."

Whitney dropped to her knees beside Bo and started to pick at the edges. "We have to unravel the seams to loosen it," she said, her deft fingers moving quickly.

Bo started on the other side. "Thank god for all those curse-word embroideries, Whit."

While they worked, Alma crouched beside Delilah. She leaned in so Delilah's head could lay on her shoulder, and she gently pushed the blood-splattered hair from her eyes.

Together, Whitney and Bo loosened the seams, splitting the blanket into two halves. Bo grabbed the half that hadn't been completely soaked through yet and pressed it against the sharp metal edge of the lantern, casting ghostly patterns on the walls. She grunted as she pushed, her knuckles white as she held the fabric taut. The blanket half ripped down the center, the jagged metal poking through. Whitney grabbed the other edge and pulled until they had freed a long strip of fabric.

"Lilah," Bo said as she scooted toward her. Alma gently guided Delilah's head upright so Bo could wrap the fabric around her neck. Delilah groaned as Bo pulled, tighter and tighter, until the fabric dug into her wound. Instantly, splotches of blood started to soak through.

"What do we do?" Whitney asked. Even in the lantern light, Bo could see her entire body shaking. "I don't know what to do. I don't—"

"Shh." Alma stood and wrapped Whitney in her arms. "We'll figure it out."

But as Bo looked around the cellar, she wasn't sure how they could get out of this. William had locked the door on the way out. They were trapped here, and Delilah could only lose so much more blood.

Bo sidled up next to Delilah and laid her head on her shoulder. She could still feel the faint flutter of her pulse beneath the skin. It took everything in her not to cry. "I don't know what to do," she said, her voice shaking.

"There's Jude," Whitney offered, but Bo could tell that even she didn't believe it.

Bo scoffed. "Like that traitor is going to do anything to help us. Where is she anyway?"

Whitney sighed and sank to the floor beside her. "Probably with Bennett somewhere. I left her in front of the house before I went to find Alma." She turned. "Alma, I am so sorry I brought you into this."

Alma threaded her fingers through Whitney's and kissed the top of her hand. "You didn't know," she said.

The room fell silent except for the sound of Delilah's labored breaths. Bo grabbed Delilah's bloody hand and squeezed. *Hang on.*

She closed her eyes, trying to picture the sunflowers lingering just outside the cellar. She imagined them bent toward the doors, scraping the metal with their petals, speaking in frenzied whispers. *Get out. Get out. Get out.*

Tears pricked the corners of Bo's eyes. If only she could thrust her hand through the ceiling and touch them, beg them to help stanch the blood, to save them all.

The sound of metal on metal echoed through the cellar, making Bo's bones reverberate in her body. She winced as the door creaked open and pale light spilled in. A shadowy figure peered inside.

And a riot of yellow petals wafted into the room like snow.

CHAPTER THIRTY-FIVE

The first petal grazed the tip of Whitney's nose before fluttering to the top of her thigh, where Alma's hand gently rested. She brushed it off before the next one fell, and then the next.

Her heart hitched in her chest as she watched the figure descend the stairs. *Please let it be Jude*, she thought. *Please let her change her mind.*

But it was Bennett's voice that rang through the cellar. "No," he whispered, staring at Delilah in horror. He dropped to his knees beside the bloody remains of the blanket. "No! Please wake up, please."

"What are you doing here?" Bo growled.

Bennett didn't look at her. He cupped Delilah's chin in his hand. "I'm so sorry," he said, his voice cracking. "I'm so, so sorry." He climbed to his feet and slid his hands under her arms.

Whitney jumped up, suddenly electric with rage. "What do you think you're doing?"

"Taking her to the hospital," he answered. As he started to lift,

Delilah's eyes fluttered open. She frowned and mumbled something, but Whitney couldn't make out the words.

Her mind flashed to that bumpy ride in the back of the Hardings' truck after the statue had pummeled her at the memorial. She'd felt the hum of the road beneath her as she swung in and out of consciousness in the back seat. Jude's delicate fingers had woven through her hair as she cradled Whitney's head in her lap. *It's going to be okay. You'll be okay.*

She'd opened her eyes at some point on the ride. The back of Caleb's and Bennett's matching blond heads bobbed in time with the curve of the road, and an endless mob of cornstalks whizzed by the windows. When they'd pulled over, green and yellow pressed in all around them.

Where are we? she'd heard Jude ask.

The hospital, Bennett had answered, matter-of-fact. Whitney had winced as she lifted her head. The only thing she could see, besides the corn and the flowers, was a dilapidated old house.

The rest was a blur as Caleb lifted her over his shoulder and carried her inside. The house was mostly empty. Whitney remembered thinking, *This isn't what most hospitals look like,* before dropping out of consciousness. There was a flurry of whispers, then the sharp taste of something acrid on her tongue as one of them tipped a plastic cup to her mouth. The *shh, shh, shh* of gauze as they wrapped her shoulder.

Whitney hadn't remembered much after that. She hadn't even thought about the car ride or the hospital again until this moment.

But had her sister known? She had to have known.

Jude hadn't been injured, or panicked, or drugged. She'd let them drag Whitney into that gross old house and call it a hospital, when it clearly wasn't.

Whitney wouldn't do the same to Delilah.

She stepped between Bennett and Delilah. "You're not taking her anywhere."

His eyes narrowed. "I'm trying to help her. Don't you *want* that?"

Whitney pushed him. "Get away from her."

"Whitney," Alma said softly from somewhere in the dark.

"No, he's lying." She pushed herself fully in front of Delilah so he couldn't touch her. "He's not going to take her to the hospital. He's going to take her to some haunted house in the middle of the fields and finish what his uncle started."

Bennett's eyes grew wide. "You remember."

"Whitney, what did he do to you?" Bo was suddenly pacing, her fists clenching and unclenching as if she were ready for a brawl.

"There's no hospital nearby," she said softly as her brain tried to snap the pieces into place. "The Hardings just pretended. They took me to some abandoned house instead, and . . . I think they drugged me so I wouldn't remember." The realization dawned on Whitney as clear as a spring morning. "They're never going to let us leave Bishop. We're going to be trapped in this town until they kill us all, one by one."

The air hung heavy in the room around them. Bennett choked out a sob. "I'm so sorry," he said, staring at Delilah. "I had no idea what I was doing. I—I was just following my brother and my uncle, and I didn't even think—"

"You *didn't* think." Bo stopped pacing and stared at Bennett with the kind of look that made Whitney's whole body chill. "You just did all these horrible things that you knew were wrong because your family was doing it? You *lied* about taking Whitney to the hospital? You let them cut up your girlfriend and you led Jude on and—"

"I didn't lead her on!" Bennett said, running his hands over his eyes. "I care about Jude. I always have. But this . . . *thing* inside me kept bringing me back to Delilah. It wouldn't let me *not* be with her, like it would whisper things to me whenever I thought about it. Things like, *You're giving up on everyone* and *You'll ruin everything we've built.* So I just . . . kept doing it."

He looked pathetic standing there, the peach-tinged light turning his skin a queasy shade of burnt orange. Whitney held back the urge to feel sorry for him. He'd done this to himself. "You did nothing, and now we all have to pay for it," she growled.

"I'm trying to fix it," he said softly, pulling something from his pocket. He held out a small box to the light. It was a first aid kit.

"*Pfft.*" Bo scoffed. "Screw you for even bringing that. She's dying! Look at her. She's bleeding out!"

Bennett swallowed. "Please, just let me do this." Before Bo could respond, he sank down in front of Delilah and started to work. His fingers shook as he readied a needle and surgical thread. "Help me," he said, the needle hovering just over Delilah's wound.

Whitney slid to the floor beside him. Her stomach flip-flopped as she looked closely at the cut. It didn't seem that deep, but the clean line across her neck was a deep crimson, and the skin around it had already started to turn pink and puffy.

"Pinch it together," Bennett said, his lips quivering.

Alma gently placed both hands on Delilah's shoulders, even though her eyes were closed again. Whitney took a deep breath. And then she pressed the widest part of the wound closed.

Delilah's eyes snapped open. She started to yell, but Alma squeezed her shoulders harder. A bead of sweat formed on Bennett's brow as he worked, expertly weaving the suture needle in and out, in and out, leaving behind a trail of zigzagging black thread. Bo frantically paced, wringing her hands until they were splotchy and pink.

When he got to the end, he leaned in so close to Delilah that his cheek was flush with hers. He paused there for a moment before biting through the nylon string. "There," he said, tying it off. "That'll help."

Delilah looked up at him with woozy, lovesick eyes, and Whitney cringed. She couldn't possibly still love him after all of this . . . could she? She'd thought the same thing about Jude, though, and look what had happened.

She glanced over at Alma, whose hands still pressed into Delilah's shoulders, though she was looking at Whitney. Even in the temporary stillness of that small, dank space, Whitney's pulse fluttered. She'd only known Alma for days—hours, really—but her heart remembered what the beginning of love felt like. It was like muscle memory. Once you'd done it, practiced it in thoughts and whispers and kisses, you knew when you were about to take off running again.

Even only having known Alma for hours, it would be hard for Whitney to unravel herself from her. Of course it would be even harder for Delilah, who had tethered herself to Bennett for years.

Delilah's dark lashes fluttered as she breathed heavily. Bennett's face was so close to hers that their noses were almost touching. She cleared her throat. Her voice cracked.

"What did you say?" Bennett asked. He reached his hand toward Delilah's cheek, but thought better of it.

"*You . . . did . . . this,*" Delilah whispered, her voice raspy.

Bennett dropped his hand. "I'm going to fix it, I swear to you. I'm so sorry, I—"

"Sorry doesn't mean shit now," Whitney snapped. "It's too late. How are you going to fix this, Bennett? You think your uncle and your brother are just going to *let us go*?" She let out a laugh. "No way. We're dead."

Bennett wiped his eyes. It took everything in Whitney not to slap him and tell him to stop crying. In the corner, Bo still paced.

Delilah scooted herself upright and whispered, "*Get . . . out.*"

Bennett started to mumble. "I just . . . I thought."

"You heard her," Bo interrupted. She stopped pacing and slid into the sliver of space between Bennett and Delilah, arms crossed over her chest. "She told you to get out."

Bennett looked like a deflated balloon as he tried to glance over the brick wall that was Bo standing in front of him. Finally, he grabbed the first aid kit and stood. Without a single word, he ascended the cellar stairs.

The doors slammed open before he even touched the handles. More petals—hundreds of them—fluttered into the room on the wind. Whitney's mouth dropped open as the petals swirled around them, a beacon of brightness in the dark.

"Hello?" Bennett said, climbing another stair. "Who's out there?"

The only reply was a gust of wind, followed by another mass suicide of petals.

Whitney tipped her head to look through the door. There was nothing but gray predawn sky and the field grass cresting the opening.

Bennett continued up the steps, swatting petals out of his eyes. He stepped onto the grass and turned to shut the doors.

A shovel swung into view, making a sick *thwunk* as it connected with the back of his head. Bennett let out a muted whimper before dropping into the grass.

CHAPTER THIRTY-SIX

The shovel vibrated under Jude's fingers as she made contact. It sank into the back of Bennett's neck like a carving knife slicing into a pumpkin. He hit the ground and didn't get back up.

Jude let out a breath as she dropped the shovel. She stuck her head into the cellar. "You all okay?"

Four pairs of eyes glinted in the dim light. Whitney stepped onto the bottom stair and squinted. "Jude?"

"*Yes*," Jude hissed. "Come on, let's get out of here."

But only Whitney took another step forward. Her face looked haunted as she looked up at Jude. "How . . . why should we trust you?"

She fought the knot forming in her throat. "Whitney . . . I'm your sister."

"But you betrayed us! You let the Hardings take me into that fake hospital! You betrayed Delilah for Bennett. He said you weren't a problem, that you were on 'their side' now."

Jude had always longed for that telepathic twin thing, but she'd never wanted it more than she did right now. She wanted to inject

Whitney directly into her brain so she could see how Jude had been intimidated by the Hardings without realizing it at first, how Bennett had used her, tied her wrists so tightly that her fingers went numb and called it love. She wanted her twin to feel the same agony that Jude felt, just for a second, so she could see that there was no way Jude could stay here anymore.

That she was ready to run.

"Give me the knife." Bo appeared in the light, her face gaunt and angry. Tendrils of dried blood climbed up her freckled arms like ivy vines. She held out her hand.

"What knife . . ." Jude trailed off, remembering the knife she'd found beside the cellar after they'd dragged Bo inside. It was still in her pocket, the bloodstained handle sticking out at the hip.

"I don't know if we can trust you," Bo said, slowly ascending the stairs. "I need the knife."

As collateral, Jude thought. *So they have something to fight back with in case I take them to the Hardings.* "Okay," she said, slipping the knife from her pocket. "Take it."

Bo snatched it from her hand and stuck it into her own pocket. She glanced behind her. "Lilah, can you walk?"

There was a groan and a shuffling sound, and Delilah appeared at the bottom of the stairs. Jude gasped. "Delilah, what happened to you?" She regretted the words as soon as they left her lips. She knew what had happened to her.

The Hardings had happened. And it was all her fault.

Bo shot daggers at her as she backtracked down the steps to hook her arm around Delilah's waist. Whitney emerged first, careful to exit the cellar as far away from Jude as she could, followed by Bo half carrying an exhausted Delilah. Alma tailed closely behind.

"Is that . . . smoke?" Alma asked, squinting at the sky. They all turned slowly toward the aroma. Jude pulled in a breath. It *did* smell like someone was having a bonfire, but it was the middle of a sweltering summer night.

"Doesn't matter. We've got to find a way out of here," Bo said. She glanced up at the Harding house. "They're going to find out we're gone." It was a statement, not a question, and Jude knew in her bones that it was true.

"Where should we go?" Alma asked.

The girls grew silent. After a minute, Jude said, "The house? We could grab some supplies, get the keys to the car and try to drive out of here?"

Bo shook her head. "That car barely worked when our moms used it. I doubt it'll start up now."

"We still need supplies," Whitney said. "A backpack of essentials. And then I guess we just . . . make a run for it."

Make a run for it. Jude imagined them weaving through the sunflowers for miles, and then maybe they could find the old house the Hardings had used for a hospital. There had to be medical supplies there. And then . . .

Where?

Jude couldn't picture what lay ahead for them. But it didn't matter anymore; whatever was out there had to be better than this. "We'll go grab some things—a first aid kit, water, some food—and head out through the sunflower field behind the house."

The girls all glanced at one another, as if deciding if they could trust Jude's plan. Jude's heart climbed into her throat as she watched them silently deliberate in front of her. Finally, Bo nodded. "Fine. Let's go." She started off, careful not to let go of Delilah's waist.

Whitney turned to Alma. "Are you sure you want to do this?" she asked, clasping her hands around Alma's shoulders. "You don't have to, you know. I've already dragged you too far into this."

Alma reached up and touched Whitney's cheek with her hand. "Whitney. There's nothing left for me here. I want to go with you."

Whitney blinked. Her mouth broke into a hesitant smile. "Okay. Okay, let's go."

Together, the three of them ran across the yard, toward the street until they saw Bo and Delilah up ahead. "You can't trust the cops," Whitney hissed as they approached downtown. "They're with the Hardings."

"We'll take the side streets until we can get to the gravel path," Bo whispered back. "Then to the house. And then we run like our lives depend on it."

Because they do, Jude thought.

The smell of smoke grew stronger as they got closer to Main Street. A pillow of smoke clouded the sky, casting a gloomy haze over Bishop. When they turned the corner, blue-and-red lights washed over the houses in front of them.

"Cops," Alma whispered.

"And the fire truck," Jude added.

"But we aren't near the Nursing Care Center yet," Whitney said.

Bo pointed. "Looks like they've got a bigger problem at the moment."

Jude glanced at the smoke, which had expanded into a looming presence in the few minutes they'd been running. Now there were flames licking the sky just beyond her line of sight. "Oh god, there's a fire at the police station," she whispered.

Whitney's eyes snapped to Alma's. Her mouth dropped open. "Oh my god. A *fire.*"

Alma's eyes widened. "They never got it under control."

Whitney quickly explained what had happened with the cops, how she'd found Eleanor's master plan buried beneath the old oak tree and finally put it to use. She'd never considered what would happen if they couldn't contain the flames at the station. She hadn't thought that far ahead.

"There have to be cops and firefighters all over downtown right now trying to contain it," Bo said, watching the flames snap above the graphite roofs. "We need to get past town and head to the path while they're busy."

Jude nodded. The gravel path that circled the edge of town and led them back to Old Fairview Lane would be the safest route. They almost never bumped into anyone on it, and it pressed in so close to the sunflower fields that they could easily sneak into the mob of yellow if they heard someone coming. "Let's do it."

They raced through the streets running parallel to Main, weaving in and out of yards, pausing behind dilapidated garden sheds and chicken coops so Delilah could catch her breath. The smoke grew into an oppressive haze, clouding Jude's vision as they tried to navigate their way back to the path. The wall of gray around them muddled everything; Jude swore she heard the quick pattering of footsteps trailing close behind at one point, but when she looked behind her, no one was there. Shouts trailed behind them like fairy-tale monsters in the woods, snapping at their heels.

The wind picked up as they pressed on, but it wasn't a light, subtle breeze. It went from dead air to a ravaging, gnashing thing in seconds, making Jude's eyes instantly water. Her chest tightened as panic coursed through her.

The Hardings must know.

Ahead of her, Delilah stumbled.

Jude raced to catch her before she dropped to the ground. She hooked her arm around Delilah's waist and lifted. Delilah let out a puff of air as she tried to stand. Her face was as pale as milkweed, the skin under her eyes swollen and bruised. Delilah didn't have much more in her. They had to move quicker.

"Whitney! Alma!" Jude shouted. "Help me carry her."

Whitney lifted one leg, careful to shift most of the weight to her good arm. Alma took the other, while Jude and Bo wrapped each of Delilah's arms around their shoulders. The four of them walked as fast as they could without jostling her too much.

You'll never get out, the wind hissed in Jude's ear.

She shook her head. *It's not real,* she told herself. *It can't hurt you.*

Jude felt the gravel path under her feet before she saw it. She let out a breath. They'd made it. They were going to make it.

She felt Bo push forward a little harder. "We're almost there."

Delilah started to cough as the wind raged. The smoke was everywhere now; it pressed in on all sides, dimming the sunflowers to a muted yellow. Every breath Jude took felt like a stone in her lungs, and what little oxygen she could catch was quickly swept away by the wind.

This is your fault, the wind hissed again. This time, it was tinged with the echo of a familiar voice. *You betrayed them. You don't deserve them.*

You're worthless.

"Stop," she whispered to William's voice. It was the same tone she'd heard on the wind that day in the clearing when Whitney had been trying to communicate with Eleanor through the weather vane. She'd thought it was Eleanor then, but now she knew better. Now they all knew better.

The wind was never going to lead them toward safety, toward love. It was an extension of the curse, the land, the Harding family, and she'd trusted it over her own voice for too long.

She gritted her teeth as the wind pushed against them head-on. It felt like running through molasses. The sunflowers were bent over, what was left of their petals shaking violently. Jude's steps were labored as the gravel swirled around her, clotting her lungs and filling her mouth with dust.

"Got 'em!" A voice yelled from up ahead. Only when Jude squinted her eyes to look, the person it belonged to wasn't very far away at all.

Sheriff Ableman stood in front of them, both hands on top of his hat to keep it in place. He was flanked by Bishop's two other cops, blocking them on the path. The sheriff's mouth twisted into a grin. "Y'all didn't get very far, did you?" He picked up his radio and pressed it to his lips. "William? We found them. We're on the path a few blocks from Old Fairview."

Jude's stomach dropped as the wind softened, just enough for William's voice to echo through the radio. *"Roger. We'll be up there shortly."*

The wind picked up again, lashing them from all sides until they were pressed up against one another in the middle of the path. Delilah shivered in Jude's arms.

The cops inched forward. As he approached, the sheriff slowly reached toward his holster and wrapped his fingers around his pistol. "If you all just stay put, we aren't gonna have any problems."

Jude's pulse rocketed through her veins.

They were trapped.

Delilah tipped her head onto Jude's shoulder. "Leave me," she whispered.

"No," Jude said, squeezing tighter. "We're not leaving you."

Leave her, the wind hissed.

Sacrifice her.

Stop this once and for all.

"*NO,*" Jude yelled. "You're not real!"

You could have me, Jude, a new voice on the wind whispered as it brushed her ear. It sounded like Bennett.

Jude clenched her eyes shut. *Get out of my head. Get away from me.*

An image of her mother appeared behind her eyelids: her mother kissing William Harding behind Bishop High as the sun dipped below the horizon.

Maybe she'd thought she'd loved him, or at least liked him enough to kiss him. And maybe he really had liked her back. Or maybe he was just pretending so he could kill her, or Indigo, or Cori. But it didn't really matter in the end. Whatever Ava had felt toward William hadn't held her back from helping her friends. From leaving this place for good.

"Go away, Bennett," she whispered through gritted teeth. "You don't own me anymore."

Jude dropped Delilah's arm and charged forward. Whitney let out a guttural sound behind her as she pushed the sheriff off-balance. He stumbled back, arms pinwheeling. "*RUN!*" Jude screamed. "Get into the field! Go!"

Whitney swung Delilah's arm around her shoulders. Together they bolted past the cops and into the thicket of sunflowers lining the path.

Sheriff Ableman righted himself. "Get back here!"

Jude started to run.

He pulled the trigger.

CHAPTER THIRTY-SEVEN

The first shot rang through the air, slicing through sunflowers and sending loose petals into the air. They rained down on Delilah's head like ash.

The second shot snapped from the barrel of Sheriff Ableman's gun, but it never reached the fields.

Jude let out a feral scream from somewhere behind them.

"NO!" Whitney yelled. She dropped Delilah's arm and started to run back. Bo couldn't hold Delilah's weight on her own. Like rainwater, Delilah oozed to the ground, where she sank into the mud between the stalks.

"I'm going with her," she heard Alma say from somewhere above her. Footsteps echoed as she ran away.

Bo hovered somewhere nearby; Delilah could feel her. She'd always been able to feel Bo, even when she didn't want to. "Shit, shit, shit," Bo said softly as she started to pace.

Delilah winced as she turned over so her back was flat against the ground. Sunflower stalks poked up around her arms and legs, almost like they were thumbtacks pinning her to the earth. She let out a shaky breath and sank in deeper.

In the hollow of her lower back, Delilah could just make out the hum of a heartbeat. Its gentle rhythm pulsed against her spine, lulling her into a dark slumber.

Everything in her ached. She could barely breathe with the wind and the smoke swirling around her, and the acrid scent of burning petals had chased them into the fields. It would be so easy to just let go. Give herself up to the heartbeat and the monster it belonged to.

Delilah closed her eyes and let herself drift.

She felt her heartbeat slow as the earth clutched her, pulling her under. Deeper, deeper, until her mouth filled with damp soil and her pain began to ebb.

You're here, the land said, yet it didn't. It wasn't speaking so much as it was *transmitting* on some kind of frequency that Delilah could hear now.

You've finally given in.

Yes, Delilah thought, and just the thought of letting go released the last of her pain. Her neck didn't hurt anymore, her ribs weren't bruised, her heart wasn't broken. Or if it was, she couldn't feel it anymore. She couldn't feel anything at all.

It was only a matter of time, really, the land said. *You had to fulfill your mother's destiny.*

Delilah felt her eyebrows twitch beneath the dirt. *Mother.* The word rolled around in her head like a marble. She'd known that person before. It had been someone important.

I chose her blood. She did not concede like I'd thought.

Concede?

She fought and she left with only the clothes on her back.

That seems so hard, Delilah thought. *So much work.*

Yes, child, it is. The land echoed through her bones. *Let me take care of you now. It's time to rest.*

Delilah's ears popped as the earth pressed in all around her.

It slowly squeezed her neck, harder and harder, until she felt her stitches snap.

There it is, the blood. The land shivered with excitement. *I'm so parched.*

Delilah let go.

She felt her blood flow from her veins, feeding the soil as it slurped hungrily. She tried to move her fingers, but she couldn't anymore. They felt delicate and whisper-thin, like the beginnings of roots.

Sunflower roots.

At least I can watch the girls, she thought, *when I'm a flower.*

The land paused its feasting. *Oh no. They're next.*

No. Delilah tried to move, but nothing happened. *No, you can't.*

Another voice cut through her mind, this one as clear as glass. *Lilah, you can still get out.*

Her mother was here.

Like back in the cellar, Delilah could sense her hovering above the earth like a ghost, speaking to her from the sunflowers. She was *right there,* and yet so far away. Delilah's heart longed for her.

There will always be more, Lilah, her mother whispered. *It'll never stop until we make it stop.*

How? Delilah thought.

You can't! The land growled. It tightened its grip. *This curse is ancient. It will never stop.*

Break the curse, sweet girl, Indigo said. *Do what must be done.*

Delilah felt the hum of her own pulse as her heartbeat picked up speed. Suddenly, her fingers twitched; she could feel them again. Tendrils of sunflower roots stretched toward her, whispering against her thighs, her neck, her cheeks. They wrapped around her like a weedy cocoon, cutting her off from the soil.

And then they pulled her upward.

Up, up, up through the cracked earth until she broke the surface. They unraveled slowly, giving her a moment to catch her breath.

"DELILAH!" Bo yelled, pulling away the last tendrils still draped over her chest. Tears rolled down her face. "I don't know where the others are, and I thought you were . . . I thought you were . . . You're *alive*."

Delilah rolled onto her side and coughed. Clumps of dirt fell from her mouth.

Bo dropped down beside her and pressed her hand into her back. "Are you okay?"

After a moment, Delilah spat out the gritty taste in her mouth. She wiped her lips with the back of her hand, streaking dirt across her cheek. "I will be."

She wrapped one arm around Bo and latched on to the sunflower closest to her to help her up out of the mud. As soon as her fingers connected with the stalk, something surged through her, recharging her like a battery.

It wasn't the sharp bite of pain she'd grown familiar with from every time she touched Bennett. This felt like a balm, the soothing thrill of coming home, of drinking sweet tea with Whitney on the front porch. Of combing out knots from Bo's perpetually tangled hair, of finishing a Sunday crossword puzzle in pen with Jude.

With one touch, Delilah could feel it all—every woman who had been sacrificed to feed this cursed land, their dreams, their fears, all the possible futures that were stolen. It all felt *familiar*, as if she'd been carrying around their legacy her entire life. These lost women wove through her veins, marinated in her bones, whispered their warnings in her restless dreams. And suddenly she knew: it had been *them* who had been with her all along, warning her about Bennett and the Hardings. It had been their collective pain, their murders she felt a hundred times over, every time Bennett touched her. They'd been trying to protect her all along.

Delilah held back a sob. Some part of her had always known. Of course she'd spent the past two years avoiding the sunflowers. She'd spent every moment knowing in her bones that they were all in danger, that the sunflower fields were fertilized with the blood of the dead. That eventually, this thing would pick them off, one by one, until they were buried beside their ancestors. She'd spent every waking second keeping track of the other girls, herding them like lambs back to the house, where she could ensure they were safe. She'd built her entire life around a fear she hadn't even known she had. Who could she have been without this fear nestled deep beneath her ribs?

She hadn't gotten the chance to find out.

This time, when her mother appeared, her translucent hands were covered in plaster as if she were in the middle of a project. She stood before her, an echo of what she once was, her expression unreadable. But Delilah wasn't the only one who could see her.

"Indigo," Bo choked out.

"Mom," Delilah breathed. "Are you . . . are you a ghost?"

Indigo smiled gently. "I'm an awakening."

Bo trembled beside her. Delilah grabbed her hand and threaded their fingers together. Slowly, Indigo turned toward the endless field surrounding them. The sunflowers shuddered, but not from the wind. They moved and swayed with their own rhythm, in their own time, their petals whispering.

"What are they saying?" Bo asked softly.

There were so many voices that Delilah couldn't make out their words, but she could feel the urgency of their messages pressing in. They wanted something from the girls—no, they *needed* something.

Delilah felt the Hardings arrive before she heard the truck doors slam shut.

"William and Caleb are here," she whispered to Bo.

The entire field shuddered in a silent scream. Indigo turned back to them. Again, her mouth made a rose-colored ring as she spoke a single word.

Bo, she said, before disappearing among the petals.

CHAPTER THIRTY-EIGHT

Bo froze at the sound of her own name.

The sunflowers quivered. *Bo,* they whispered.

Bo. Bo.

Bo.

"I don't know what they want me to do," she said as she stood there, frozen among them. Her entire body felt numb as she stood there, watching this muted yellow graveyard pulse with urgency.

"We have to go," Delilah whispered. "The Hardings are coming."

"But Jude," Bo said, glancing back through the stalks. "And Whitney and Alma. I don't know what happened—"

We'll keep them safe, the sunflowers whispered. *Hurry, hurry.*

"Let's go," she said, grabbing Delilah's wrist. Together, they wove through the stalks, tracing their way back toward the house.

"Come out, come out, wherever you are," William called, his voice tinged with malice. Bo pulled in a shaky breath. His heavy footsteps stomped too close behind them.

The wind picked up again as they started to run. The smoke was so thick now that Bo could barely make out the shape of the stalks as she and Delilah zigzagged through the field. Every breath felt like a weight on her chest, the scent of burning petals singeing her nostrils as she ran for all of their lives.

The outline of the house cut through the fog. If they could just keep going, run past the house and into the sprawling fields beyond, they could pull the Hardings far away from wherever Jude and the rest had ended up. If the men hadn't already found them.

As they got closer, the smoke darkened. Delilah coughed heavily beside her. Bo waved her hands in front of herself to try to cut through some of the wall of gray.

The house was on fire.

They jerked to a stop. The house on Old Fairview Lane was engulfed in flames. Smoke billowed from all the windows, and even the old tree that had crashed through the porch was charred and lifeless.

"Look." Delilah pointed to the field past the house.

It was all ablaze. The trail of houses leading back to downtown were all on fire, as if the sparks had caught on the wind and hopped from structure to structure until they reached the edge of town. Bo turned to Delilah. "We have to go back the other way."

"But the Hardings," Delilah said, coughing.

We'll keep them away, the sunflowers whispered. *Hurry, hurry.*

Together they raced back through the field, making a wide loop to avoid drawing the Hardings back to the spot along the path where Jude and the others could still be. "Bo, where are we going?" Delilah yelled.

I don't know, she thought, but she couldn't bring herself to say the words aloud. *I don't know, I don't know, I don't know.*

All at once, the sunflowers parted, and a path yawned open in front of them. Standing on both sides was a parade of ghosts.

There were old women with wrinkles in their ethereal skin, young women with wispy hair trailing down their backs. There were women in bonnets and gingham skirts, and women who didn't look much older than Bo. They all turned their heads. *Hurry, hurry,* they whispered.

They ran. Bo clasped Delilah's hand like it was a life raft as they raced along the path that kept opening before them, guiding them to some unknown destination. Behind them, the sunflowers snapped closed like a curtain as soon as they passed through.

Footsteps followed, quick and angry. Bo thought she heard Caleb yell, but she couldn't be sure through the wind and smoke. She pumped her legs harder.

The ghosts continued along the path, whispering in their petal-soft voices.

Keep going.

You're almost there.

Avenge us. Avenge us.

Avenge us.

It felt like they had run for hours, but the fields stretched on and smoke still clotted their lungs. Bo started to feel loopy. Was this some kind of trick of the eye, some relentless maze Bishop had set up for them? Would they run until their legs gave out, until they dropped into the dust and lived among the ghosts?

Was it even possible to leave this place?

"The clearing!" Delilah yelled. "Up ahead!"

Bo saw the open plot of land peeking through the stalks. The path opened wider before them, leading them directly to it. She slowed. "Why are they leading us back into town?"

Delilah paused beside her, pulling in heavy breaths. They stood among the flowers and the ghosts, their toes just cresting the edge of the clearing. It was empty now—William had removed the remnants of their mothers' shattered memorial. But the incessant windstorms had churned the soil like butter in a barrel, unearthing more than dust and bonfire ash.

They were all there. All of Bishop's dead and lost, parts of them that had long been buried and forgotten. Bo took a tentative step forward. Beneath her sneaker was a wallet-size photograph, faded and soft at the edges. A chubby baby smiled up at her, toothless and blissfully unaware.

There were more, so many more. A single pearl earring. A tarnished bracelet with a broken clasp. A sliver of green fabric poking out of the earth like a pale shoot in the spring. All the slivers of life, of living and breathing women with hopes and dreams and people they had loved, whom William and his ancestors had forgotten, or didn't care to look for. They'd made the cuts, let the earth swallow them up, and smoothed dirt over what was left behind of the women's bodies without considering what they'd left behind of their lives.

And when it all started to come to light, they tried to smother them with stone.

"It's time to come out now." William's voice echoed through the clearing. The creepy singsong voice was gone; he wasn't playing with his prey anymore. "You can't escape us. You can't outrun us."

Bo's heart sank. It wouldn't matter how fast or how far they ran. It wouldn't matter how much of this place burned to the ground. This town wouldn't let them go so easily. The Hardings would never stop trying to find them. Their mothers' disappearance had haunted William. Driven him wild to the point of constructing statues of them in the clearing to hide the bloody messes they'd made there. He could have constructed *anything* in that clearing, and yet he'd erected stone likenesses of their missing mothers—the only women who had escaped him.

And yet.

Bo took a step into the clearing. "Our mothers escaped."

Both William and Caleb's heads snapped in her direction. Patches of red bloomed on William's neck. "And they never came back for you," he spat. "They left you here and they didn't care what happened to you." Beside him, Caleb looked pale and shaky. Bennett wasn't there at all.

Delilah let out a puff of air from somewhere behind her, like she was a balloon that had popped. But Bo felt something more feral rise within her.

The ghosts of Bishop crowded around her, lining the clearing with their ethereal presence. *They weren't ready,* the ghosts whispered in unison.

They weren't ready to break the curse.

The Hardings didn't seem to notice the web of ghosts closing in around them. William shoved Caleb forward. "Do it, son. Finish this."

"But the land hasn't asked for her yet," Caleb said, stumbling in front of Bo. "We have to keep her alive until it's the right time."

"*Do it now!*" William screamed. "*Finish this.*"

Caleb's eyes connected with Bo's for a split second, stained with fear. And then he lunged.

Delilah screamed. Bo grabbed her wrist and yanked her back into the sunflowers, crashing through the shivering stalks, the smoke threading through their hair and clothes and lungs as they ran.

You're the one, the ghosts whispered. *You can break the curse.*

Bo stopped. Delilah slammed into her, her eyes wild with panic. "Go!"

Bo shook her head. "No. We can't keep running." She looked Delilah in the eyes. "There's only one way out."

Two years ago, Cori, Ava, and Indigo had done the best they could. They'd found a way out and they took it, but they hadn't been able to put an end to the curse. Now it was their turn. Now it was Bo's turn.

Bo knew what she needed to do.

The knife felt heavy in her pocket. She wrapped her fingers around the handle and slid it free.

She would do this for all of the women of Bishop, dead and still living, but mostly she was doing this for them—Delilah, Whitney, and Jude. The Hardings would *never* take them from her. Ever.

"Come here, Caleb," she called, her heart pounding in her chest. "I'm ready."

CHAPTER THIRTY-NINE

There was so much blood.

It splattered the sunflower stalks, covering their leaves with scarlet flecks. As Whitney got closer to where she'd heard Jude scream, the blood flecks reached all the way to the petals.

"Jude!" Whitney yelled. She dropped to her knees. Her sister was curled into a ball among the stalks, a pool of dark blood spreading beneath her. "Jude," she said again, a panicked scream clawing its way up her throat. "*Jude*."

Alma broke through the stalks, her breath heavy. Her lips parted when she saw Jude. "Oh god. No."

Whitney swallowed the urge to scream. She gently placed her fingers on Jude's neck. *Please be alive, please.*

Jude groaned. Her eyes snapped open. "Whit," she said.

"What happened? Where are you hurt?"

"It's just my leg," Jude croaked. She tried to push herself upright. "I can still move." She winced as she dragged her injured leg in front of her.

It was hard to see exactly where Ableman's bullet had entered her leg, with so much blood and dirt smeared over her skin, but Whitney could tell it was somewhere close to her calf. Standing would hurt. Running would hurt more. "Jude, you don't have to—"

Whitney paused at the sound of sunflowers rustling. A soft *click* echoed through the field.

Sheriff Ableman was coming with his gun.

Whitney looked at Jude, her eyes wide. "There's no other choice," Jude whispered. "Help me up."

Together, Alma and Whitney flanked Jude. They lifted her out of the mud and started walking, careful to avoid rustling the leaves as best they could. They'd only gone a few steps when Whitney realized they would never make it. They would never outrun the sheriff and the other cops. They didn't even know where they were going—Bo and Delilah had disappeared, and the Hardings were surely lurking somewhere close by.

Whitney.

Her name rang as clear as daylight through the smoke. She jerked to a stop.

Eleanor stood before them, wearing the same sweatshirt she'd had on that last night at the bonfire, only now, it was a ghostly white. *She* was a ghostly white. "Eleanor," Whitney whispered. Her whole body went numb.

Beside her, Jude pulled in a sharp breath. "I can see her."

"Me, too," said Alma, breathless.

The sunflowers shuddered, then shifted to reveal a path opening behind Eleanor. She waved a translucent hand. *Follow me.*

They followed as Eleanor led them down the path. The sunflowers snapped closed behind them as they pushed forward, creating a thick wall of yellow. Ableman yelled from somewhere behind them, and the footsteps picked up speed.

Every muscle in Whitney's body clenched as she tried to run. "You've got this," Alma whispered. Whitney nodded, tears streaming down her face, as she pushed forward.

The path opened up to the edge of the clearing. Eleanor stood at the threshold between the open land and the thicket of sunflowers, pointing to something jutting out of the ground.

Jude squinted. "Is that . . ."

"The weather vane," Whitney whispered.

She swooped down and pulled what was left of it from the ground like a forgotten weed. That day she'd led them all to the clearing to talk to Eleanor seemed like a lifetime ago. She could still remember the desperate feeling clinging to her like fog when the weather vane had snapped in her hand, cutting her off from her only source of hope. She'd kicked it into the fields when she'd realized it could never be fixed.

But now she knew. It had never been Eleanor speaking to her; she'd just wanted it to be so badly that she'd convinced herself of it. How could she ever have thought Eleanor would be an almost-whisper on the wind? She was here now, and she was so much more than that. She was light, and she was love, and she was all the memories they had made together, tucked forever into Whitney's heart.

The stalks parted as Ableman and the other two cops trampled through. As soon as he saw them, he raised his gun. "Come on now. Let's make this simple."

Alma moved so quickly that Whitney didn't have time to think. She dropped Jude's arm and lunged toward the sheriff, clawing at his skin and forcing his arm to jerk up toward the sky. He pulled the trigger. The gun let out a *bang* as he stumbled back.

Whitney swung.

The weather vane cracked against Ableman's skull, his canvas hat only softening the blow slightly. His eyes rolled back before he dropped to the ground.

Jude limped forward and scooped up his gun.

The two cops trailing him froze. "Put your hands up," Jude snarled. Their hands lifted in the air, eyes bouncing between the three girls. Whitney, with the weather vane still clenched in her fist. Alma, with the sheriff's blood caked under her fingernails. And Jude, pointing the pistol in their direction, her finger hovering over the trigger.

They stayed like that until Whitney snapped. "*GO,*" she yelled.

Slowly, the cops stumbled backward, until they must have felt safe enough to turn around and run full speed ahead.

Whitney let out a breath. She glanced at the endless green and yellow around her. Eleanor's ghost had disappeared, the path had closed, and they were in the middle of nowhere.

She heard the rustle of someone moving through the flowers.

"Come on, Bo, it doesn't have to be like this." *Caleb's voice.* It was close.

Whitney hunched down and crept through the stalks, listening, as Alma held up Jude while they trailed behind her. Pieces of Bo came into view from several feet away. A sliver of matted blond hair. Dirty T-shirt. The glint of the knife in her hand.

The flowers groaned as Caleb came closer. "Why are you making this hard, Bo? You know I'm gonna find you," he said, though the wobble in his voice didn't sound so sure. Whitney watched Bo's hands tighten.

"Just make it easy already. You don't have to fight everything. If you would have just stopped fighting that night, it would have been a whole lot better for the both of us."

Bo released a feral scream as she lunged. There was the glint of the knife and a blur of motion and a *thwick, thwick, thwick* sound as Caleb screamed and screamed until he stopped.

More footsteps, heavier this time. "Caleb?" William called. "What's going on? Oh my—"

Bo didn't hesitate. The sunflowers shuddered as she lunged again, the *thwick, thwick, thwick* of the knife echoing again through the field. Whitney felt the earth reverberate beneath her feet as the second body dropped to the ground.

The only sound was Bo's breathing, haggard and shaky.

Whitney wove through the stalks until she found Bo, hunched over in a tiny ball in the dirt. She glanced up. Her hair was matted with blood, her face splattered with it. Whitney crumbled at the sight of her. She would help Bo wash the blood away, but the marks it would leave behind would last forever.

"Bo," she said softly.

Bo started to cry.

Whitney ran to her. She wrapped her in her arms and held her close to her chest. After a moment, another pair of arms surrounded them, and another, and another.

Delilah pressed her cheek to Bo's, tears cutting through the dirt on her cheeks. Jude leaned on them, draping herself across their backs like a blanket, and Alma curled up close to Whitney, her nose pressed into the nape of her neck.

They stayed like that for a long time.

CHAPTER FORTY

The sunflower fields were even denser than Jude had imagined. They stretched on forever as the five of them marched silently toward a destination they couldn't picture.

At some point, the smoke began to fade as they left the fire behind them. Alma was the first to find the gravel path. "Look at this," she said, stepping onto the path that cut through the sunflowers like a river. Jude followed, leaning heavily on her sister, as the pain in her calf streaked through her like lightning. Pebbles stuck to the bottoms of her blood-soaked shoes.

She knew this path.

They followed it until it led them straight to a dilapidated old structure in the middle of a field. It was smaller than Jude remembered, more worn around the edges. It had never even been painted—the wood siding was sunbaked and warped, the single window in the front covered with a plastic tarp.

How had she trusted Bennett so much that he had been able to convince her that *this* was the hospital? She wanted to believe Bennett had cast some spell on her, made her see things that weren't really there. But the truth was, she had wanted to believe it. Some part of her thought if she believed this little lie, then it would be easier to believe that he really did love her, too.

Whitney stood beside her as they paused in front of the building. "This is where they took me," she said. It wasn't a question. It was a confirmation.

"Yeah," Jude said. "This is it."

Whitney let out a little puff of air. "How—"

"I don't know, Whit," Jude said. Tears pricked the corners of her eyes. "I didn't . . . I couldn't see him clearly. I really messed up."

Jude's sister turned to her. She chewed her lip. "It's going to take me a minute to forgive you, you know."

A tear streaked down Jude's cheek. "Yeah. I know."

Whitney nodded, then threw open the door and stepped inside.

The innards of the building were just as pathetic as the frame. It was a single room, with a freestanding cabinet and an old cot in the corner. If Jude looked at the floor hard enough, she could almost see speckles of rust-colored blood in the grooves of the floorboards. But she tried not to look at that. "There's got to be some kind of bandages in here," she said.

Jude popped open the cabinet. It was filled with rolls of gauze in neat little rows, bins of peach-colored pill bottles—oxycodone, Tylenol, codeine—and IV bags topped off with saline solution. There was even a pair of crutches propped up against the cabinet, ready to use in case the Hardings ever brought someone here who needed them to keep up their charade.

All those times the cops had picked up half-dead women and rushed them out of town for treatment, had they taken them here, too? Drugged them so they wouldn't question the sunlight bleeding through the cracks in the walls or the way the unfinished floorboards left splinters in their feet, and then left them here to die?

Or tossed them into the fields like feeble prey for a monster.

"Sit," Alma said, guiding Jude toward the cot.

She limped toward it and sat, gripping the frame so she wouldn't sink into the center. Whitney guided Delilah to the cot, too, and forced her to sit. The left side of Jude's body pressed into Delilah's right side, their legs and arms so close they were almost entwined. Bo sat in the corner closest to the door, her arms wrapped tightly around her dirt-streaked legs.

As Alma and Whitney dug through the cabinet for supplies, Jude turned to Delilah. "I wish I could explain everything, but I can't. I don't know why I did the things I did, or why I was willing to risk our relationship over Bennett." Jude swallowed. "All I know is that I'm so, so sorry. And I don't expect you to ever forgive me."

Delilah looked at Jude. "I know what you mean. About Bennett. He just . . . was really good at making people see what he wanted them to see."

"Do you think it was because he was a Harding?"

Delilah sighed. "Yeah. But I also think it was because he was Bennett." She pressed her shoulder against Jude's. "We're okay now."

Jude touched her temple to Delilah's. They sat like that as Whitney and Alma came back with trays of antiseptic and bandages and rows of pills. "I'm going to see if I can get the bullet out," Alma said, picking up a pair of forceps. "It's close to the surface, and it's in the muscle so it might not bleed as much."

"Okay," Jude said, pinching her eyes shut. She felt Delilah's fingers squeeze hers.

The pain was white hot and sharp at first, but then it dulled into a persistent ache. Delilah never let go of her hand as Jude clenched her jaw, trying to stifle a scream.

"There," Alma said, letting out a long breath. There was a *clang*. Jude opened her eyes to see the bullet, covered in her blood, lying in the corner of the metal tray. Alma let out a sigh of relief. "Thank you for all those medical shows, shitty satellite TV."

The room grew silent as Whitney and Alma worked, except for the occasional groan from Jude while Alma tried her hand at stitching her up, along with Whitney's *Sorry, sorry, sorry* whispers as she applied antiseptic to Delilah's neck.

Alma pressed a small white pill into Jude's palm, and then Delilah's. "It's going to be painful to walk, and I don't know how far we have to go. This'll help." They swallowed the pills down. "And you'll definitely need these," Alma said, handing Jude the crutches.

Jude slid off the couch and tucked the crutches under her arms. She wobbled over to Bo. "It's your turn," she said.

Bo lifted her head from her knees. The skin beneath her eyes was puffy and purple. "I'll be fine."

"Bo, come sit," Delilah said, gesturing toward the cot.

Bo grumbled as she pulled herself to her feet, but she didn't fight them any further. She dropped onto the edge of the cot, her gaze on her shoes, but really she was somewhere else entirely.

"Can I touch you?" Delilah asked softly.

Her eyes fluttered shut. She nodded, but when Delilah's fingertip gently grazed her temple as she tucked a strand of matted hair behind her ear, Bo flinched. "This looks like it hurts," Delilah said. Bo didn't say anything.

Whitney grabbed a chemical ice pack from the cabinet and snapped it so it would start to grow cold. She handed it to Delilah, who gently applied it to the swollen purple knot jutting out of Bo's head. Alma grabbed a pen flashlight and turned on the light with a *click*. She trained it over Bo's right eye. "They taught us how to check for head injuries at the Nursing Care Center, in case anyone fell in their rooms," Alma said, moving the light across her face. "It looks like you might have a concussion."

Bo just nodded. She wasn't all here, and it wasn't only because of the injury.

Jude squeezed between the girls and sidled up beside Bo on the cot. She wrapped her arms around Bo and pulled in her so close that she could smell the sweat and earth and blood on her skin. Whitney went back to the cabinet and retrieved a towel and a bottle of water. She poured half of it into the towel and gave the other half to Bo, who absentmindedly drank from it while Whitney tried to wipe the bloodstains from her skin.

"We should get going," Bo said after a while. "They're never going to stop looking for us."

Whitney slowly stopped dabbing at Bo's skin. Delilah's eyes flicked to Jude's. *Does she even know what she did?*

Bennett had been smashed in the head with a shovel. William and Caleb were dead. Ableman was probably dead, too, and the cops who had been with him were sniveling cowards who weren't about to risk their lives to chase the five of them out of town. Especially when there was a fire raging and they could be heroes by helping to put it out.

"Yeah, we'll get going," Jude said. "Why don't we just take a minute, though—"

Bo jumped off the cot before she could finish. She headed out the door of the makeshift hospital without another word.

The girls scrambled to take whatever they could fit in their pockets—aspirin, antiseptic wipes, bandages. They each grabbed what was left of the water and tucked them under their arms, with Whitney carrying an extra bottle for Jude, before following Bo into the miles of sunflowers surrounding them.

The ghosts had all but vanished, and the berating voices that used to plague Jude had disappeared with the wind. Now it was just them, and the flowers, and the heaviness of what they had done hanging in the air around them like a fog.

They walked in silence for what felt like hours. As the medicine threaded through Jude's veins, she forgot what the stinging in her leg had felt like back at the building. Now it was more like a memory; she could feel the niggling sensation of something being *off* around her calf, an echo of pain, but not the pain itself.

She kept going.

The sun crested over the horizon, the morning sky bleeding into lavenders and corals. It was becoming more and more difficult for Jude to maneuver the crutches around the thick stalks as her entire body began to ache with exhaustion. They would have to stop somewhere soon.

And then they just . . . stopped.

One minute Jude was in the field, and the next she wasn't. She stared at the expanse of dusty land yawning open before her. There was another clearing, and up a little farther, a road. A *real road*—one that had been paved smooth, like someone had actually expected people to drive on it.

"I don't . . . where are we?" Whitney asked, hugging a half-empty water bottle to her chest.

"Where are we supposed to go now?" Bo stepped into the middle of the road, which stretched through the field in both directions.

Jude followed her. She looked one way and saw nothing but flowers and corn. She glanced the other way. Nothing but more of the same.

"Look," Delilah said softly.

Sunflower petals whispered on the lightest breeze. They wafted from the field, parading past them in a single line, and continued floating down the road.

CHAPTER FORTY-ONE

Delilah.

She turned back and glanced at the fields at the sound of her name. It only took Delilah a moment to realize the sound was coming from somewhere up *ahead*.

Delilah.

Her mother's voice.

"This way," she said, waving on the rest of the girls. Together they walked down the road in a single file line as the sunflower petals twirled in the gentle breeze before them. Indigo didn't speak another word as they marched through the predawn light.

Delilah was just about to turn around and tell the girls she might have made a mistake when she saw a soft glow just up the road. "There's something up there!" she yelled.

Excited murmurs followed her as she started to run. A single petal broke off from the others, flipping and twirling in the air, as a small building with a steepled roof appeared before her, milky white light spilling from all the windows. A faded sign hung on the front door: LITTLE PRAIRIE MARKET.

The petal landed gently on the rust-speckled doorknob.

Delilah turned back. The rest of the girls hovered around her, their eyes shining like those of wild animals in the woods. They were all battered and blood splattered, their expressions hollow as ghosts'. They had no clean clothes, no car, no money, and no idea where they were going. Whatever—or whoever—was in the Little Prairie Market was their last hope.

Bells jangled as Delilah stepped inside, and a blast of air conditioning smacked her in the face. It smelled a bit like mothballs and a cheap vanilla candle, and the shelves lining the center rows were stuffed full of trinkets. There were rows of porcelain angels with chipped wings, fake flowers laden with dust, and an entire section of snow globes. Delilah picked up the heaviest one and shook it. Flecks of incandescent glitter swirled around a tiny plastic yeti inside.

"Sodas are in the cooler to the left, and we don't sell alcohol," a woman's voice shouted from the back of the store.

Delilah followed the sound of shuffling boxes until she saw an older woman no taller than five feet, her salt-and-pepper hair cropped close to her head. She glanced up at Delilah, a roll of stickers tucked into her fist. "Can I help you?"

The rest of the girls crowded into the aisle behind Delilah, all bloodied and battered. The woman's eyes widened. She dropped the stickers into the box at her feet. "Oh my. Come. Come on."

They followed her into a stuffy storage room in the back. Instantly, it reminded Delilah of the one at Rose and Rain, where Gale-Ann had led her so she could comb through all the phone numbers, searching for the one her mother had written on a faded receipt. That dank room had started this mess. Maybe this one could end it.

"What happened to you girls?" the woman asked once they were all tucked inside. "What do you need? Water? I have some right here." She started to dig through boxes like a rabid bear digging through trash.

"It's okay, ma'am," Delilah said. "Please. We just need help finding someone."

The woman stilled. She turned slowly toward them, her eyes scanning each of them from head to toe. "You came from that wicked town, didn't you?"

Delilah's whole body went numb. "You know about Bishop?"

Her jaw clenched. "Yes, I know about Bishop. There's been rumors around these parts for years, but I'd never heard of anyone actually *from* that place until a couple years ago."

Bo let out a puff of air from somewhere behind her. "Two years ago?"

"When those other women came in here, a mess, just like you all are now. I'm Esther, by the way," the woman continued. "Ah, there's that water."

Esther handed them dusty bottles of water, twisting the caps to crack the seal before she set them in their hands. Delilah tried to calm her heartbeat, which had started to roller-coaster in her chest. "Esther, how many women came in here two years ago?"

Her eyebrows knitted together as she twisted off another cap. This time, she poured the water into her own mouth. "Three," she said, wiping her mouth.

"*Three,*" Delilah whispered. She glanced at the rest of the girls, who stared at Esther with wide eyes. "What did they look like?"

"One had dark curly hair. One was tall, thin, with a lot of freckles. Another one had short hair cut kinda like mine," Esther said. "You know them?"

"*Yes,*" Whitney said, her voice trembling.

The next question got caught in Delilah's throat: *Where are they now?*

Because Esther's answer to that question could change everything. If she told them that she didn't know, that they'd moved on from this place without telling anyone where they were going, the girls would have nothing left. The past two years of agonizing and longing would suddenly come to an end, and Delilah wasn't completely sure that this all had been worth it. It *had* to be worth it.

As if reading her mind, Esther's face softened. "They're okay, honey. In fact, you can see for yourself. They live right up the road."

Slowly, Delilah turned. Jude stood with the crutches behind her, shaking like roof shingles in the wind. Whitney clung to Alma, eyes shining, and splotches of pink had already started to bloom on Bo's cheeks.

They're alive.

They're right down the street.

"Esther, thank you," Delilah said breathlessly. "Which way do we go from here?"

"Take a quick right out the door, then a straight shot down. It's the first house you'll come up to. If you start seeing a lot of houses, you're all the way in Fowler, and you've gone too far."

"Thank you," Delilah said again, squeezing Esther's hands. She spun around and rushed out the storage room door.

"Wait, do y'all want to take your waters with you?" Esther called after them.

But Delilah was already running, her footsteps making the porcelain angels shake on the shelves. "No, thanks!"

Whitney threw open the shop door, the bells still jangling as she jumped down the steps. Alma followed, mindful to stay close to Jude as she hobbled toward the road. Delilah ran. She ran until her heart thrummed through her veins, until her muscles burned. This time, when the wind threaded itself through her hair, she welcomed it. It felt like freedom.

As their footsteps smacked the cement, Whitney let out a laugh that echoed in the summer air around them. It was a precious thing, so rare since Eleanor died that Delilah had almost forgotten the sound of it. She let out a laugh of her own. Tears streamed down her face as she laughed so hard that the muscles in her neck pinched against her stitches.

Bo.

Delilah jerked to a stop. Alma, Whitney, and Jude kept going up ahead. She spun around.

Bo was far behind, her silhouette just barely visible in the tepid glow from the single streetlight. She jogged back.

"Hey," she said, sidling up to Bo. "What's wrong?"

Bo shook her head, but almost instantly she sighed, as if she already knew that Delilah wouldn't stop asking. She stopped walking. "What if, when I tell my mom what I did, she . . . she doesn't want to be around me?"

"Oh, Bo." Delilah scooped her up like a stray cat on the side of the road and held her close to her chest. "That will never happen," she whispered into Bo's hair.

"You coming?" Jude's voice called from up ahead.

Delilah pulled away. She stared into Bo's eyes and watched her face crumple as Delilah told her, with her thoughts, all the things she'd always wanted to say.

You're the bravest person I know.

I've never looked up to you more than I do right now.

I love you. I love you.

I love you.

They held hands as they raced down the street, trailing behind the rest. It wasn't long before the glow of a porch light greeted them. The rest of the house came into view, piece by piece: a sprawling front porch, just like the one on Old Fairview Lane. A steepled roof of a different color. Terra-cotta pots tucked into every corner of the porch, the flowerbeds, the windowsills, each one filled with something fragrant and blooming.

And a single sunflower flush with the porch, standing tall as if guarding the place. Delilah swore she saw it shiver as they stood together at the foot of the steps.

The front door flung open. A silhouette stood in the frame, but Delilah knew.

She knew it was her mother.

"*MOM!*" she yelled, running up the stairs.

"Delilah?" Indigo said softly. She stepped onto the porch. "Oh my god, *Delilah*. Cori! Ava! Come here quick!"

Delilah threw herself into her mother's arms like she was five years old and had scraped her knee on the gravel driveway. She squeezed Indigo extra tightly so she could feel her mother's shoulder blades and sun-warmed skin and the solidness of her. The realness of something she'd dreamed of for so long.

"Mom," she whispered.

CHAPTER FORTY-TWO

When Bo woke, she wasn't in the house on Old Fairview Lane, but it felt just the same. The walls were a creamy white instead of plastered with floral wallpaper, and early morning light splashed every corner of her mother's modest bedroom. The kitchen hummed with activity beneath her, voices Bo had only heard in her dreams the past two years falling into the soothing rhythm of everyday life.

They had found their mothers three days ago, and still, Bo couldn't find the words that everyone else seemed to sink into with ease.

Indigo and Delilah hadn't *stopped* talking since they'd found each other again. Well after the sun had sunk below the horizon, Bo could hear them speaking in their room across the hall in urgent whispers, like one of them could disappear again at any second. Whitney and Jude had settled into an amicable rhythm, too, with Jude taking up the mornings on the sun-soaked porch, reading with Ava while Whitney curled up between her and Alma on the couch in the evenings.

Bo had barely said anything to her mother.

It wasn't that she didn't want to—Bo had dreamed of all the things she'd talk to Cori about again one day, if she ever got the chance.

What were you like when you were my age?

What did you want to be when you were my age?

Did you feel as angry as I always do?

She wanted to ask her about growing up in Bishop, and if a boy had ever hurt her like Caleb had hurt her, and when was the last time she'd talked to Bo's father, and what had really happened that last day, the last time Bo saw her. Each night, Bo crawled silently into a sleeping bag on the floor instead of lying in bed next to her mother, whispering her questions into the dark.

She pushed the sleeping bag to her ankles and climbed to her feet. An old ballet-pink T-shirt hung to her thighs, but fortunately, their mothers had made a trip to Fowler's single clothing store to get them all new underwear. Cori had bought her a size too small. It was the size Bo had worn before her mother left.

Morning scents wafted up the stairs—coffee and dish soap and a sunbaked breeze. Delilah's laugh echoed through the house like a tinkling bell. Bo bypassed the kitchen and went out the front door.

Cori sat in front of one of the garden beds, a riot of garden tools surrounding her. The day had just begun, but there were already beads of sweat clinging to the back of her neck. She glanced up from the wilting tomato plant she had been trying to rehab. "Morning."

"Morning." Bo made her way to the porch steps and sat, careful not to flash her new underwear, although there weren't really any neighbors around to see. "What are you working on?"

Cori sighed. "This tomato plant just doesn't want to produce. I've tried fertilizing it, watering it more, watering it *less*, pruning it. It won't bloom." She held a spindly vine between her fingers. Where there should have been a smattering of yellow flowers and a bulging tomato, there was nothing at all.

"Maybe it's just not ready," Bo said softly. "Maybe it needs a little more time."

Cori looked at Bo for a long time before gently dropping the vine. "I know you're angry with me."

Bo shook her head. "I'm not—"

"Don't lie to me, sweetheart," Cori said, her face crumpling. "We've been apart way too long for that."

Bo closed her eyes. "I don't want to be mad at you. But you *left me*. You knew what that place was capable of, and you *left me there*. And I know what you all told us about how Indigo had figured out William had something to do with it, and how he was targeting Ava and he might have killed her. But you weren't a part of that, Mom. You had nothing to do with William or the Hardings. You could have just . . . stayed."

Cori looked up at the single sunflower planted in the bed. Her eyes shone with tears. "It wasn't that simple. I knew Ava and Indigo were in danger, and they refused to leave without me. Indigo told me she'd 'rather stay and risk dying' than leave me alone in that town. Plus, she had a point: once William found out they were gone, he'd know that I knew something, too. And it would only be a matter of time before he killed me. Or worse: killed you."

She dabbed at the delicate skin beneath her eyes. "I didn't want to leave you, baby. God, I didn't want to leave you. Following Ava and Indigo out the door that day was the hardest thing I've ever done in my life. But I knew if we had a chance at living a real life—*all* of us—I had to go. I was always, always going to come back for you."

"But you didn't," Bo choked. *Damn it.* She didn't want to cry. It was easier to be mad.

"Look," Cori said softly. She waved her arm toward the wall of sunflowers across the road, the same labyrinth of petals they had both walked through for miles and miles. "They wouldn't let us go back."

Bo blinked. "The . . . sunflowers?"

Cori nodded. "They cleared the way for us to leave, but once we had escaped, the sunflowers wouldn't let us come back. They knotted together. Every time we tried to push through, they pushed back, and there were thousands—*millions*—more of them than us. They kept whispering to us. *You have to stay. You have to stay.* I can't tell you how many times I sat there on the side of the road and just begged, Bo. I pleaded with them to let me come back to you, but they told me that if I went back, I'd never get out alive, and neither would you. So I just talked to them. I whispered back to them. I told the flowers everything I wanted to tell you—*Look closer, run, fight back.* And I prayed that somehow you could hear me."

A knot formed in Bo's throat as she watched the sunflowers sway in the light. They'd saved the girls the night they'd escaped Caleb and William and Bishop, but they'd also been trying to save them for *years* before it ever came to that. She remembered the sunflower tipping through the window while Bo searched through the town records. *Look,* it had whispered.

How they'd hovered over her while she lay half dead and beaten in the field and told her to *Get up, get up, get up.*

How, when she'd been on the gravel path that pressed up against the sunflowers, she'd heard the faintest echo of her mother's voice as the wind carried it through the petals. *Run.*

"It wasn't enough, Mom. I *needed* you." Bo swallowed. "I turned into a monster without you there."

Cori brushed the dirt from her hands and joined Bo on the steps. She cupped her daughter's face with both of her soil-streaked palms and forced Bo to look at her. "What happened out there?" she asked gently.

Bo told her. She told her about how Evan had died, and how the last time she'd seen him she'd told him to piss off. She told her about the night in the cellar and what Caleb had done to her, and how her rage had spread like a wildfire ever since, burning down everything she touched.

And finally, she told her about what had happened in the field.

Cori never took her eyes off Bo as she told her about the sound of footsteps following, circling. How everything in her hurt. The sound the knife made, and how Bo could only remember slivers of it, but she could still feel the weight of the blade in her hand every time she closed her fist.

When she was finished, she couldn't bear to look at her mother's face. She squeezed her eyes closed and let her tears fall into Cori's open palms. "I'm so sorry," she whispered.

"Bo, look at me."

Bo opened her eyes. Her mother's face appeared, and to Bo's surprise, she didn't look disgusted, or even angry. She pressed her forehead to her daughter's. "A monster is someone who hurts people for their own gain. You didn't do that, sweetheart. You made a sacrifice and you used that anger so that no one else would have to do what you did, and you freed us all. That's called being a hero."

"Mom, I . . ." The rest of the words dropped away like leaves from a tree. She started to sob.

"Listen to me," Cori said, wrapping Bo in a hug so tight that it made her ache. "I am damned proud of you. Because of you, anything is possible now. For all of us."

Anything is possible.

Bo let the words roll around in her mind. *Anything.* She hadn't been able to think of anything except survival for so long, the idea that she could do anything, or be anything, or go *anywhere* felt absurdly surreal, like something she'd read in a fantasy book long ago.

Cori unwrapped her arms from Bo's shoulders and glanced back at her garden. "Maybe this tomato plant was never going to work out because it wasn't meant to be. Maybe the soil and the nutrients wanted to put all their attention on growing something else, something even more magnificent this time."

Cori looked up at the sunflower. Bo followed her gaze. Its cheery yellow halo tipped toward the sunlight, soaking in the endless possibilities a single day could bring.

"Maybe it'll grow even bigger now," her mother said.

Maybe it would.

Maybe she would.

CHAPTER FORTY-THREE

Whitney had tried not to think about Bishop at all over the last couple of days, but as she helped her mom make dinner, her mind kept drifting back there.

It had taken less than a day for the news of the fire to spread throughout the state. Whitney had woken to her mother and Jude curled up on the sofa, watching the news on an old TV. The woman on the screen was blurry around the edges, but her voice was clear. "State police are stunned by the wreckage of a fire gone rogue in the central Kansas town of Bishop," she said as fuzzy lines cut across the screen. "According to authorities, multiple bodies have been found. The town appears to be abandoned at this point. Stay tuned for updates as they develop."

"Hand me that pepper," Whitney said to Jude, who tossed her a bell pepper as big as her fist. She didn't make eye contact. Whitney hadn't exactly forgiven her sister yet, and Jude knew it, but she had started to thaw. Jude had messed up, but she had also come back for them. She had ignored the danger that Bennett presented, but she had also smashed him in the head with a shovel to free them. It was, at best, complicated.

"Hey," Whitney said softly. She reached for Jude's hand and squeezed. "Thanks."

Jude's eyes fluttered. Her mouth crept up in the corners. "Of course."

Whitney released Jude's hand and turned back to the kitchen faucet. She let the water run over the pepper's delicate skin. Every time she blinked, she saw the first sparks of Eleanor's lighter as she lit it with a *snap*. The scent of lighter fluid and charred wood flooded her memories.

She'd been the one to start that fire. She hadn't stuck around to help put it out.

Whitney turned off the faucet and set the pepper on the cutting board in front of her. She hadn't known the fire she'd started to free Alma would spread so quickly. Really, it was William's fault—he'd been the one controlling the wind, making it rage across town while he searched for them. That was what had caused it to spread so fast, burn the whole place to the ground. Ruin homes. Take lives.

That was what Whitney told herself as she cut the pepper into thin ribbons. It was the same thing her mother had told her, over and over, since they'd watched the news.

Whitney, love, this is not your fault.

"Can I help?" Alma sidled up beside her, her bare shoulder grazing Whitney's. Every nerve in Whitney's body lit up like a Christmas tree.

She didn't regret what she'd done.

"Sure," she said, rolling an onion to Alma. "You can help me chop."

They stood together in silence as their knives made soft *thwick*s through their vegetables. Jude hummed something from the other side of the kitchen as she stirred a pot, while their mother pawed through the pantry, her long skirt billowing in the breeze from the open window.

Whitney closed her eyes and let the sounds of the kitchen fill her. *This* was what she'd been waiting for without even knowing.

They worked like that until the light from the windows turned to coral. The four of them floated past each other like ships on water, careful to acknowledge each one's space without crashing their rhythm.

There was a knock just as Whitney placed the last dish on the table. The front door creaked open. "Hello?" someone called.

Whitney peeked her head around the corner. "Oh! Esther. Come in."

Esther walked into the house, a paper shopping bag tucked under her arm. Ava greeted her. "I'm so glad you could come," she said, wrapping the old woman in a hug. "Please, take a seat. Everyone, it's time for dinner!"

One by one, they filed into the stuffy "dining room"—if you could even call it that. There was an old table that Indigo had repainted in a vibrant emerald green, and a hodgepodge of mismatched chairs surrounding it. But most important: there was room for them all.

Alma sat on Whitney's left side, while Esther sat on her right. In front of them dozens of dishes of all shapes and sizes decorated the table. There was Ava's roasted red pepper pasta in a Tupperware bowl that had seen better days and a salad made from the butter lettuce in Cori's garden, the greens glistening with oil and vinegar. There were sautéed onions and a creamy mushroom sauce and freshly made pasta still speckled with flour.

"Alma," Ava said softly. She reached across the risotto and wrapped both her hands around Alma's. "I'm so glad you're here. I've been waiting a long time for Whitney to bring home someone she cares about so I could meet her."

Whitney almost fell apart right there, but it was Alma's face that held her together. She was looking at Ava with the same reverence

Whitney felt toward her mother. It was the face of someone who knew how precious the gift they'd just received was. "I'm so glad to be here," she said, her eyes shining.

As dishes were passed and the tinkling of forks on plates filled the air, Whitney glanced over at Bo, who was shoving a forkful of pasta into her mouth. It was the first time Whitney had seen her eat since they'd arrived. Beside her, Cori gently rested her hand on top of Bo's and squeezed.

They ate until their stomachs bloated, until their laughter had started to fade and the sky turned the color of an oil slick. When everyone had set their forks on their plates and leaned back in their chairs, Indigo spoke. "I just want to thank you, Esther, for all you've done for us. Letting us stay in this house these past two years. Taking care of us when we had nothing. Sending the girls our way when they finally arrived. This is all because of you."

"Hear, hear," Ava murmured, lifting her drink. The rest of them followed suit, clinking their glasses and murmuring their gratitude.

Esther took a long drink from her glass of wine. "It's nothing, truly," she said, setting down her glass and dabbing her mouth. "We have to look out for one another. What gets me, though, is that the people who ran that horrible place just got off with no consequences."

Whitney watched as Cori squeezed Bo's hand even tighter. "I wouldn't say there were no consequences," she said gently.

Esther huffed. "Even if they're dead now, that's not good enough. They should've been rotting in prison from what I hear about that place."

Whitney stole another quick glance at Bo, who had suddenly become reinvested in her half-empty plate. Esther continued, "Did you see the news this afternoon? They found two more bodies out in the fields. An older man and a younger one."

Whitney's pulse quickened. "Just two?"

Esther looked at her for a long moment. "Yes, just two," she said slowly.

Whitney nodded, pretending to busy herself with a leftover mushroom on her plate. She'd hit Sheriff Ableman with the weather vane not far from the spot where William and Caleb had died. He must have woken up at some point. Maybe he'd gone back into town to help stop the fire from spreading even farther. And then there was Bennett. He hadn't budged after Jude had smashed him with that shovel.

Whitney could only hope he'd burned up with the rest of the town.

Stop, she told herself. *You can't turn into one of them.*

It was something she'd been chanting to herself every day since they'd gotten here. She couldn't let the cops and the Hardings and the whole damn town harden her heart, no matter what they'd done to Eleanor. She needed to keep her heart soft and open.

She had a good reason to.

"I'll clear the plates," Whitney said, pushing out of her chair.

She grabbed a stack of cups and plates and headed into the kitchen. As she lowered them into the sink, something just outside the window caught her eye.

Eleanor.

She dropped the last of the dishes with a *clang.*

Whitney ran out the back door and down the cement steps. Eleanor's ghost stood before her, only this time, she wasn't wearing her old sweatshirt. Instead, her body was mostly a blur of opalescent light. Only her face was clearly defined.

"You're here," Whitney whispered.

Eleanor's ghostly hand reached toward her. She stroked Whitney's face with the back of it, though Whitney felt nothing but the breeze.

It's time to rest, Whit, she whispered. *Be happy now.*

A tear rolled down Whitney's cheek as she closed her eyes. "I won't forget about you."

Eleanor drew her hand away, and Whitney felt the absence of her more than anything else. She opened her eyes to see Eleanor smiling. *That's more than enough.*

And then she was gone.

Whitney stood in the dark, grass caressing her ankles as invisible crickets chirped from the fields. She let out a long, slow breath, and with it, she finally let go of Eleanor, too.

"Whitney? Are you out here?"

Alma. Whitney spun around to find her on the steps, the warm light from the kitchen making her glow. She ran.

"Alma," she breathed, wrapping her arms around her.

Whitney kissed her.

She felt Alma melt in her arms like butter in the sun. Her lips felt like the electricity in the air before a storm, and when she threaded her hands through Whitney's hair, Whitney's whole body felt like it was orbiting somewhere in outer space.

She could do this forever with Alma.

And she planned on it.

CHAPTER FORTY-FOUR

Jude sat on the front porch with a glass of iced tea and stared at the sunflowers. After a week of this, she'd stopped expecting anyone to come running out from the stalks, whether to capture her or kiss her.

The cops weren't coming.

And Bennett wasn't, either.

She had given up the idea of a relationship with Bennett Harding. She knew, in her bones, that they would never be together, and they *shouldn't*. Bennett was a mess of a person, and to be honest, she wasn't that much better.

But still. Some niggling part of her insisted that he was still alive. And if he was . . . that meant whatever monster marinated in the earth below Bishop was still alive, too.

So she watched. And waited.

The other girls had started to talk about their futures with the kind of hope that could be easily shattered. Jude mostly listened as Delilah flipped through college pamphlets, their glossy coating reflecting the lamplight, dreaming of the kind of East Coast school with ivy pressed up against the windows. And just yesterday, Whitney had casually mentioned how she'd always wanted to drive up the California coastline, feel the kind of breeze that was laced with nothing but salt water. "Yeah," Alma had said, her eyes dreamy. "Let's do that."

Even Bo knew where she wanted to head next. Jude had overheard her talking to Cori in the living room one night after dinner, telling her that she wanted to go somewhere that was nothing like Kansas. "Somewhere with mountains, maybe."

"That sounds nice," Cori had said. "Maybe I'll go with you."

The screen door opened and the sound of ice cubes clinking against glass wafted out, followed by Ava in a gauzy skirt. "Can I join you?" she asked, sipping her own glass of iced tea.

Jude patted the spot next to her on the steps, and Ava sat, her skirt pooling around her ankles. "You've been out here quite a while."

"Mm," Jude said, sipping her iced tea. "I guess I have."

They sat in silence for a long time, ice cubes snapping inside their glasses as they melted in the heat. After a while, Ava said, "Have you thought about what's next for you?"

Jude shrugged. "Honestly, I can't think of anything I want to do or any place I want to see yet. It's like . . . like Bo and Whitney and Delilah are so clear on what they want, but I just . . . everything just feels murky."

"You know, Jude, you're still *so young*. And I don't say that to be dismissive—I mean that you've already lost so much, you haven't even had a chance to *be* seventeen. And what if, for a little while, that was all you did?"

Be seventeen. Hadn't that been what she'd been doing back in Bishop? She'd spent an entire summer hooking up with a boy in sheds and cellars and sunflower beds, drinking honey-colored liquor in red plastic cups.

And that was pretty much it.

Jude let out a breath as she watched the sunflowers dance in the breeze. That was *it*. She'd spent the better part of her life longing for Bennett, chasing him even after he was unavailable, hoping he'd somehow change his mind. Even now, she didn't know if what he'd told her was true, that he had been in love with her all along, but the curse inside him forced him to be with Delilah. From the other side of this sunflower field, it seemed like an easy way to have one girl in your pocket while leading on the other.

Jude closed her eyes. "I just . . . he really messed me up. I don't even know who I *am* when I'm not . . . when I don't want him."

She felt her mother's soft skin brush against hers as she slid her arm around Jude's shoulder. "I know, sweetheart. I know. I was in love with a Harding at one time, too."

Jude opened her eyes. Ava continued, "And when I found out Indigo had been seeing him, too, oh—I thought I would die from that kind of pain. But, truly, it was the best thing to happen to me. To all of us, really. Indigo helped me see the truth about William, that town, all of it." She looked at Jude. Her lip quivered. "And now you're free, too."

The tears came hot and fast down Jude's cheeks. "I wasted so much time," she choked out.

"No, no, no." Ava pulled her in tighter. "You're only seventeen, Jude. You have *time*. All you have to do is be seventeen now."

"But where would I even do that? Be seventeen?"

"Right here, if you want," Ava said gently. "I have my teaching job in Fowler. You could stay here with me for a while until you figure out where you want to go. It's going to take a bit, anyway, for us all to figure out exactly where we're going next, now that we can go anywhere."

"I can go anywhere." Jude tried out the words on her tongue, but they still didn't quite fit together, like a puzzle missing a piece. Technically, it was true. She could pack up the few things she'd collected and take off for New England, or the California coast, or the Colorado mountains. But there was still one piece missing.

There was one thing left to say.

Jude set down her empty glass and hopped off the porch. She crossed the road and headed to the fields.

This late in the summer, the sunflowers were taller than she was, their bulbous heads so heavy that they hung limp on their stalks. Crows had already started to peck out their seeds in preparation for winter.

The sunflowers in Bishop had looked like this, too, on the night Bennett had met Delilah. Jude remembered the way the seeds had made little divots in her back while she was in the field with him earlier that day.

"I deserved better than you," Jude said to the sunflowers. Her hands curled into fists by her sides. "You almost broke me. You almost broke all of us."

Above her, the sunflower dipped its head in shame. "Whatever's coming to you, or whatever's already come, you deserved it, Bennett."

Jude turned back toward the house. Her mother was waiting for her on the porch. As she started across the road, a gust of wind curled itself through her hair.

I know, it whispered.

BISHOP

The land had been satisfied for so long that it had forgotten how painful thirst could be.

Days stretched into weeks. It no longer felt the footsteps of the townspeople on its dusty paths, could no longer feel the weight of tires and hooves as they caressed the ground. All was still and silent.

At first, the land fed on what it could find. Some were dead, lost to the fire that had burned all that the travelers had worked so hard to build. It pulled them deeper, deeper, and sucked the blood from their marrow.

Others had left the land behind, including the very last traveler, the youngest boy. He had woken from his injury and stumbled to the truck. It had watched as he had fumbled for something inside, smearing his own precious blood while trying so hard to abandon this place.

He left just before the house burned to the ground.

Once what was left had been sucked dry, the land cried out.

More, it whispered, but there was no traveler to hear its cries.

Time stretched on. The land grew weaker as its thirst grew more urgent. It began to crack under the unrelenting sun, the air still heavy with the scent of singed petals. Eventually, it stopped speaking at all, for it had so little energy left, and it could not be wasted on unheard cries.

But then: a miracle.

The land felt the boy approach. He had come from a far-off place where he could not hear its cries, but now he would hear and he would kill and he would finally, finally relieve it of this relentless thirst.

But the boy traveler's thoughts were not on killing quickly. They were not on killing at all. As he walked across the barren, deserted town, he was only thinking of one thing.

The girl.

That wretched girl who had ruined it all. If he had just locked her in the cellar with the others instead of sparing her, this all could have been different. The land wouldn't be in so much *pain*.

He thought of her as he approached the clearing. *She deserved so much better,* he thought.

The boy traveler closed his eyes. "I know," he whispered. "I'm going to make it right."

He did not hesitate with the knife. The cut was swift and shallow, a slash across the palm. His cursed blood drip, drip, dripped into the soil.

The land whispered, *More.*

"There is no more," the boy said. "This is the last blood you will ever taste."

He dragged his boot across the place where he'd made his sacrifice. "I denounce this curse. I am no longer bound to you, monster." He paused for a long moment. "You can die out here."

NO. The land tried to scream, but it was too weak. It tried to tremble and quake, to kick up dust and summon the winds, but they were no longer listening.

The boy walked across the town once known as Bishop, pausing only to examine the remains of the last house at the edge of town.

"I'm ready," he said.

The sunflowers parted.

The boy began the long walk toward the unknown.

ACKNOWLEDGMENTS

This is the first book I've written in a long time that feels like me. I can't tell you exactly when and where I lost myself on my writing journey, but I can tell you who helped me come back into myself, all the way, with newfound confidence and acceptance.

Victoria Marini, you've witnessed me at my creative lows, and yet you still held space for me to do the work. Somewhere in the past decade, you've also become my friend on top of my agent, and there is no other way I'd prefer it. Thank you for pushing me, consoling me, and telling me to stop trying to make this book into a portal fantasy. Seriously. Dodged a bullet there.

And my editor, Mara Delgado Sánchez. I knew the second I sat by you at that hot pot restaurant that you were someone I wanted in my life. I was right. Thank you for not only threading your brilliance into this story, but inherently trusting me to tell stories about girls and women that aren't always easy to hear. Truly, I couldn't do this work without you. Plus, my crystal collection would definitely suffer without your influence.

To the entire team at Wednesday Books and St. Martin's Publishing Group: y'all are incredible. The behind-the-scenes work you did for this book and do for every book is awe-inducing. Thank you for every single email, cover concept, genius idea, and attention to detail you put into this story.

And let's be honest, this story wouldn't even exist without the love and support my community has given to me. Aimée Carter, thank you for reminding me that it's okay to take myself and my writing seriously. Becca Mix, thank you for always being a soft place to land when this business is especially hard. Kristin Lord, thank you for inspiring me to dream bigger and want more. My OG coven, Heidi Schulz and Emma Trevayne, your love and magic spells have always been a balm while I went to the edge of my depths for this story. And my spooky writing coven: it's so lovely to have a place to show up to and just be *me*.

When I'm not coming completely undone writing my books, I also run a business, and I literally could not have done both without Kay Smith and Sheyla Knigge. You both saved me more times than I can count, and you generously offered some of your creativity and brilliance for this business, for which I am eternally grateful. And to the Unearthed community, particularly Naomi Ansano, Shelly Jay Shore, Chris Forshner, Kat Enright, Karis Rogerson, Adi Davis, and Elizabeth Aguilar: I can't think about this beautiful thing we've built together without crying. Thank you for that gift.

The men in Bishop are pretty awful, but I'm extremely lucky to have three good men in my life that have never minded when the spotlight is on me. In fact, they're the ones who actively push it in my direction, all while holding space for me to shine. Austin Light, thank you for being a constant source of comfort and stability for this chaos being, and for all those long walks in Michigan, North Carolina, and NYC to talk out plot problems. Zack Martin, thank you for reminding me to laugh at myself, especially on the hard days. And Matt. There isn't a person out there who could possibly make a better partner in life. Thank you for saying yes when it would be so much easier to tell me no.

To every neighbor who offered to watch my kids, the grandparents who kept them overnight, friends old and new who called and texted to offer support: I see you, and I bow to you. Books are so much easier to write when you have good people in your corner.

And finally, for you, sweet reader. For all the daughters and granddaughters that are still carrying the weight of their caregivers' very human failures: I know. It's so heavy. You can set it down now, love. There's freedom on the other side.